THE ULTIMATE PRIZE

"All the legends agree that the Grail, in whatever shape it is in, brings health, wisdom, and immortality to those who partake of it."

Turcotte thought about it. "But if the Grail is in the Black Sphinx with Lisa, then rescuing her is one and the same thing."

"Yes," Yakov said, "but I wanted to be sure you were thinking clearly. Because that means that she is not the important thing down there, no matter what your heart tells you. Not important to the bad guys, the guys in the black hats, and, I must say this, not important to us. If it comes down to it, we must get the Grail before we get her. Do you agree?"

Turcotte looked up, met Yakov's dark eyes, and lied. "I agree."

ROBERT DOHERTY

AREA 51
THE GRAIL

A DELL BOOK

Published by
Dell Publishing
a division of
Random House, Inc.
1540 Broadway
New York, New York 10036

This is a work of fiction. Names, characters, places, and incidents either
are the product of the author's imagination or are used fictitiously. Any
resemblance to actual persons, living or dead, events, or locales is
entirely coincidental.

Copyright © 2001 by Robert Mayer.
Cover art by Chris Moore.
Cover design by Fiorillo Design.

Dell® and its colophon are a registered trademark of
Random House, Inc.

ISBN: 0-440-23495-6

Printed in the United States of America

Published simultaneously in Canada

February 2001

10 9 8 7 6 5 4 3 2 1
OPM

AREA 51: THE GRAIL

PROLOGUE: The Past

AVALON, ENGLAND
528 AD

Thick clouds were gathering over the island, lightning flickering, followed by thunder seconds later, as if the gods were displaying their displeasure over the scene below. A large plain in western England stretched as far as could be seen in all directions. In the center was a shallow lake out of which jutted a long, steep island like an earthen rampart, a magnificent Tor, over five hundred feet high. At the very top, a stone abbey with one tall tower dominated the land and water all about. Next to the abbey, a dozen men in armor were gathered round their leader who lay next to the tower's east wall.

The king the knights called Arthur was dying, of that there was no doubt among the few surviving men. The wounds were too deep, the loss of blood too great. Despite the king's weakened state, his right hand still firmly held the pommel of his sword Excalibur. A coating of blood failed to hide the bright sheen of the blade's finely worked metal and the mystical runes carved on the surface.

Arthur lay on his back, his armor dented and battered. His bright blue eyes looked up toward the dark heavens. He was a large man, a fiercesome warrior, over six and a half feet tall and solidly built. Red hair streaked with gray topped his head. Despite spending most of his life in the field at war, his skin was fair and pale.

Several of the knights were looking to the east, in the direction of Camlann, where they had come from. The day had started with some hope of peace in the civil war splitting Britain. Arthur's forces and those of Mordred had been drawn up on opposing sides of the plain at Camlann. Under a flag of truce the two leaders had met in the high grass in the middle of the field, out of earshot of their followers. What transpired between the two held the fate of all the other men who waited, sweaty hands on the pommels of their swords and the hafts of their spears.

It appeared to end well as the king and Mordred shook hands. As Arthur turned to return to his troops Mordred struck a dastardly blow with a hidden dagger, wounding the king. Arthur spun about, pulling Excalibur out of its sheath. He slashed down, striking Mordred on the shoulder, cleaving through the armor. The wounded men staggered back as both armies thundered forward into the fray.

Arthur's knights drew him back from the front lines, as did Mordred's. Again and again, the armies charged until the field was strewn with the dead and dying.

Few on either side were still alive when they left. War-hardened though they were, none of the knights had ever seen such a blood lust descend on both sides in a battle, not even when they had fought the crazed Scotsmen of the north—and this battle had been between Englishmen, knights who had sworn an oath to a code of conduct. But today no quarter had been given, wounded slain where they lay, unarmored auxiliaries hacked to pieces, suited knights dragged from their horses and pounded to death, blades slammed through visors or under the armpit where they could get through the armor.

At least Arthur had struck Mordred a grievous blow

with Excalibur before going down; they had all seen that. They could only hope the boy-bastard was dying or already dead.

None on the Tor knew who had won or if the battle was even over yet. Shortly after the king had been seriously wounded, his inner circle of bodyguards, known as the core of the Round Table, had placed Arthur on a pallet and dragged him away while the battle still raged. No courier had come with word of victory or defeat.

They felt the dark, rolling clouds overhead threatening a vicious storm to be a portent even though Merlin was not there to read the signs. Where the sorcerer had gone in the days before the battle was a mystery, and there were many who now cursed his name. Regardless, they knew the Age of Camelot was done and the darkness of barbarism and ignorance would descend once more on England.

The knights turned in surprise as the thick wooden door in the side of the abbey creaked opened. They had pounded on the door without success when they'd first arrived by boat thirty minutes ago. They'd brought Arthur here because of the legend—that on the isle of Avalon dwelt the Fisher-King and his chosen knights; men who were immortal and who could bestow the healing gift on those they deemed worthy. And would not King Arthur, of all who walked the Earth, be worthy?

But on arrival they had found an apparently deserted island, with the tower locked tight.

In the now open doorway stood a man framed by light from behind. Robed in black, the man's hands were empty of weapons, his face etched with age, his hair silver. He was breathing hard, as if he had come a long way. Despite his non-threatening appearance, the knights stepped aside as he gestured for them to part, allowing him access to the king—all except the knight closest to Arthur.

"Are you the Fisher-King?" Percival asked as the man came close. He was always the boldest in strange situations or when the king was threatened. Percival's armor was battered and blood seeped out from under his left arm where a dagger had struck just before Arthur sustained his final wound. Percival's right hand gripped his sword, ready to defend Arthur, to amend for not taking the blow that had downed the king. He was a stout man, not tall but broad of shoulders, with dark hair plastered to his head with sweat. A thin red line ran along one cheek where a blade had struck a glancing blow.

The stranger paused. "No, I am not a king."

"Are you a monk?" Percival persisted, leery of allowing a stranger next to the king.

"You may call me that."

Percival looked over the man's cloak, noting the trim on the ends of the sleeves, the chain around his neck. "You dress like Merlin. Are you one of the priests of the old religion, the tree worshippers? A sorcerer of the dark arts?"

The man paused. "My line has been here on Yniswitrin, what you call Avalon, since the dawn of time. But we worship no gods and practice no sorcery."

"You're a Druid?" Percival persisted. "It is said the Druids have been on this island forever. That they sing the eternal song here, but we found no one when we arrived."

"There is no time for questions." The man knelt down, placing his wrinkled hands over the king's bloodstained ones.

"Can you heal him?" Percival was now the only one close; the others stood near the edge of the Tor, attention split between what was happening to their king and the water to the east, from which news of victory or the promise of death in defeat would come. They had no doubt that if Mordred's side won, there would be no mercy.

"The healers—such as they are—will arrive shortly, I believe," the monk said.

"What healers?" Percival demanded.

"There are things beyond you. You waste precious time. Let me speak to the king in private for a moment—to give him absolution in a way only he will understand."

"You said you worshipped no god," Percival argued.

"You brought him here, now let me do what is necessary," the monk snapped. He raised a hand toward Percival and struggled to control his voice. "I mean him no harm."

Arthur spoke for the first time. "Leave us, Percival. There is nothing to fear from this man."

Reluctantly, Percival joined the other knights.

The monk leaned close so that only Arthur could hear his words. "Give me the key."

Arthur's eyes turned to the man. They showed none of his pain. "I have heard of you. You are Brynn, are you not?"

The monk nodded.

Arthur continued. "You are the Watcher of this island. It was one of your people who started all this. Merlin."

Brynn shook his head. "We called him Myrddin. He is a traitor to the oath he swore. He is not of my people any longer. You, of all people, should know well how there can be traitors among a close-knit group. My group has been scattered for many, many years."

"What do you want?" Arthur asked.

"The key. I will keep it safe."

"My people will keep the key safe," Arthur replied, his eyes shifting up to the dark clouds. "Merlin gave it to me to offset the Grail. It was never intended to be used, and it hasn't been. You don't even know what it really does."

"Merlin should never have unearthed the key or the Grail," Brynn said. "He is one of those that upset the balance in the first place."

"I tried to do good," Arthur said. "To rectify what was done. To restore the balance."

There was a commotion among the knights watching the water, cries of alarm that Brynn and Arthur could hear.

"And what if the others get here first?" Brynn hissed. "A ship bearing Mordred's insignia has just been sighted offshore approaching quickly. Would you give *them* Excalibur and what it controls? I promise to keep the key safe inside the Tor. They will never find it. And when your people come at the anointed time, I will give it to them. Remember—we only watch, we do not choose sides."

"No?"

Brynn placed his hand on Arthur's forehead. "You will be dead soon."

"I will not give it to you."

Brynn's hand slid down and with two fingers he snatched at Arthur's left eye before the king could react. Between his fingers dangled a small sliver of blue; a contact lens, incongruous with the armor and other accoutrements. Arthur blinked and his eyes opened wide, revealing a red pupil within a red iris. The pupil was a shade darker than the iris and elongated vertically like a cat's.

Brynn cocked his head, indicating the knights. "I will show them what you really are. You cannot allow that. What good you *have* done, what you are so proud of, would be washed away with that truth. You will be remembered as a monster, not a king. Not as the leader of the Round Table, which you worked so hard to establish."

Arthur closed his eyes, pain finally beginning to show on his face. "What about the Grail?"

"Mordred's men had it briefly, but they did not know what it was or have time to take it to him. He too lies dying. One of my order was in their camp and recovered the Grail. He will take it far from here. We will return everything to the way it was."

"Do not lie to me."

"I swear on my ring—" Brynn held a metal ring in front of the king's face, a ring with a human eye, etched on the surface "—and on my order and on my son, the next Brynn, the next Watcher of Yniswitrin, that I speak the truth."

One of the knights cried out from the Tor's tower, warning that the ship bearing Mordred's colors was about to land.

Arthur's voice was low, as if he were speaking to himself. "That is all I sought by coming to England. To reinstate order, and maybe help your people a little."

"Then let me finish it," Brynn argued. "Let me restore the truce, Artad's Shadow."

The king started at the mention of his true identity. "You must keep that secret. I have worked very hard for a very long time to keep that secret from men."

"I will if you give me the key. There is not much time. I must get back inside the Tor to keep Mordred's men from getting the key."

Arthur's hand released its grip. "Take it."

Brynn placed Excalibur under his robe, tight against his body. As he prepared to stand, Arthur grabbed his arm. "Keep your word, Watcher. You know I will be back."

Brynn nodded. "I know that. It is written that your war will come again, not like this, but covering the entire planet. And when that happens, I know you will return."

A weary smile crossed Arthur's lips. "It is a war beyond the planet, Watcher. Beyond the planet in ways you could not conceive of. Your people still know so little. Even on Atlantis your ancestors knew nothing of reality, of the universe. Merlin was foolish to try to take the Grail. Its time has not come yet."

"We know enough," Brynn said. He stood and quickly walked through the doorway. It swung shut behind him with a solid thud.

Percival approached the king. "Sire, the enemy approaches. We must move you."

Arthur shook his head, his eyes closed tightly. "No. I will stay here. All of you go. Spread the story of what we tried to do. Tell of the good, of the code of honor. Leave me here. I will be gone shortly."

The protests were immediate, Percival foremost among them. "Sire, we will fight Mordred's traitors to the death. Our lives for yours."

"No. It is my last command. You will obey it as you have obeyed all my other commands."

Only then did Percival notice the sword was gone. "Excalibur! Where is it?"

"The monk has it." Arthur's voice was very low now. "He will keep it safe until it is needed again. I will return. I promise you that. Go now! Escape while you can and tell the world of the good deeds we did."

One by one, the surviving knights bid their king farewell and slipped into the storm, disappearing over the western side of the hill until only Percival remained. He came to the king, kneeling next to him. "Sire."

Arthur didn't open his eyes. "Percival, you must leave also. You have been my most faithful knight, but I release you from your service."

"I swore an oath," Percival said, "never to abandon you. I will not now, my Lord."

"You must. It will do you no good to stay. You cannot be here when they come for me."

"I will fight Mordred's men."

"I do not speak of those slaves who blindly obey with no free will."

Percival frowned. "Who comes for you, then?"

Arthur reached up and grabbed his knight's arm. "There is something you can do, Percival. Something I want you to do. A quest."

Percival placed his hand over the blood-spattered one of his king. "Yes, Lord?"

"Search for the Grail."

"The Grail is but a legend—" Percival began, but Arthur cut him off.

"The Grail is real. It is—" the king seemed to be searching for the right words. "It is the source of all knowledge. To one who knows its secret, it brings immortality. It is beyond anything you have experienced, what any man has experienced."

A glimmer of hope came alive in the despair that had shadowed Percival's eyes since removing Arthur from the field of battle. "Where is this Grail, my Lord? Where should I search?"

"That you must discover on your own. It is spoken of in many lands and has traveled far—here and there— over the years. But trust me, it does exist. It will be well guarded. And if you find it—" Arthur paused.

"Yes, my Lord?"

"If you find it, you must not touch it. You must guard it as you have guarded me. Will you do that for me?"

"I do not want to abandon you, my Lord."

"You will not be abandoning me. I go to a better place. Do as I have ordered."

Slowly and reluctantly, Percival stood, bent over, his hand still in the king's. "I will begin the quest you have commanded me to pursue."

Arthur tightened his grip. "My knight, there is something you must remember in your quest."

"Yes, Lord?"

"You can trust no one. Deception has always swirled about the Grail. Be careful." He released Percival. "Go now! I order you to go!"

Percival leaned farther over and lightly kissed his king's forehead, then stood and departed.

Arthur was alone on the top of the Tor. Only then did he open his eyes once more. He could hear yells from the eastern slope—Mordred's mercenaries and mental slaves climbed the steep hillside, but his eyes remained focused at the sky above, waiting.

A metallic, golden orb three feet in diameter darted out of the clouds and came to an abrupt halt, hovering ten feet above Arthur. It stayed there for a few seconds, then without a sound, sped to the east. There were flashes of light in that direction, screams of surprise and terror, then silence from the rebel warriors. Arthur was now the only one alive on the Tor.

The orb came back and hovered directly overhead. Arthur looked past it, waiting, holding on to life. Finally, a silver disk, thirty feet wide, flat on the bottom, the upper side sloping to a rounded top, floated silently out of the clouds.

The disk touched down on the Tor's summit next to the abbey. A hatch on the top opened and two tall figures climbed out. They made their way down the sloping side. The shape inside their one-piece white suits indicated they were female, yet their eyes were not human, but the same red Brynn had revealed in Arthur's.

They walked to where the king lay, one standing on either side. They pulled back their hoods, revealing fiery red hair cut tight against their skulls. Their skin was pale, ice-white, unblemished.

"Where is the key?" one asked in a low-pitched voice.

"A Watcher took it," Arthur said. "I gave it to him. We must hide it to restore the truce."

"Are you sure, Artad's Shadow?" one of the women asked. "We can search for it. The Watchers cannot be trusted. Merlin was one of their order."

"I am sure," Arthur cut her off. "It is the way I want it to be. Merlin, no matter what evil he stirred up, was trying to do a good thing. Have you heard of the Grail's fate?"

"Mordred's mercenaries had it, but they didn't know what it was. A Watcher in the area took it. We can take the Grail from him."

"No."

The two creatures exchanged glances.

"The truce must be restored," Arthur continued. "It is not time yet." Arthur slumped back, satisfied that at least that part of what Brynn had told him was true. He knew he could not tell them of the quest he had given Percival. It was the only thing he could think of to get his favorite knight off the Tor. If Percival had been here when the others arrived, he would have suffered the same fate as Mordred's men. Arthur knew his knight

would never track down the Grail, but it gave the man a
purpose and he had found that such a quest worked well
with men like that.

"And Aspasia's Shadow?" Arthur asked.

"Mordred too dies in this life, but Guides are there to
pass Aspasia's spirit on."

A spasm of pain passed through Arthur's body.
"Let's be done with it then. I am very tired. Remember,
I am only a shadow also."

The two women looked at each other once more, red
eyes meeting, then the first nodded and spoke. "The
spirit of Artad must move on."

"The spirit of Artad must pass on," the second said.

Arthur nodded. "My spirit must pass on."

The second woman knelt beside him, a short black
blade in her hand. It easily sliced through the dented armor on Arthur's chest with one smooth stroke, revealing
a padded shirt underneath. With a deft flick of the knife,
the cloth parted, revealing his chest. Lying on the flesh
was a gold medallion shaped like two arms extended
upward in worship with no body. She cut through the
thin chain holding the medallion and held it up for the
other woman—and Arthur—to see.

"We take your spirit, the spirit of Artad," she said to
Arthur.

The king nodded weakly. "The spirit of Artad
passes." His head bowed down on his chest, his lips
moved, but no sound emerged.

"Are you ready to finish the shell that sustained this
life?" she asked.

Arthur closed his eyes. "I am ready."

"Is there anything since the last time you merged
with the *ka* that you need to tell us?"

Arthur shook his head, knowing that remaining silent
when his spirit passed on would leave no memory of

Percival's quest, which would guard the knight for the rest of his life. It was his last thought.

The black blade slammed down into his exposed chest, piercing his heart. The body spasmed once, then was still. The woman stood and placed the blade back in its sheath.

The first woman extended a gloved hand, fist clenched, over the body. The fingers moved, as if crushing something held in it. She spread her fingers and small black droplets the size of grains of sand fell onto the king, hitting flesh, armor, and cloth. Where it fell on the latter two, they moved swiftly across the surface until they reached flesh. Where they touched skin, they consumed, boring through and devouring flesh, bone, muscle, everything organic. Within ten seconds nothing was left of the king but his armor and clothes.

With the ceremony complete, the two women swiftly retraced their steps to the craft they had arrived on. It lifted and swiftly accelerated away, disappearing into the storm clouds.

The heavens finally let loose with rain, announcing its arrival with a cacophonous barrage of thunder, lightning playing across the top of the Tor. A large bolt struck the high tower of the Abbey, shattering stone and mortar, spraying debris over the remains of the king.

CHAPTER 1: The Present

THE GIZA PLATEAU, EGYPT

Deep under the Giza Plateau, Lisa Duncan placed her hands on the lid of the Ark of the Covenant. A surge ran through her body, a feeling of power. A red glow suffused both of the cherubim-sphinxes on either end of the Ark and extended over the lid, encompassing her.

She could no longer hear those outside the veil that surrounded the Ark. Her world was the Ark: the gold under her fingers. She grabbed the edge of the lid. She felt suspended in time, beyond the reach of everything she had ever known. She lifted the cover. A golden glow blazed out, overpowering the red as the lid went up. It locked in place, revealing the chamber inside.

Of the seven wonders of the ancient world, only one remains in the modern world. Located on the Giza Plateau, southwest of Cairo, stand the three large pyramids of the Pharaohs Khufu, Khafre, and Menkaure; they are symbolically guarded by the Great Sphinx, whose stone visage peers to the east, into the rising sun and over the Nile River, the lifeline of Egypt through time immemorial.

All four structures have been weathered and battered by time: the hand-smoothed limestone facing of the three great pyramids had long ago been looted for building materials, diminishing some of their majesty, but until the building of the Eiffel Tower, they had held reign for millennia as the tallest man-made objects on the planet.

As one comes upon them from the Nile Road, the middle pyramid of Khafre appears to be the largest, but only because it was built on higher ground on the Giza Plateau. The Pharaoh Khufu, more popularly known as Cheops, was historically credited with building the greatest pyramid, farthest to the northeast. Over four hundred and eighty feet tall and covering eighty acres, it is still the largest stone building in the world. The smallest of the three is that of Menkaure, measuring over two hundred feet in altitude.

The sides of all three are perfectly aligned with the four cardinal directions from northeast to southwest, largest to smallest. The Great Sphinx lies at the foot of the middle pyramid—far enough to the east to also be out in front of the Great Pyramid, behind the Sphinx's left shoulder.

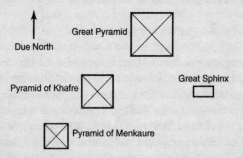

As long as men have stood on the plateau, dwarfed by the immense structures, they have been one of the greatest mysteries of the ages. Egyptologists had come up with dates and origins for the three pyramids and the Sphinx, but the data, upon close examination, was woe-

fully incomplete. Not a single mummy was found in
any of the pyramids, casting doubt on the age-old theory they were large mausoleums. Up until recently,
every chamber discovered was empty. Even more puz-
zling was the distinct lack of any documentation concerning the architectural development of the pyramids
or Sphinx. Not even among the numerous stone and pa-
pyrus documents from the various Egyptian dynasties.

The recent revelation that aliens—the Airlia—had
visited Earth in the distant past, and never left, had
thrown the accepted version of human history into dis-
array, including the reason why the pyramids and
Sphinx were built. Peter Nabinger, one of the original
members of the team that had penetrated the secret of
Area 51, had come up with his own explanation of the
pyramids' purpose before his death in China: when
sheathed in the original smooth limestone their radar
signature had been immense, able to be picked up far
out into space. Thus, he reasoned, they were a beacon,
designed to bring a spaceship close. That was stage one,
the attention-getter. Then Nabinger had found stage
two, the accompanying message written on the face of
the Earth in the form of the Great Wall of China itself,
spelling out the Airlia High Rune word for HELP.

Unfortunately, Nabinger had not lived long enough
to unravel the riddle of the Sphinx. With the aid of another archaeologist, Professor Joseph Mualama from
the University of Tanzania, Lisa Duncan had discovered
that the Sphinx was a surface marker for what lay
buried deep beneath, where she had just opened the lid
of the Ark of the Covenant.

Almost a half-mile directly below the Great Sphinx
was a cavern, just short of a half-mile in diameter with
curved walls. Light came from a bright orb on the ceiling, a mini-sun that had burned for millennia ever since

the object that rested in the center of the floor was first hidden.

Here lay a replica of the Great Sphinx. Its skin, however, was not made of stone, but a flawless black metal that absorbed the light. The head was larger, the nose not shot off like its cousin on the surface. The eyes of the Black Sphinx were blood red with elongated red irises that glowed from some inner power.

The Sphinx's paws extended almost sixty feet in front of the head, which rose seventy feet above the floor of the cavern. The body stretched one hundred and eighty feet back, making the entire object almost three hundred feet long. Between the paws, just under the chin, stood a statue over nine feet tall, shaped like a man, but with subtle differences—the body was too short proportionally, the limbs too long. The largest difference was the head, with polished white skin, ears with long lobes that ended just above the shoulders, and two gleaming red eyes set in the long narrow face. The stone that covered the top of the head—imitating hair—was also red.

In front of the statue was a group of soldiers armed with the latest weapons awaiting further orders. In the corridor that led from below the statue to the chamber inside of the Black Sphinx stood their leader, known to Middle Eastern intelligence agencies as the terrorist Al-Iblis. What he sought, Lisa Duncan had in her hands.

Two bodies lay on the floor near him. Both had borne the name Kaji, father and son. Both had been Watchers, entrusted with the secret the Black Sphinx held. Facing Al-Iblis stood Professor Joseph Mualama, the archaeologist who had picked up the torch passed on by Nabinger, trying to make sense of the ancient mysteries and legends. It was from his searching on the path of the famous explorer Sir Richard Francis Burton, that he had been able to lead Duncan to the Great Sphinx. From there the elder Kaji had led them to the Black Sphinx before being killed along with his son by Al-Iblis, ending the line of their family that had watched the Giza Plateau for millennia.

Al-Iblis turned as one of his men ran up to him rattling off something in Arabic about incoming helicopters. Barking commands, Al-Iblis led his soldiers toward the tunnel leading to the surface, dragging Mualama along with them.

Lisa Duncan's face reflected the glow coming from inside the Ark. Resting on a cradle of black metal lay a golden hourglass figure, eighteen inches high by eight wide at each end. The middle was an inch wide. It was a thing told of in tales and legend:

The Grail.

Immediately Duncan saw where the legend that the Grail was a cup came from, but beyond its form, both ends appeared to be solid. She reached in, surprised at how steady her hands were, and picked it up. The Grail was heavy, as if solid.

She sat down cross-legged on the floor next to the Ark, and placed the Grail in front of her. She simply stared at it for several minutes. She could see why so many legends had grown up around the object. The surface was translucent, emitting a slight golden glow. It seemed to be made of the same material as the guardian computer. There was a strong sense of power emanating from it.

She held her hand out, six inches over the flat top. Her skin tingled. She lowered her hand until it touched the metal and held it there for several seconds. She jerked it back as if scalded as the surface shimmered brightly for a second. The top irised, revealing a six-inch-wide opening. Cautiously, Duncan leaned forward and peered down into it.

Four inches into the Grail was a small, perfectly round depression, about an inch and a half in diameter. Duncan frowned, then, very slowly, she dipped the fore-finger of her right hand into the opening. The tingling sensation grew stronger as she touched the depression, but nothing else happened.

She pulled her finger out of the Grail. After ten seconds, the opening closed. Duncan thought for a while, then turned the Grail over. She touched the flat side that was now up and wasn't surprised when it also irised open, revealing another small depression, identical to the first one.

Something went in those depressions. But what? Without conscious thought, her hands strayed to the two empty pockets on the *essen* she wore. Where the *urim* and *thummin* stones were supposed to be. The pockets were only about two inches wide and three inches deep, just big enough for stones an inch and a half in diameter.

Lost in the Grail, what she didn't see right away were the fine black wires clipped into the lid of the Ark that ended in what appeared to be tiny carved rose petals.

AIRSPACE, MEDITERRANEAN SEA

Mike Turcotte slapped the back of the magazine of 9mm bullets against his kneecap, relishing the jolt of pain and the sound of the rounds settling tight against the metal casing. He did it once more, even harder.

He slid the magazine into the well of the MP-5 sub-

machine gun and let the bolt slide forward, chambering
a round. He felt emotionally detached from the members of the Special Forces A-Team gathered around
him, from the Russian agent Yakov, to the Chinese archaeologist Che Lu, to every person inside the alien-
made bouncer speeding through the air toward Egypt.

Weapon ready, he let it hang from his shoulder on the
sling. Then he paused, taking a deep breath. Turcotte
stretched his right hand out in front, opening the palm,
stretching the scar tissue.

"Pain is too emotional," Yakov said.

Turcotte was startled. "What?"

Yakov shook his head and didn't repeat the statement, and another voice filled the void.

"Sir, the Egyptians are refusing permission to enter
their airspace." Captain Billam had been monitoring the
radio since they departed Mongolia.

"Screw them," Turcotte said as he clenched his hand
into a fist. "Any word from Area 51 on Duncan's exact
location?"

"Negative," Billam replied. "Last word was the Giza
Plateau. Nothing since. But we do have an intelligence
report that the entire plateau has been sealed off by the
Egyptian military."

Yakov placed a large hand on Turcotte's shoulder.
"My friend, I do not think this is a time we should—
how do you say?—'Shoot first and ask questions later.'
We do not know exactly where your Doctor Duncan is.
We may be able to get this craft to Giza, but what then?
Once we go outside, we will be fair game."

Yakov was a giant of a man, almost seven feet tall
with a thick bushy beard hiding his lower face. He had
been a member of Russia's Area 51 team called Section
IV, and now that the aliens had destroyed his home
base, he had joined Turcotte and Duncan's small group,

searching for the truth about the aliens and their follow-ers, trying to foil their plans.

Yakov leaned closer. "Also, you have a wounded man on board. It would be best if we got him to a hospi-tal, yes?"

Turcotte could feel the gaze of every man—and the wizened, dark eyes of Che Lu—in the bouncer on him. He refused to look at them, instead staring down be-tween his feet through the floor of the bouncer at the blue water of the Mediterranean flashing by below them. Human scientists had yet to figure out the Airlia technology that allowed someone inside to see out, yet kept the outside opaque to observers. Turcotte knew it was one of many things humans didn't understand about the Airlia. He felt as if he and his fellow men and women were children who had stumbled upon a grown-up's cache of technology. They had discovered many things over the years; some could be used but their true purpose never understood. More unsettling to Turcotte was what they hadn't found yet—or even more disturb-ing—the other uses for things they had but didn't know about yet.

Ever since uncovering the secrets of Area 51—the alien mothership and atmospheric craft, called bounc-ers, hidden there—Turcotte felt like he and the others in his small group had constantly been reacting, never ahead of the various forces at play in the civil war among the Airlia and their semi-human minions.

On one side were the Airlia led by Aspasia, whom Turcotte had killed when he destroyed their fleet com-ing from Mars trying to claim the mothership. The death of their leader didn't seem to have slowed their forces, though. Their human servants were Guides, men and women whose minds had been altered to obey by direct contact with a guardian computer. The Guides' headquarters was a place called The Mission, its present location unknown.

The Guides and their followers were being drawn to Easter Island where a guardian computer that shielded the island was using nanotechnology—machines crafted at the atomic level—to convert both humans and machines to Aspasia's cause.

On the other side were the Airlia led by Artad. Turcotte strongly suspected that Artad lay in suspended sleep underneath the great Chinese tomb of Qian-Ling, and he had just handed over the "key" to the lowest level of that ancient tomb to one of Artad's followers, a human/Airlia clone named Elek. This group was known as The Ones Who Wait. Turcotte had a feeling they weren't going to be waiting much longer.

The leader of the The Ones Who Wait, Lexina, and some of her people were heading to China to unlock the lowest level and uncover whatever—or whoever—was hidden there.

And both sides, as they had clearly shown in the past several months, cared little how many humans were killed in the pursuit of their goals. So far Turcotte and his partners had uncovered evidence that both sides had greatly affected human history with such things as initiating the Black Death in the Middle Ages and manipulating forces of the SS during World War II. It kept Turcotte awake at night wondering how much more of the history he had been taught in school had been manipulated behind the scenes by the aliens and their creatures.

Every walk of life seemed to be infiltrated by one or the other of these alien groups, making it nearly impossible to trust anyone. Already there had been numerous instances of betrayal and even assassination. He trusted only Lisa Duncan, and now he was being told to abandon her.

His eyes finally rested on Master Sergeant Boltz, who had been wounded during the rescue operation in Moscow. The team medics were working on him, but it was obvious he had lost a lot of blood.

Turcotte's thoughts were interrupted by Captain Billam, the A-Team leader. "We'll go in, sir. Whatever you say."

Turcotte felt a wave of gratitude for the captain's support.

"We're crossing into Egyptian airspace," the bouncer pilot called out. "We've got multiple bogeys on radar closing on our position. Egyptian jets. We can outrun them easily enough, but if we land . . ."

Turcotte turned to Che Lu, eyebrows raised, deferring to age to help him make his decision.

"Giza is a large place," the old Chinese woman said. "I have been there several times to study the mysteries. There are secrets there yet to be uncovered. Such a thing takes time."

In Ranger School, Turcotte had been taught one thing above all else—any action, even the wrong one, was better than doing nothing.

"Lock and load," Turcotte ordered.

As the special forces men checked their weapons, Yakov shook his head and removed his long, heavy coat, sure he wouldn't need it on the Giza Plateau. He eased next to Turcotte and lowered his voice. "This is not a good idea, my friend."

"If we wait, we may not have another chance," Turcotte said. He turned away. "I want to do a low-level fly-by," Turcotte told the pilot. "I'll show you where to put us down."

Everyone started as an Egyptian jet flashed by less than fifty feet away.

"Hold on," the pilot advised as he accelerated and dove at the same time. The bouncer was now just above the desert floor, startling an occasional group of villagers as it raced overhead approaching Cairo.

The pilot gained a little altitude as they hit the city limits, but he was still so low that everyone cringed as he shot the craft between two high-rise buildings, then was above the Nile, scraping by just above the boats.

They could see the top of the Great Pyramid now, off to the right. Then the other two pyramids. Everyone stumbled as the bouncer abruptly slowed. Turcotte knelt, looking through the floor as they went over the Giza Plateau. He saw the ring of troops and armored vehicles surrounding the plateau, the troops a good distance from both the pyramids and Sphinx. Then he spotted a cluster of people between the legs of the Sphinx, a tall black figure among them.

"There." Turcotte had one hand on the pilot's shoulder, the other pointing at the Sphinx. "Put us on top of the head. Have your rappel slings ready."

He jumped to his feet, grabbed the ladder that led to the top hatch, and climbed up.

"We have helicopters inbound," the co-pilot announced.

Turcotte threw the hatch open and climbed out, clinging to the lip of the hatch as the bouncer arrived at the massive head of the Sphinx, edge touching the top. Turcotte slid down the smooth skin of the alien craft and landed on the ancient stone. He unslung his MP-5 and edged out to where he could see down.

He could see Mualama in the center of a group of armed men in unmarked desert camouflage. A figure in a black robe was next to the archaeologist, looking up. No sign of Duncan. Turcotte grabbed a sling rope and looped it around a snap link on his harness. Then he tucked the steel butt of the submachine gun into his shoulder as the rest of the A-Team deployed on the top of the Sphinx.

"Choppers are less than a minute out," the co-pilot informed him through the FM-radio. "From the north."

The men below had their weapons trained up, while Turcotte and his had theirs pointing down.

"An international incident," Al-Iblis called out. "Americans invading Egypt. Excellent. I couldn't have planned it better myself."

"Where's Duncan?" Turcotte demanded.

"I suggest you surrender your weapons." Al-Iblis ignored his question.

"Helicopters thirty seconds out," the co-pilot announced. "Egyptian gunships."

Turcotte lowered his voice so only the members of his team could hear. "Flash-bangs on three, then board the bouncer."

"You do not have much time," Al-Iblis said. "I control the forces here."

"One," Turcotte said. He stood, letting the submachine gun dangle on its harness, both hands held up as if surrendering.

"Two." He could hear the inbound helicopters and knew he was probably in the sights of a mini-gun.

"Three."

Six black canisters were tossed, arcing down from the head toward the men below.

Al-Iblis's eyes widened in surprise—surely they wouldn't kill Mualama with grenades!

The flash-bangs went off. One was enough to deafen

and blind anyone within twenty feet. Six, in the enclosed space between the Sphinx's paws, was devastating.

Turcotte jumped off the head of the Sphinx, letting the line slide through the snap-link, rappelling down. The members of the A-Team were clambering up the side of the bouncer toward the hatch when the first gun ship made its run spraying bullets at the rate of three thousand rounds a minute. Two SF men were hit, torn to shreds, bodies tumbling past Turcotte as he went down. He saw them fall but kept his concentration on what he was doing as he flexed his legs and sprang out, pushing his right hand out to release the rope brake on the snap link.

He hit the sand between the paws, all the men around him blinded, hands over their eyes, blood coming out of ears deafened by the detonations. He ran to Mualama and wrapped his arms around the equally stunned archaeologist.

"Go!" Turcotte ordered into the boom mike.

The bouncer lifted, half the survivors of the team inside, the others clinging to the side. Turcotte dangled below, his arms gripping Mualama tightly.

A second gun ship fired a quick burst before the bouncer was out of range and another green beret was hit, his body caught in the cargo netting that lined the bottom edge.

CHAPTER 2

NGORONGORO CRATER, TANZANIA, AFRICA

The lion had been in one place for two hours watching the grazing herd of gazelle slowly make its way through the high grass. The big cat was old, several steps slower in just the past year, and because of that, it was hungrier and more patient that it had ever been. Just two years ago, the lion would have sprung from its hide and chased down a tender youngster, culling it from the herd.

Now it watched with narrowed eyes as one of the herd wandered away from the main group. An old grandfather—the flesh would be stringy, the lion knew, but it would be meat. Over a week had passed since the last kill and there was little interest in being finicky.

Muscles tensed, claws grabbed into dirt just a little deeper as the lion prepared to spring. Another five feet and he would be assured of a kill. Suddenly the herd froze and all heads turned, not toward the lion's hide, but to the sky near the rim of the crater, behind the lion.

Then they began galloping away. The lion slowly uncoiled from its spring position, its meal rapidly disappearing toward Soda Lake in the center of Ngorongoro Crater. The large shaggy head twisted and peered up, searching for what had startled the herd. Yellow eyes blinked, making no sense of the strange flying creature that had just cleared the edge of the crater.

It was far larger than any bird the lion had ever seen, over ten meters long, and slightly less than half that wide. A long, arced neck stretched up from the body to a serpent's face with large jaws filled with black teeth. The eyes were dark red. Two short wings extended from each side, but they were stationary, not flapping like a bird's.

The lion forgot about hunger and pride as it bolted after the gazelle in a desperate attempt to get away from the dragon.

Inside the flying machine unearthed from the Airlia cache in the upper levels of the Qian-Ling tomb in China, the human-Airlia clone, Elek, had his hands on the controls, slowing forward speed and bringing the craft to a hover.

Below the dragon, stretching twelve miles from rim to rim, Ngorongoro Crater was a throwback to a time before man made his presence known in the wild. Teeming with animals, it was isolated from the land around by the two-thousand-foot-high crater rim that surrounded the over one hundred square miles inside. The rim of the crater was over a mile above sea level. The center of the crater was covered in water, Soda Lake.

There was a flash of light to the right and Elek pivoted the dragon, known as Chi Yu in Chinese legend. The display screens in the cockpit located just behind the chest of the machine registered a second flash and Elek moved toward the light.

"Do you see me?" The voice over the radio was sexless, easily belonging to a man or woman.

"I see you, Lexina," Elek confirmed as he brought Chi Yu to a landing near the source of the light.

Three figures waited. In the center was Lexina, the head of The Ones Who Wait. For decades she had tried to maintain Artad's side of the truce, first from the secret base in Antarctica and now from the remains of an Airlia base underneath the crater. Now there was no more truce for Lexina to try to maintain—recent events had seen to that.

It was time for action.

The back ramp, underneath the dragon's tail, dropped down. Lexina, followed by her companions, walked on board.

"The spirits have passed on." Elek nodded to the other two—the recently cloned and reborn bodies of Gergor and Coridan, two members of The Ones Who Wait. The previous Gergor and Coridan had received a fatal dose of radiation in the process of destroying the Russian Area 51 on Novaya Zemlya Island.

"The spirits have passed on," Lexina echoed as she took a seat to the side of his. "Now let us make sure that Artad's true spirit has not passed on." She extended a long, thin hand. "Back to China."

THE GREAT SAND SEA, WESTERN EGYPT

Turcotte's arms were ready to give out as the bouncer finally slowed and descended toward the desert floor. As soon as his feet hit the soft sand, he let go of Mualama, who promptly collapsed onto his back, eyelids rapidly blinking over unseeing eyes.

"You'll get your sight back when the effect of the flash-bangs wears off," Turcotte told him as the bouncer settled down next to them. He could see the body hanging in the cargo netting, a stream of blood down the smooth side of the bouncer.

"Where are we?" Mualama sat up.

"In the desert," Turcotte said. "Where's Duncan?"

"In the Black Sphinx, underneath the stone one. She's with the Ark. She is safe for the time being inside—Al-Iblis cannot get to her there."

The hatch swung open and Yakov appeared, followed by Captain Billam. They went to the body, untangling it from the webbing.

Turcotte got to his feet and took Mualama's arm, helping him up. "We need to get on board." He could sense Yakov's eyes upon him, but he avoided meeting the Russian's gaze as he guided Mualama up the side of the bouncer and inside.

"I lost three men at the Sphinx and we left two bodies behind," Captain Billam informed Turcotte.

"I saw," Turcotte said.

"Where to, sir?" the pilot of the bouncer asked.

"Duncan is underneath the Sphinx." Turcotte was checking the function on his MP-5. "If—"

"We cannot go back there," Yakov said flatly.

"They're disorganized now," Turcotte said.

"No, there's more of them now," Yakov disagreed.

"We can't abandon her."

"We can't get to her," Yakov said.

"She is safe for now," Mualama interjected. "She is with the Ark, and it does not allow anyone not wearing the proper attire close to it."

Turcotte had no idea what Mualama was babbling about.

"We need to go back to Area 51," Yakov said.

Turcotte glanced at Captain Billam. His team had lost almost half its strength.

"I don't see what we can do," Billam said. "We don't have a plan. We don't know exactly where this place is that Doctor Duncan's being held."

"Sergeant Boltz has lost a lot of blood," the team medic informed him from where he was working on the NCO wounded in the assault at the Kremlin.

Reluctantly, Turcotte removed the magazine, pulled

the bolt back to eject the chambered round, and put the
MP-5 down. "Head for Area 51."

THE GIZA PLATEAU, EGYPT

Duncan heard a noise, the slightest of movements. Her
senses were running on super-alert, every input magni-
fied. She reluctantly put the Grail back in the Ark's cradle and turned. The four sphinx heads mounted on the
poles that held up the white veil surrounding the Ark
had all turned toward the chamber's entrance. Their
ruby eyes were glittering, as if they were alive.

Duncan was a slight woman, her slender body
weighted down with the garments she had on. She wore
the robes of the ancient one who had tended to the Ark.
The costume was elaborate and precisely layered. First,
a white linen robe; over it a sleeveless blue shirt that
Mualama had called the *meeir*; then the *ephod*, a coat of
many colors fastened by two stones at the shoulders; the
essen, a breastplate encrusted with a dozen precious
jewels of various colors; and over her short black hair a
crown, made of three metal bands. Each band represented two things, according to Mualama: the three
worlds of existence, heaven, hell, and the Earth, and
the three divisions of man, spiritual, intellectual, and
physical. At least those were the legendary representa-
tions.

It was this clothing that had allowed her to pass the
inspection of the four heads. Airlia technology was built
into the clothes and accoutrements, technology that
mated with the guard system of sphinx heads and had
allowed her to pass unscathed.

She turned from the Ark, which rested on a

waist-high black platform. The Ark, of the Covenant
was three feet high and wide and slightly over four feet
long. It was gold-plated and the two long poles that had
been used to carry it were poking out on either end
through the rings on the bottom of the Ark—just as it
had been described in the Old Testament.

The most intriguing aspect were the two "cherubim-
sphinxes" on the lid. They were shaped exactly like
miniature versions of the head of the Black Sphinx,
with ruby-red eyes. As soon as she had entered the veil,
both had turned and fixed their inhuman gaze on her, as
had their cousins on the top of the veil poles. A sophisticated, automated defense system that had existed for
millennia to guard the contents of the Ark.

Duncan walked to the veil and slid through. A tall
man in a dark robe stood in the tunnel entrance—
Al-Iblis, Duncan had no doubt. Two men in unmarked
desert camouflage with automatic weapons stood behind him. Al-Iblis was tall, a couple of inches over six
feet. A hood left his face in shadow, the glint of dark
eyes the only thing visible in that dark pocket.

"Give me the Ark," Al-Iblis said.

"Where is Professor Mualama?" Duncan asked.

"I'm holding him outside. If you do not give me the
Ark, I will have him killed."

"Then kill him," Duncan said coldly.

A long silence followed that statement.

"You don't even know what you have," Al-Iblis finally said.

"I have the Ark which holds the Grail."

Al-Iblis laughed, a sound like worn brakes going
downhill. "You have no clue what the Grail is, do you?"

"I know I have it and you don't," Duncan said. "If I
give it to you, then I have nothing. That would be stu-
pid. I don't believe you are someone to be trusted."

"Then I will take it from you." Al-Iblis gestured and the two men dashed forward, weapons ready.

They made four paces when the two veil-pole heads on that side released a flash and bright red beam that struck each man in the chest. There was a sharp sizzle, and both men fell to the floor, a hole burned neatly through their chests.

"That was even stupider," Duncan said.

"They matter nothing," Al-Iblis said. "There was always the chance the security system might not work after all these years. Even Airlia technology has the potential for failure. Come here. Give me the garments so I may get the Grail. If you do not, I will have your friend killed very slowly. I have men trained in causing pain."

"If I give you the clothing or the Ark, then I will be the next victim of those men," Duncan said.

Al-Iblis reached inside his robe and pulled out a 9 mm pistol. "I could kill *you*," he said to Duncan as he took aim at her, his hand perfectly steady and on target.

"Then you would leave these—" she ran her hand down her body "—here with my body and these clothes are the only way someone can get close enough to open the Ark. Nothing will change."

Al-Iblis nodded. "All right. A standoff. I have much experience at that. I have dealt with kings and prophets and heads of state. I will raise the ante elsewhere then." Al-Iblis paused before he left. "Perhaps you do have an idea how important the Grail is?"

"Perhaps," Duncan said.

"Who are you?" he asked her. "Why have you sought the Grail?"

She met his gaze and held it. "Who are *you*?" she asked in turn.

"They currently call me Al-Iblis."

"Who are they?" Duncan had heard the name, but she knew little about the man behind it.

Al-Iblis considered the question, as if it had never been asked before. "The people of the desert. Nowadays, intelligence agencies also use that name for me because they think I am a terrorist. As usual, they are clueless. In past time, prophets, seers, men who claimed to be wise and weren't as bright as they thought. Caliphs and ayatollahs. Women who claimed to be—" He paused suddenly.

Duncan took a step forward. "What do *you* call yourself?"

"You want to know who I am? Perhaps more importantly, you should ask *what* I am. The end to all this is coming, so it doesn't matter if I tell you. Then, perhaps you will understand how powerless you are and accept the inevitable and align yourself with me. It is the only smart choice."

The tall man pulled his hood back, revealing a pale, narrow face with black eyes set like stones on either side of a hatchet nose. He smiled, revealing long teeth, almost predatory. "This body is just a garment, like those clothes you wear now. The body allows me to walk the Earth. I am a Shadow."

"A shadow of what?"

"More a shadow of who."

"Who?"

"You can call me Aspasia's Shadow."

Duncan shook her head. "Aspasia is dead. He was killed aboard his Talon spacecraft."

"The original being known as Aspasia was killed. As I told you, I am a Shadow. I had his entire consciousness imprinted many years ago." His hand went to his own chest and rested there for a second. "And because I—my consciousness—have been alive all those years,

I am more than he ever was. Wouldn't you agree?" He didn't wait for an answer.

"It is best he finally died. He was—" a twisted grin crossed his face "—out of touch? Antiquated? Like the gods of ancient Egypt, which, of course, he and his followers were. He, and his, would be out of date in this new millennium. I will lead my people to victory."

"Your *people* also died with Aspasia," Duncan said.

"No, *my* people—the Guides, The Mission—have struggled with me for millennia here on Earth while Aspasia and his followers hid on Mars. We have earned the right."

"The right to what?"

"To rule. To become the Gods that Aspasia and his once were. Gods for a new age, a new world where technology is more important than faith—and we have the technology."

"And the Airlia on Mars? The ones left behind there who control the guardian at Cydonia? Do they give their allegiance to you?" Duncan asked.

"Left behind?" Aspasia's Shadow smiled once more without humor. "They know nothing of what it means to be left behind, almost powerless, for thousands of years. They slept while I struggled and fought here and died again and again only to be constantly reborn. Now they have no choice but to obey me."

"There is always a choice," Duncan argued.

"Free will?" Aspasia's Shadow shook his head, indicating what he thought of that concept. "You are very ignorant and naive and know nothing of what you speak. You talking about free will is rather ironic if you are what I think you are."

"What do you mean?"

Aspasia's Shadow shook his head. "You will either discover what you are looking for or you won't; it is not my concern. There are larger issues than the things you think you are concerned with."

That made no sense to Duncan, and she wondered if he was trying to confuse her. "How did this all start?" she asked.

"How it started isn't important," Aspasia's Shadow said. "The end is all that counts. And that is coming very soon."

"Why did the Airlia come here?"

"That is not important."

"Why are *you* here? Why is the Grail so important?"

"You have no idea what you have," Aspasia's Shadow said. "If you—"

"I know more than you think," Duncan cut him off, tired of his threats and his declarations of her ignorance.

"You are not who you've pretended to be," Aspasia's Shadow said. "I should have known of you, the one who uncovered Area 51, who stopped Majestic-12. Your Captain Turcotte killed Aspasia and stopped the fleet, but you were the one who started it all, who put Turcotte in place to do those things. Does he know he is being used? Does he know who you really are? Do *you* know who you really are?" He didn't wait for an answer. "There have been others like you before, those who upset the delicate balance and caused great grief and death. You've hidden well, Doctor Duncan, but you cannot hide anymore."

"You babble," Duncan said. "You are old and need to be put down like a mad dog."

A cruel smile curled Aspasia's Shadow's thin lips. "You try to bait me. Very good. But I have lived a long time and met enemies much greater than you and defeated them all. I am still here and they have long ago turned to dust."

Duncan crossed her arms on top of the *essen.* "So

you think. But I'm where you want to be. Did you talk to those old enemies like you talk to me? Did they hold what you want?"

"But will it do you any good?" Aspasia's Shadow asked. His eyes went up and down her, noting the garments. "Do you have everything you need?" Once more he didn't wait for an answer. "When you find you don't, we will talk again."

Aspasia's Shadow turned and disappeared into the tunnel that led out of the Ark chamber. Duncan went back inside the veil and looked at the Grail. Once more she put her hand over one end. It opened and the empty depression appeared. She knew that was what Aspasia's Shadow had meant when he'd asked her if she had all she needed. The stones were needed for the Grail to work and the alien creature had known it. Did he have them? And if he did, how could she get them from him? Or were they hidden as so many other Airlia artifacts had been?

The chamber around her seemed smaller than before, the weight of the plateau above a palpable presence. She was safe for the moment, but she now knew she was also powerless.

Duncan stood by the veil, the four bodies her only company. She looked up to the top of the chamber, but her mind went further, through the rock, to the surface, into the sky. She knew Mike Turcotte would come for her. The thought did not give her as much comfort as it had a few days ago. She turned back toward the Grail, troubled by the words of Aspasia's Shadow.

There was something lurking at the edge of her subconscious trying to come forward, but she couldn't draw it out. Her eyes rested on the Grail, sensing in it a key to unlock whatever it was that was hidden in her mind.

CHAPTER 3

AREA 51, NEVADA

Flat brown desert floor, broken abruptly by steep, rock-strewn mountains, made for uninviting terrain in the southern center of Nevada. A hundred and twenty miles northwest of Las Vegas, nestled between seven-thousand-foot mountain ranges, lay Groom Lake. It might have once held water, but now the flat lakebed contained a seven-mile-long concrete runway, the longest in the world. Many had thought that Area 51 had been located at Groom Lake because of the remote and desolate nature of the surrounding countryside—a good place to hide things the government didn't want prying eyes to see.

Actually, the opposite was true. In the early days of World War II, military reconnaissance teams found hidden in a massive cavern under Groom Mountain something so startling and foreign to the planet that the government immediately knew it had to keep the discovery secret. The alien object was so immense—over a mile long and a quarter mile at its widest—that there was no way to move the alien mothership, at least until the drive system for it was figured out.

As more alien artifacts were discovered, the greatest being the nine bouncers, the installation at Groom Lake grew in size and secrecy. The site was labeled on the Nellis Air Base reservation map as Area 51. Until the uncovering of Majestic-12, the ruling body at Area 51 since its founding, the United States government never admitted the base even existed, even though photos of the surface facilities were posted on the Internet. But today, as Mike Turcotte could see out of the side of the bouncer, secrecy seemed to be the last thing on anyone's mind.

News vans were parked all around the edge of the Groom Lake runway. It was a far cry from the days when even climbing one of the mountains surrounding the Area 51 complex could land a person in jail or much worse if they were picked up by Landscape, the inner security force of Majestic-12. Despite the presence of the media at the previously highly classified facility, Mike Turcotte felt that they were as far from the "truth" as they had ever been.

The bouncer floated down the side of Groom Mountain, the large hangar doors sliding open. As soon as it touched down, Turcotte was first out of the hatch, followed by Yakov, Che Lu, and the rest of the A-Team. Mualama's sight had slowly returned to him during the flight, and he followed the old Chinese woman off.

As Turcotte appeared, reporters and cameramen flowed through the open doors, surrounding the bouncer. Sliding down the side of the bouncer, Turcotte was met with a thicket of microphone booms. He knifed his way through, trying to reach Major Quinn, who was standing behind the reporters clamoring for information about what was going on with the Airlia, the Guides, The Ones Who Wait, The Mission, the nuclear explosion in China, and Lisa Duncan's location.

"Get these people out of here!" Turcotte yelled to Quinn.

The Major raised his hands and pointed at the two military police officers who were trying to control twenty times their number. "That's all I have."

Turcotte spun about. Captain Billam was exiting the

bouncer with his team behind him. Master Sergeant
Boltz, the team sergeant wounded in Moscow, was being hauled out on a stretcher. Che Lu was almost hidden
among the hulking team members.

"Clear this hangar," Turcotte ordered Billam.

Seeing the hesitation in Billam's face, Turcotte
pulled his 9mm pistol from its holster. That gained him
a couple of feet of space as the closest reporters and
cameramen pressed back away from him.

Turcotte fired twice into the air, aiming out of the
hangar toward the desert. A moment of silence descended on the crowd, followed by the curses of the media representatives, threatening lawsuits. Turcotte
lowered the pistol and aimed it at the closest reporter.
"You have thirty seconds to get out of this hangar."

The reporter opened her mouth to say something,
then noted the look in Turcotte's eyes and how steady
his hand was. She turned and pushed her way out of the
circle. The others followed. As soon as the last one was
out of the hangar, the large doors slid shut.

"What the hell is going on?" Turcotte demanded of
Quinn. "Where is security?"

The major hardly looked like a warrior. Slight of
build, with thinning blond hair and large glasses
perched on his nose, Quinn was what Turcotte called a
screen watcher—someone who sat on their ass all day
and looked at computer screens. But he had been help-
ful in the fight against the aliens and their followers and
had been an ally in the transition from Majestic-12's secret rule at Area 51 to the present regime.

"That *is* our security." Quinn indicated the two Air
Police.

Turcotte had first been assigned to Area 51 to be part
of the elite security force that protected its secrets. The
facility had been secured by top-of-the-line personnel

and equipment. Even after Majestic-12 was deposed, security had remained tight, guarding against actions by either group of Airlia minions. The goal was to prevent Area 51 from suffering the same fate as the Russian Section IV base that had been destroyed at Novaya Zemlya.

"What's going on?" Turcotte asked.

"I had all my air police, except those two, and all my special security personnel from Landscape and Nightscape who passed the review panel, pulled on orders from the Pentagon this morning. I've been trying to get through to somebody—anybody—to get the orders rescinded, but there's a lot of confusion in Washington. I'm getting a major runaround. No one knows what's going on. I've backended some requests and will have more people here soon, but in the meanwhile, we have to make do with what we have."

"I see the long arm of The Guides acting here," Yakov said. He shrugged his large shoulders. "Or The Ones Who Wait. Both groups undoubtedly have your higher echelons of government and military thoroughly infiltrated and compromised. They want Area 51 vulnerable. They destroyed my country's Area 51; yours is next." The Russian had the bag over his shoulder containing what they had managed to pilfer out of the Russian Archives on their raid, minus, of course, the Spear of Destiny, which they suspected acted as a key to the lowest level of Qian-Ling.

"What about Doctor Duncan?" Quinn asked.

"Mualama knows where she is," Turcotte said. He wanted the bouncer inside the secure hangar before they off-loaded the team member's body. "Let's seal this place."

Quinn gave the necessary orders and the bouncer floated in, the large doors sliding shut behind it. Then Quinn gestured for them to follow him toward the large

freight elevator that led to the Cube—command and
control central.

"We've been looking at Burton's manuscript. It's in a
language no one can recognize."

"Hakkadian," Mualama said. The African archaeologist had spent most of his life following the path of Sir
Richard Francis Burton around the world, finding clues
here and there that led him further in pursuit of a "lost"
manuscript of Burton's. Mualama had told them that it
detailed all that Burton had learned of the aliens and
their minions on the planet.

"What exactly is Hakkadian?" Turcotte asked.

"A distant forerunner of Arabic," Mualama answered. "Last spoken in ancient Babylon. Burton was
an extremely amazing man. He spoke *twenty-nine* languages fluently."

"The only things we could read were the foreword
and a letter put on top of the manuscript by his wife,"
Quinn said. "Pretty amazing stuff."

"Where exactly in Giza is Duncan?" Turcotte
pressed.

"Directly under the Great Sphinx." Mualama quickly
told them of the Black Sphinx and the chamber hidden
inside.

The doors to the elevator opened and they walked toward the Cube. They paused as a red light suddenly began flashing.

"What's that?" Turcotte asked.

"Security sensor," Quinn said. "One of you is
bugged."

Turcotte's first instinct was to look to Che Lu. She
had been under the control of The Ones Who Wait at
Qian-Ling, although he wasn't certain why they would
want to bug her. It wasn't as if the location of Area 51
was a great secret anymore.

"Go through one at a time, please," Quinn said.

Turcotte went through first and there was no alarm. Che Lu was second, and again, nothing. Mualama followed and still no red light. Turcotte stared hard at the Russian—after all they'd been through to have this happen—but again he had the same question as with Che Lu: why? And when could this have happened?

Yakov stepped through and the red light began flashing. Quinn picked up a small handheld detector and ran it over the Russian's body. He paused when he was at the back of Yakov's neck. "It's there."

"How?" Turcotte asked.

"Whatever it is," Yakov said, "it was not there last time we came through here. So it must have been placed on me since then."

"Katyenka," Turcotte said. It was hard to forget someone who had tried to kill him. She had been a GRU operative, Yakov's former lover, but actually working for The Ones Who Wait who had ambushed them in Moscow.

Yakov nodded. "Yes. She had opportunity and reason." He took his heavy coat off.

Turcotte shook his head and tried to make light of it. "I can't leave you alone for a moment, can I?"

"It makes sense. It is how those soldiers found us in the Archives," Yakov said. He ran his fingers through the thick lining near the collar, then paused before pulling out a small black object about a quarter inch long. "Here it is. Nothing very exotic. Standard GRU issue. Range about three miles, but very intense so they could track us through the tunnels under Moscow." He tossed it on the floor and smashed it with his boot. "Shall we continue?"

Turcotte paused, considering the Russian. It was indeed most likely the bug had been planted by Katyenka,

but there had been much deception and betrayal since
he'd arrived at Area 51 and he could not be certain. For
a moment, Yakov's arguments to leave Egypt and come
back here took a slightly different angle.

"Are you coming?" Yakov and the others were
waiting.

Turcotte shook himself out of his suspicions and followed as they headed to the Cube. The main room of
the Cube measured eighty feet by a hundred. Banks of
computer screens gave it a similar appearance to mission control at NASA, but Turcotte noticed that three
quarters of the chairs in front of those screens were
empty.

"More ordered cuts in personnel," Quinn said, noting
his look. "Someone's really trying to hamstring us.
Again, I'm trying to backdoor requests."

Turcotte knew Quinn was an expert at manipulating
government and military bureaucracy. With the proper
passwords, the right communication channels, and experience, he could get just about anything eventually. It
was something he had done while working for
Majestic-12—a valuable asset that both Duncan and
Turcotte had thought necessary to keep at Area 51.

Turcotte turned his attention to the front wall where a
twenty-foot-wide-by-ten-high screen displayed a pleth-
ora of information.

"What's hot?" Turcotte asked, trying to make sense
of the various displays.

Quinn sat down in the chair that used to belong to the
head of Majestic, or MJ-12 as some called it. It was on
a raised dais in the back of the room and oversaw everything that went on. There was the quiet hum of machinery along with the constant slight hiss of filtered air
being blown into the room. The entire complex rested
on huge shocks and was hung from large springs,

allowing it to sustain a nuclear surface blast. Turcotte had just prevented such an incident by bargaining with The Ones Who Wait, giving them the Spear of Destiny.

"The NSA is tracking that flying dragon thing that holds The Ones Who Wait who took the key from you in Mongolia," Quinn said.

"That 'dragon thing' is called Chi Yu," Che Lu said. "It is part of the lore of my land. When the yellow emperor Shi Huangdi ruled the northern part of China, Chi Yu ruled in the south. They fought and Shi Huangdi subdued the beast and took it prisoner."

"Which in reality—" Turcotte began, but Che Lu cut him off.

"I believe that Shi Huangdi was Artad, one of the alien leaders. And Chi Yu must be a machine fashioned by the other side—The Guides—to fight and terrify so many years ago. Shi Huangdi captured it during their battles and it must have been inside Qian-Ling."

"Is this machine back at Qian-Ling now?" Yakov asked.

"Negative." Quinn typed into the keyboard and then pointed at the main board. A map of eastern Africa appeared. "See the red dot? It stopped at Ngorongoro Crater briefly and is now heading northeast on a track that will take it to Qian-Ling. It's assumed the Chinese will pick it up on radar and try to intercept. ETA at Chinese border in eighteen minutes."

"Why did it go to Ngorongoro Crater?" Yakov wondered.

"I found the scepter key there," Mualama said. "And history records Burton spent quite a bit of time in East Africa exploring."

"It will be interesting to see how my government reacts to these events," Che Lu said, which earned her a hard look from Turcotte. On the international scene,

China had always been an enigma, and with the advent of the discovery of the Airlia the country had cut itself off completely. Because of all the betrayals Turcotte had seen recently, a small part of him had to wonder if it was just coincidence that Che Lu had opened up Qian-Ling just after the Airlia had been discovered. And then Mualama had uncovered the key right after that. And Yakov had been wearing a bug when he arrived here.

"If The Ones Who Wait bring Artad up from the low-est level," Turcotte said, "it will be interesting to see how *everyone* in the world reacts. We still don't know the truth about what happened among the Airlia." He turned to Quinn. "What else?"

The major hit another command. The map changed to show the southeast Pacific. "The shield is still pro-tecting Easter Island. What remains of Task Force 78, with the addition of Task Force 79 and the aircraft car-rier USS *Stennis*, has backed off to a range of three hun-dred kilometers north of the island. We've lost all contact with the submarine USS *Springfield*. It is as-sumed it has been taken inside the shield and is lost to us. Official policy now is to stand off and watch, which doesn't please the Navy much.

"However," Quinn continued, "the last transmission from *Springfield* had some interesting data in it." He hit a switch and a large map of Easter Island appeared on the screen. "We think they found a hole in the shield wall. When the *Washington* hit the island, it tore up a big part of the ocean floor as it bottomed out. We think there is a very small gap in the shield where it cut through the floor."

"Can we get in?" Turcotte asked.

"Possibly," Quinn said. "But, as I said, official policy is to stand off and do nothing."

"That doesn't do Kelly Reynolds any good," Turcotte said. "Can you get some SEALs?"

"I can't even get us MPs at the moment," Quinn said.

"That's because the Pentagon knows who's asking and what they're for," Turcotte said. "We still have the ST-8 clearance by presidential decree, right?"

Quinn nodded. ST-8 was the highest clearance possible and meant that orders issued using it had to be followed as if they came from the National Command Authority.

"Then I'll just issue an order to get us some SEALs."

"To do what?" Quinn asked.

"Infiltrate Easter Island." Turcotte pointed at the screen. "It's a job the SEALs are trained for. Go in under the shield, see what's going on, rescue Kelly, and get back. I'll bet there's a SEAL team on board one of the ships of Task Force 79. Plus, I don't think the Navy will put up too much of a fight over the mission. I've got a feeling they want to know what's happening to the *Washington* and their people."

"It's worth a shot," Quinn said.

"And the Giza Plateau?" Turcotte had already moved on to more pressing issues.

"Satellite imagery shows it wrapped up even tighter with troops since your assault. The Egyptian government has closed it off and is complaining to whoever will listen that the United States violated their sovereignty."

"We have to go back," Turcotte said.

"That might be difficult," Quinn noted.

"Of course it will be difficult," Turcotte said. "But there's always a way."

"What about the manuscript?" Mualama said.

Quinn stood. "It's in the conference room."

Turcotte paused. "I need a minute."

Quinn nodded and went into the conference room. Yakov put a large paw on Turcotte's shoulder. "Are you all right, my friend?"

"No," Turcotte said.

"I would have been worried if you said you were," Yakov said. "No one is all right. Only the smart people know that though. Especially now."

"Especially now," Turcotte acknowledged. "Give me just a minute and I'll join you."

"Da."

Turcotte waited until Yakov and Che Lu disappeared. He walked down the hallway to the latrine. There was no one inside. He sagged back against the door, feeling the exhaustion of constant tension in every fiber of his being. He slid down to his knees, then sat on the floor, his back still against the door. He put his right hand out, opened it wide, and stared at the scarred flesh. He could see the pregnant woman who died just before he grabbed the red hot muzzle of his team leader's gun in Germany as if it had just happened. Another second earlier and she—and her unborn child—would still be alive.

The fingers of his left hand traced over the scar tissue in the palm of his right hand, remembering his failure. And his most recent failure had cost the lives of three men. Finally, he stood. He shoved the door open and went to the conference room. Inside was one other person beside Quinn, Mualama, Che Lu, and Yakov. Larry Kincaid was their authority on space operations. He was looking through a pile of photographs. Kincaid stood and shook hands as he came in.

Quinn stood near the end of the table and pushed a button on a lectern. A piece of the wood paneling slid up, revealing a six-by-six-foot video display. Turcotte sat in the leather chair at the head of the conference table, Yakov to his right, Che Lu to his left, Mualama next to her. The screen turned white, and then two lines scrolled up to the center and stopped.

"This is the prologue to Burton's manuscript which we've scanned into the computer," Quinn said.

THE PATH OF A TRUTH-SEEKER
BY SIR RICHARD FRANCIS BURTON

Quinn leaned over and indicated a key on the keyboard embedded under the top of the table at Turcotte's position. "You hit this to scroll up."

Turcotte pressed it.

THE SEARCH FOR LEGENDS

Prologue:
I, Richard Francis Burton, have lived a long and wondrous life that now winds its way into darkness. What is written on these pages was accumulated over the last thirty-six years when my life took a turn that I could never have imagined. I have tried to organize it as well as I can and I leave it to my beloved Isabel to finish my work after my death. Without her, I would never have been able to complete it; indeed my life would not have been worth living without her light spirit to keep me from falling into the darkness of all I have learned.

My involvement in the tale began when it reached my ears, in the city of Medina, in the year 1854 of the Christians after the birth of their Lord, that there was a man who knew much of the secrets of the world and the ancients. He was not spoken of favorably but with fear. That did not dissuade me. I had learned early in my life that one must often travel into darkness to get to the light.

I sought out this man, spoken of only in whispers as Al-Iblis, and was granted an audience. Some said he was a sorcerer, others a creature of the night whom mothers talked of to scare their children into going to bed on time. Others said he was a religious leader, but of what sect no one was certain.

I could sense much evil in his presence, but he overcame my fear by hinting of strange and wondrous things. He pointed me to Giza, to the plateau of the three great Pyramids and the great Sphinx. He told me to seek out a man named Kaji, who knew further secrets and could show me something my eyes would not believe. He gave me a medallion which he said would gain me an audience with Kaji.

Al-Iblis wanted me to return to him, to tell him what I had seen, but I knew even as I left his palace I would never be back there and never wanted to be in his presence again.

He was right in his hints, for at Giza, under the guidance of Kaji, I saw something hidden under the earth, in the bowels of the plateau; something so strange as I can still hardly believe it, and was told a tale even stranger, that every effort of my life from that moment to this as I write, the darkness of death not far from me, has been dedicated to tracking down the Truth. It became my tariqat; my spiritual path leading to the truth.

I barely survived that first step as Kaji tried to leave me to die under the plateau, but that tale will be told elsewhere.

The beginning of this path, I eventually learned, revolved around intelligent creatures who were not men, who were not even of this planet. These came to

*our Earth from the stars before the dawn of recorded
history and fought among themselves for millennia,
in the process changing much of mankind's history,
most often for the worse.*

*I have learned much of these creatures—the
Airlia—and their followers who walk among us.
Once I overcame my shock at being told of their existence and seeing the proof in the Black Sphinx hidden under the Giza Plateau, I set out to learn as
much as I could about them.*

*Over the years I have traveled far, read, seen, and
heard much. What has fascinated me most are the
Legends that man has woven to explain things that
could not be explained any other way at the time.*

*Artifacts from these Airlia have become part of
the lore of many lands, being given various names.
Most have been called no more than literary devices
by scholars with no basis in fact. I had always
thought such thinking naive. Now I know it to be.*

*What I have discovered is that the Legends are
real, and they date back before the shadows of what
those same scholars call the beginning of history.*

*On these pages I will write of the Grail, the Spear
of Destiny, Excalibur, the Ark, and other objects
shrouded in myth and legend.*

*Much of what I write on these pages cannot be
proven. Most comes from documents that I have
translated with great effort from tongues that have
not been spoken for a very long time and from another tongue that scholars insist does not exist despite all evidence to the contrary. Other information
comes from tales told to me in shadowy rooms by
men and women, and even those who are not completely human, whose veracity may indeed be ques-
tioned, but I believe it all because of the pieces of the*

tale I have seen with my own eyes. And because of the efforts that were made both to aid me and to hinder me in this path, too much effort was made to stop me, for there may be some truth in what I have learned, truth that others want to keep buried.

The story begins before Rome was founded, before the Greeks etched their letters on stone tablets, even before the pyramids themselves were built—before the dawn of recorded time.

Turcotte hit the scroll key, but nothing happened. "That's it?" He turned to Quinn.

"That's all of Burton's prologue," Quinn said. "Inserted behind those first pages were several written in a different hand."

Mualama leaned forward. "Do you know of Sir Richard Burton? His life? The controversies surrounding him?"

"Not really," Turcotte replied. He was anxious to be moving, to be planning a second assault on Giza and rescue Duncan. He didn't understand Mualama's fascination with an old manuscript.

"Burton translated the Kama Sutra," Mualama said. "And the Tale of the Thousand and One Nights. He was more than a writer and translator of other's written works. He was a famous explorer. A man who dared to travel where others feared. He searched for the source of the Nile hidden in the heart of Africa. It has been widely believed that his wife, Isabel, burned a manuscript when he died." Mualama pointed at the screen. "It appears she burned the only copy of *this* manuscript."

"The next few pages tell what happened on the night

Burton died," Quinn said, "and why she did what she did. It is most intriguing."

"Put it on the screen," Turcotte ordered. The writing that appeared was written with black ink, a thin spidery lettering:

My love is dead. His body not yet cold.

I write to warn you. If you read these words and have this manuscript in your possession, you are cursed, as my dearest Richard was.

As Richard had feared for so many years, the evil creature who started him on his path, his tarigat, came for us last night just as Richard finished the manuscript. I was making a copy, as I always did, of Richard's work. The opus was complete and Richard felt he had done all he could with the life he had been given.

The creature came in the dark. Its face was pale, its twisted body cloaked in black. The eyes—I will always remember the eyes. If my sins—and they are many according to those who say they know those things—send me to Hell, I readily expect to see eyes like that again. But is there a Hell? I wonder because I no longer believe in Heaven.

I wander. My mind is not in this. Richard lies dead just down the hallway.

But you must know of the creature who knows not death. Because if you are reading this, then the creature will eventually come for you too.

The creature wanted the manuscript; the information Richard has so painstakingly translated and gathered over the past four decades.

It came after dark. Richard was in bed, his body weakened by the disease ravaging him. I was wiping

*the sweat off Richard's brow, when I heard the heavy
wood door crash open. I ran to the top of the stairs
and saw it in the foyer. It looked up at me and I first
beheld those eyes.*

*They transfixed me. I knew Richard's guns were in
the study, but I could not move. The creature came up
the stairs, occasionally staggering to the right, grabbing the railing as if it were drunk.*

*It wore a long black cloak, the tail almost touch-
ing the floor, and underneath, formal wear, as if it
had come from a party. But the cloth was dirty and
spotted. It came close to me and I could smell the
stench of death on its breath. It opened its cloak. A
hand came out holding a surgeon's blade. It pressed
the weapon against my throat. I thought it would
rupture the skin. Never had I been so aware of the
blood that flowed through my veins, feeling that cold
steel against my flesh.*

*"Your husband, whore," the creature hissed. "I
want your husband."*

*I wanted to shake my head, but I thought it would
finish the work of the blade. "He is not here."*

*"You lie, bitch. You are a whore like all the
others."*

*I was startled when Richard's voice came from the
doorway to our room. "I always knew I would see
you once more."*

*How Richard managed to get out of bed, I knew
not. I felt, and still feel, I had let him down. I should
have thrown myself into the blade and ended it there.
Perhaps that would have satisfied the blood lust I
could feel coming off the creature. We once met a
man named Bram Stoker who spoke of creatures of
the darkness who drew blood from their victims for
sustenance. Richard had been intrigued and talked*

with Stoker deep into the night until I could no longer stay awake with them. Richard told him of Indian legends of things called vampires and other similar creatures he had heard of in our travels around the world. If such creatures existed, I knew this was one of them. But Richard seemed not afraid of this thing that stood in our house.

"Leave my wife be. She has nothing to do with this. She knows nothing."

The creature pulled the blade away from my neck, and with a movement faster than I could follow, hid the blade deep inside the recesses of its cloak.

"I don't care what she knows. She is like all women. A whore. Worth nothing. She deserves what they all deserve. Death. Worse than death."

But he took a step away from me, toward Richard, something stronger than his hate for my gender drawing him toward my husband.

"Al-Iblis." My husband said the name like it was a curse, and confirmed what unholy creature I was seeing. Richard had written of it extensively in the manuscript. I knew then what I had hoped was just a collection of tales was true. The world as I had known it and been taught by my church, my parents, my schools, was not the world as it was.

"Sir Richard Francis Burton," the creature hissed. "I had heard the queen-whore knighted you. You have traveled far since we met in Medina. But you never came back to me like you promised."

"You lied to me," Burton said.

The creature laughed, like the sound fingernails make on a blackboard, causing my skin to crawl. "I lied? I told you much truth. Enough for you to go to Giza, to find Kaji. So I lied about myself. What does that matter? You will never know the truth."

"I know more than I did," Richard answered him. "I know many of your names now."

The creature smiled, revealing yellowing teeth. "You do? Do you know what they call me now?"

"In the newspapers they call you Jack the Ripper," Richard said, a name which froze my heart. I had read of the atrocities committed by the shadow the papers had given that title to. To have it stand here in my hallway; I knew we were doomed. I had read how his hate for my gender had been displayed, most likely with the very same blade that he had held against my throat seconds earlier.

"The Ripper," the creature repeated. "They are fools. I do not rip. I cut with a precision the best of your surgeons could not even begin to imitate, but they ignore that and worry only about the death of worthless scum."

"Our surgeons try to save lives," Burton said.

"I try to save a life also." The creature pointed a thin, pale finger with a long nail at the end, at its own chest. "Mine."

"You have lived for millennia." Richard seemed more intrigued than scared. I had seen him this way before in dangerous situations, where normal men would have fled for their lives. His only interest was learning more. But this was our house, not a jungle. And this creature—there was no doubt it was more dangerous than any Richard had ever faced on any of the many continents he had traveled to. "Why are you afraid for your life now?"

"This has lived for millennia!" The creature clawed through his cloak and suit shirt, pulling out an amulet on a thin metal chain. The metal was formed in the symbol of two hands lifted up in praise, but there was no body between. "This—" the creature thumped the pale flesh of his chest, "will die soon."

For the first time I picked up something other than hate off the creature as it turned its head looking down the stairs, toward the open front door. Its voice dropped low, as if afraid of being overheard. "They track me. They want me to go with them. To pass on, they call it. But I don't want to. I don't want to die!"

"Why do you hate women so?" Richard asked. "Why do you kill them and cut their bodies?"

"I am not of woman," the creature snarled. "I was not born of woman. It is a woman who tracks me, who wants me to pass on. They are all evil. Evil. I need blood to keep me going until—I need parts of their bodies. I cannot—" He fell into silence, as if confused.

"Tell me your real name." I had seen Richard stand upright against a charging tiger in India, rifle to his shoulder, waiting until the last possible second before taking the fatal shot, wanting to see the tiger's eyes, every little detail. If the gun had jammed then, we would not be here today. He always pushed—always. It was why I had given my life to spend with him. What woman could resist such a man?

"My real name?" The creature took a few steps until it was opposite Richard in the hallway, its back to the banister. I remained frozen at the top of the landing. I could tell this was desperately tiring to Richard, his right shoulder leaning against the doorjamb. The disease that was killing him from within was making great strides in doing just that as he wasted energy. I also knew that Richard would stand and talk to the devil himself if it would give him more information regarding his tarigat.

The creature seemed to be regarding Richard's

*query as if it were some sort of riddle. "My real
name means I have to know who exactly I am." The
creature held a hand up toward the hall light as if it
could see through the flesh. "I am a Shadow. That's
what I was made to be. The Shadow of someone real.
Created to do his bidding. They once called me
Lucifer, long ago."*

*Those words chilled me. I had always known the
things Richard were uncovering would change the
accepted view of history, but Lucifer!*

*"They said I was cast out. But I wasn't cast out. I
was left behind. Do you know what that feels like? To
be made, to not even be real, and to be left behind to
do his bidding when you are more than he was?
More than he ever will be."*

*"His name," my husband pressed. "The one you
are the shadow of. What is it?"*

*"It would mean nothing to you," the creature said.
It twitched, looking to the open door once more. The
skin on its face rippled as if worms moved beneath.
"They are coming for me. The lackeys. The women.
The whores who serve The Mission. To pass the
Shadow on which means my death." He took a step
toward Richard.*

*"I need the Grail," the creature's voice went even
lower. "I need to know what you have learned of the
Grail! It is the only thing that can save me."*

"Tell me the name."

*"Aspasia," it spit the word out. "The leader of the
firstborn. I am his Shadow."*

*"Aspasia," Richard repeated. "I have heard that
name. I know who that is."*

*The creature—Aspasia's Shadow—stepped for-
ward, close to my husband. "The Grail. Tell me
where it is." It paused, searching my husband's face,*

comprehension dawning on its face. "You don't know what it is, do you? You've searched all these years and you don't even know what it is you've been looking for!"

That was the most human the creature had been, the shock punching through to its core. I turned, the faint sound of horses' hooves on the long driveway echoing through the door. The creature heard them too.

It drew the blade as it spun toward me. I didn't even have time to raise my hand. It had the knife at my throat, so swiftly did it move. "I will slice her open, spill her putrid innards so the world can see the whore she is! Where is the Grail?" The dementia was back in full force.

Heavy boots sounded on the outside stairs. Three men cloaked in black entered, followed by a tall woman similarly dressed. She held up her hand, palm out, as she stepped between the men to the fore-front. "Come with us."

The creature whirled, putting me between him and the men. "I do not wish to pass on. I want my life!"

"It was never your life to have." The leader was advancing, the others behind her. She reached the bottom of the stairs, slowly coming up. "Your life was to be a servant and you have done that well. We are all servants. Now it is time to pass on."

"Never!" He screamed a sound like a beast in pain. "I will bathe this world in blood like it has never seen. I will tell these humans the truth of their existence, rip their gods out from their chests, spit on their religions, destroy their beliefs, their petty sciences."

"You have waited too long." The woman was six steps below us when she paused. "Your mind is gone.

You should have come when I first summoned you. You have done much damage. The humans search hard for the madman you have become. We cannot let them catch you." Her voice softened. *"Come with me. We can be together once more as we were many times in the past."*

"Catch me? These people? I will never—" the creature began, but there was a solid thud and the blade slid down, lightly slicing the skin on my right arm, but missing my throat. Richard was there! A club he had been given in the far east by a native guide in his trembling hands. The creature dropped to its knees, dazed from the blow.

"Come, Isabel!" Richard held out his right hand for me, the club raised in his left. I got behind him, feeling the safe haven of his body between the creature and me.

Aspasia's Shadow rolled on the floor, snarling, came to its feet, the knife held out, the tip darting back and forth between Richard and the strange woman who now climbed to the top of the landing.

"I want to live!" it screamed.

"It is time to pass on," she said. "Remember long ago? When you were Osiris and I was Isis? We can have that again if you go with me." The woman spoke in a soothing voice, as one would to a child, and took a step closer.

"You betrayed me!" The creature leapt with startling speed. The blade slammed into the woman's throat, a geyser of red spraying the air. As the creature sought to withdraw the blade her hands, unbelievably, wrapped around his, trapping the weapon in her own body. This allowed the other three strangers to wrestle him to the ground, on top of the dying body of their leader, blood covering them all.

Richard held me tight, the club ready. I could feel him shaking with exhaustion, amazed that he could even stand, never mind defend me.

They had metal cuffs on the creature's wrists, pinning its hands behind its back, but still it bucked and twisted, trying to get free. They grabbed its legs and drug it down the stairs, not caring that its head thumped and bounced on the wood.

Richard let go of me and went to the wounded woman who lay in a spreading pool of her own blood. "They take him to The Mission, don't they?"

She didn't seem to notice him. "It is time for me to pass on," she whispered.

"I met you before in another form," Richard said.

Still she ignored him. And then, of all things, she reached up with her right hand and jabbed her fingers into the wound, ripping it further open, increasing the flow of blood. She died seconds later, revealing nothing.

One of the men reentered the house, bounding up the stairs two at a time. He knelt over the woman's body, confirmed she was dead, then reached inside her clothes and pulled out a small amulet, a figure of two arms raised in prayer, with nobody between them, the same as Aspasia's Shadow had around its neck. The man whispered some words very quickly, much like a priest at an early mass in a hurry to get to his breakfast.

He pulled something from inside his cloak, scattering it on the body. It was like black sand. I gasped as the skin began to disappear, the sand eating through the flesh, the muscle, the bone. Richard tried to step closer to see what was happening, but I held him back.

The body was gone in less than a minute; only the

clothes remained. The man gathered the clothes, tucked them under his arms, then looked at Richard and me.

"You have been foolish. We should have let him kill you, then taken him back."

"Why didn't you?" Richard asked.

"You will be dead soon anyway. And you are famous. Your murder would cause more like you to search. I would recommend you tell no one what you saw tonight. Let your secret die with you, Burton. If you do not, you will only bring grief—" here he looked at me "—to those you leave it with."

We watched as he went out the door.

I had never seen such a thing and hope never again to see it.

I must rest.

No, I must finish this. The words must be written even as Richard's body slowly cools.

You, the reader, must know of the terror of those who seek the truth. And the danger of this manuscript.

To finish the tale of this past evening, I took Richard back to his bed. He never rose again. He died three hours ago in my arms, consumed by his disease and exhausted by all that had happened. In a way, he was as happy as I had ever seen him, the visit of the foul creature just another confirmation of all he had learned over the years.

I waited until the servants arrived in the morning. Knowing they would see me, I took the copy I had made of Richard's manuscript. I stood in the garden and burned it. The servants thought me quite mad. I was still covered in blood. My arm was bound where the blade had cut me. My eyes were wild—Richard, my love, my life, was dead. I burned the cursed words. In flames went the clues, the tales, the secrets Richard had sought for so many years. I knew the servants would spread the tale and that would be my only protection from others who would come as had been threatened.

But I kept the original. I owed Richard that. I could not burn his life's passion. And I knew that someday, someone good who would fight evil would need this story. To know about the Legends and the Truth. To know what Richard had learned, what Richard had guessed about. What he had given his life to.

But it had to be hidden. And for that I knew where to turn. The Watchers would hide it for me. I will give him who Richard promised the translation of the scrolls this copy. And you who read this, wherever you are, remember Richard and me.

Turcotte's finger was pressed down on the scroll button, but the screen didn't move. He wasn't even aware he was still pressing it until the keyboard beeped several times. Slowly he removed his finger. He turned to Yakov.

The Russian stood. "I need a drink."

Major Quinn had a bottle of vodka ready. He slid it across the table to Yakov along with several glasses. The Russian filled each one to the brim and gave one each to Turcotte, Kincaid, Quinn, Che Lu, and Mualama.

Yakov raised his glass. "To Sir Richard Francis Burton and his wife, Isabel, a woman of bravery."

Turcotte put the glass to his lips and took a deep drink. He slammed the glass back on the conference table, as silence reigned for a while, each lost in their thoughts about what they had just read.

"We have to go back to Giza and rescue Duncan," Turcotte finally said. "That's our number one priority right now." He pointed at Quinn. "I want all the intelligence you can get on the plateau. And replacements for the men we lost." Then to Mualama, "I want you to write up a detailed report on how you got to the Black Sphinx—the route you took. And everything you can remember about Al-Iblis and his forces."

"What about the manuscript?" Mualama asked.

"What do you want to do with it?" Che Lu asked.

"Translate it," Mualama said.

Turcotte frowned. "I thought it was in an ancient langauge that no one knew?"

"Hakkadian," Mualama said. "I have studied it."

"Why?" Yakov asked.

"I knew Burton had studied it," Mualama said.

"Why didn't you say something before?" Turcotte asked. He could have sworn that Mualama had told them he couldn't read the manuscript earlier.

"I wasn't certain I could translate it," Mualama said. "But looking through this," he tapped the manuscript, "I think I can do a good job on it."

"You think you can do a good job?" Turcotte rubbed the left side of his head where a headache was pounding. Lisa Duncan lost in Giza, the aborted assault, Easter Island, having had to give up the spear to The Ones Who Wait. There was too much going on at once and too many conflicting signals.

Turcotte looked around the table at the group before him: Mualama, his hand on the Burton manuscript; Che Lu, her face guarded; Yakov, who met his glance and raised his eyebrows; Major Quinn, looking earnest as usual, and Kincaid with his pictures of Mars. He missed Lisa.

Turcotte needed some time to sort things out. He didn't see how translating the manuscript could hurt, but he was determined to keep a closer eye on the African archaeologist.

"Write up your report on Giza first," Turcotte said. He slapped his palm on the conference table. "We are going back to Giza. And we are rescuing Lisa Duncan."

CHAPTER 4

EASTER ISLAND

The largest weapon system ever made by man, a Nimitz-class aircraft carrier, the USS *Washington*, lay beached, bow inland, on the north shore of the island. Moai statues gazed down on the ship, which dwarfed even the largest of them, weighing over two hundred tons.

The statues appeared to be the only thing not involved in the bustle of activity taking place on board the carrier and all over the island. Small pools of black were spread out on various places aboard the ship—nanomachines, each one built at the molecular level—working on the carrier, putting it back together, in many cases making improvements over the original man-made design.

The Easter Island guardian was using nanotechnology to transform both the machines and people it had captured. Nanotechnology was molecular manufacturing. With it, the guardian could break down machinery at the smallest level and reconstitute it. It had also developed a nanovirus that could get inside the brains and bodies of humans and control them.

Along the airfield in the center of the island, men and women slaved at their tasks. Their movements were smoother now, almost natural as the current version of the nanovirus designed by the guardian computer shunted their conscious will into blind obedience to the orders broadcast by the alien machine.

The guardian used the humans to perfect the

nanovirus. Those who did not serve the experiment well were buried, to prevent disease from hurting the ranks of the slaves.

Deep under Rapa Karu volcano, Kelly Reynolds was still pressed up against the side of the guardian. The ten-foot-high golden pyramid was now the center of all activity on the island, along with propagating the opaque shield that guarded the island from the humans and their weapons on the outside.

Kelly was thirty pounds lighter than she had been when she'd arrived on Easter Island. Even the relative stasis invoked on her body by the guardian was not enough to keep the body from breaking down, consuming itself to stay alive. The guardian was hardly aware of her presence anymore. She had served her purpose and she might serve a purpose in the future, but right now the guardian had many higher priorities.

Although the guardian was hardly aware of Kelly Reynolds, the opposite was not true. Kelly had managed to divest her body of the nanovirus by slipping a command into the guardian that went unnoticed by the higher echelons of control. Kelly could still tune in to much of what was going on with the guardian, but the flow of information and commands that her mind tapped into was like trying to take a drink from a rushing mountain stream, so much went by her that she had no clue about or could not reach. She had managed to get a single message out to Area 51, but beyond that, she had accomplished little, other than try to keep track of what the guardian was doing.

One thing was clear from what she had picked up on—the rebuilding of the *Washington*, the adaptation of the attack submarine *Springfield*, and the spread of the nanovirus among the captured humans—the guardian was preparing for all-out war. It would take time for it to have its forces ready, but war was coming. She knew that those outside the shield could not see what was going on, cloaked by the alien technology.

She could also pick up some of the messages the guardian was sending out, contacting other Guides, contacting The Mission, talking to the Airlia trapped on Mars, coordinating their efforts. All with one goal in mind.

All-out war was coming. And at the end, the guardian planned only to have its chosen slaves alive.

WESTERN CHINA

The Chinese air force lieutenant had never seen a similar radar signature. It was smaller than a commercial airliner, and the way it moved about sharply indicated it might very well be a helicopter. If it was, it was a very large one.

He grabbed the mike to broadcast on the emergency band in Chinese. "Unidentified aircraft entering Chinese airspace, identify yourself. Over."

He counted silently to three, correct procedure, then keyed the mike once more. "Unidentified aircraft, you must turn back immediately or you will be shot down. This is your only warning."

The lieutenant watched the screen for three more seconds before dialing the number for the local Air Force base.

Two SU-27 fighters scrambled in response to the call, afterburners blazing. With the recent events at Qian-Ling and the fragmenting of the world's countries into Isolationist and Progressive camps, the Chinese military, particularly those stationed in the predominantly western Muslim section, had been on a high degree of alert.

Lead pilot Major Fukang Jimsar's name represented the ethnic mix of the people in that part of China. A mixture of Chinese and Mongolian, he should not have been assigned to the Kashi air base. It was standing policy in the Chinese military to send personnel to assignments outside of their home area, thus ensuring it would be more likely that they would be willing to fire on rioters and keep the civil peace. Because Jimsar was one of the few pilots trained by the Russians in the SU-27, there had been little choice.

As soon as he was clear of the runway and had some altitude, Jimsar kicked in the afterburner, accelerating his fighter to Mach 2. He checked his radar to make sure his wingman, Captain Hanxia, was right behind him, then followed instructions as the lieutenant vectored them toward the bogey infiltrating Chinese airspace from the west, out of Afghani airspace. Jimsar knew that meant it could be coming from anywhere, as the anarchy in that neighboring country left it wide open for overflights.

The bogey flew along the northern foothills of the Himalayas as the two fighters closed the gap. The lieutenant reported the intruder making a course adjustment to the north, over the Tarim Basin while also dropping in altitude, apparently trying to escape the detection of radar. But by now, Jimsar's own radar had picked up the strange image from his higher altitude. The intruder was fifty miles straight ahead.

Standing orders dictated that the pilots aim their air-to-air missiles at any intruder and, once they received a lock-on signal from the radar homing device, to fire.

There was to be no reconsidering those orders, no initiative displayed, no hesitation. The Chinese military believed in one thing above all else—obedience.

When the Chinese bought the Su-27 Flanker aircraft from the Russians in 1992, they'd also purchased 144 AA-10 air-to-air missiles to arm the craft with. Jimsar knew that renaming the missiles R27 didn't change the country of origin for the weapons. Of course, he had never uttered that thought aloud. The Chinese government was desperately afraid of the corrupting influence of foreigners, yet it didn't draw the line at buying their weapons.

At twenty-five miles, Jimsar received lock-on confirmation that the on-board radar had acquired the target. Still out of visual range, he and his wingman armed their missiles.

Twenty miles and still closing, Jimsar flipped open the small red cover over the fire button. He thought briefly of the Russians downing KAL Flight 700 and the American navy ship shooting down the Iranian airliner. He knew if he did not fire there was a good chance he would be shot down on approach back to Kashi airfield by his own anti-aircraft batteries. His only other option was to try to fly to freedom, but he had a limited amount of fuel on board—not enough to reach a decent airfield to land the plane, and without the prize of the plane he doubted he would be granted asylum in any of the countries within reach. Also, if he fled, he had been told in no uncertain terms that his family would be sent to prison for the rest of their lives.

Jimsar pressed down, and a missile leapt from beneath each wing. Seeing that, his wingman followed suit and four missiles raced forward at four times the speed of sound toward the target.

Jimsar watched the action play out on his display.

"We have multiple hits," he announced, watching the trail of his two missiles abruptly disappear. This was followed by the second two at a slightly further location, which was strange, but Jimsar didn't report that.

"Confirm wreckage location," the lieutenant ordered.

In the time it had taken the missiles to fly twenty miles, the jets had flown ten. The short conversation at Mach 2 closed the gap another five miles. The Flankers dipped down and slowed until they were cruising at a relatively slow five hundred miles an hour, less than eight hundred feet above the desert floor.

Jimsar loved flying close to the ground, the terrain flashing by, emphasizing the speed and power of the jet. His eyes were glued forward. A tall sand dune over a hundred feet high rapidly approached.

For a second, Jimsar froze in shock as the strangest thing he'd ever seen rose from behind the sand dune. At his speed all he had was a glimpse, then he was by, but there was no doubt of the form—a dragon, open mouth pointing directly at them!

"Break and circle!" Jimsar ordered.

There was no response from Hanxia.

"Break and circle." Jimsar already had the Flanker in a steep left-hand turn.

"Roger, breaking and circling right," Hanxia replied in a shaky voice.

As his hands worked the controls, Jimsar replayed the image in his mind. "It was metal," he said out loud. He forced himself to snap back to reality. "Captain!" Jimsar ordered. "We're going to circle back. Do you understand? Over."

"Yes, sir."

"It's a machine," Jimsar said as he leveled off, heading back toward the dragon. He checked his display. Nothing. The dragon had to be using the sand dune to mask its radar signature. "Keep your eyes open," he warned Hanxia as the dune came into view five miles ahead and below.

"Sir, I think—" There was a loud burst of static, a scream inside of the static, then silence.

Jimsar's action was instinctive. He rolled the Flanker hard right, dropped altitude, punched in afterburners, and pointed the nose almost straight up. His back slammed into the seat from both the acceleration and vertical attitude.

His head twisted and turned as he searched the sky from this unique perspective. He saw the dragon racing up, no visible means of propulsion, three miles away and closing both horizontally and vertically.

Jimsar pushed the stick over, going from a climb to a twisting dive that put him head-on with the dragon, now less than five seconds away. He pressed the trigger for the 30mm cannon and felt the plane shudder as it spewed eight-inch-long bullets. Every fifth round was a tracer and his hand twitched on the stick, bringing the fiery rope of bullets right into the chest of the dragon as it raced toward him.

A line of light leapt from the dragon's mouth, and came back at Jimsar's plane as fast as his bullets were going the other way. He released the trigger and rolled left into a steep dive, narrowly avoiding the beam.

He kept his afterburners on and used the descent to add to his speed before leveling off at one thousand feet and almost seventeen thousand miles an hour in speed. He headed directly for the airfield at Kashi, the battle over.

Not only did Jimsar accept he was overmatched, his fuel gauges were dangerously low because of the limited fuel he had been given.

CHAPTER 5

THE GIZA PLATEAU, EGYPT

Duncan ran her hand along the top of the Ark, feeling the thin wires coiled into the lid. At first she had thought they were artwork, but when she tugged on them, they came out. Three long filaments of metal, ending in what appeared to be a small rose-shaped object about half an inch across, each made of a different material.

She looked at the wires for a short time, something nagging at her, as if she had seen this before. She reached up and took the crown off her head. On each of the three bands of metal that comprised the crown was a small indentation, the inverse of the objects on the end of each line.

She took each lead and placed it against the indent on the band made of the same material. The first two clicked firmly in place. She hesitated on the third, not sure what it would bring forth, but she had an overwhelming urge to move forward. She pushed the last one in place and the lid glowed brightly, enveloping her in a golden light, but that was all.

Duncan lifted the crown and set it on her head.

She gasped as she "saw" the Giza Plateau from a bird's-eye view, in the midst of a lush, green land, but with no pyramid or Sphinx on its surface. The vision shifted and she saw a Talon spacecraft on the plateau, its long, lean form against the blue sky. The Talon fired a beam down into the rock of the plateau, burning deep

into it. Another Talon appeared, the Black Sphinx just
below it, held in a golden field propagated from the tip
of the craft. The Black Sphinx was lowered into the
hole that had been cut. Men and women were now getting off the first craft carrying supplies.

Duncan was overwhelmed, her mind receiving input
faster than she could process it. What she was experiencing was more than a vision. She knew things about
what she was seeing. It was as if the Ark was giving her
information in the form of memories.

She reached up and ripped the crown off her head,
then collapsed next to the Ark, her body shutting down
to protect itself.

VICINITY EASTER ISLAND

It was the worst defeat the US Navy had suffered since
Pearl Harbor. The Nimitz-class carrier USS *Washing-
ton*, the pride of the Pacific fleet, was lost. As was the
USS *Springfield*, a Los Angeles-class attack submarine.

The loss of the carrier and its battle group to the unknown force on Easter Island had effectively gutted
Task Force 78's power, as the surviving ships'—two
guided missiles cruisers, three destroyers, two frigates,
another LA-class sub, and two supply ships—primary
mission was to guard the carrier.

The arrival of the *Washington*'s sister ship, the USS
Stennis, and her battle group, had restored the combat
effectiveness of the fleet that now steamed two hundred
miles north of Easter Island, with the new title of Task
Force 79, under the control of the commander of the
Stennis, Captain Robinette.

The orders to sit tight and do nothing didn't sit well
with Robinette, nor the men and women he

commanded. When he received a mission asking for a SEAL team to infiltrate Easter Island with the dual mission of reconnaissance and rescue, all he cared was that it had sufficient clearance, and ST-8 was the highest possible. He knew that he should check in with Pacific Fleet Command at Pearl to confirm, but he chose not to, for fear they would countermand the order. Instead, he personally took the tasking to the commander of the SEAL team billeted aboard his ship.

AREA 51, NEVADA

Turcotte had been pacing in the hallway outside the conference room for the past hour after grabbing a quick meal in the base's cafeteria. Yakov sat on a hard plastic chair just outside the door, a bottle of vodka between his knees. He'd made a big show of getting the bottle from Quinn, but Turcotte noted that the level had dropped less than a half inch in the past hour, barely a wetting of the lips for the Russian.

Turcotte was ready to go, but the replacements for the men who had been killed had not yet arrived, nor did he have sufficient intelligence on the Giza Plateau to even begin planning a second rescue mission.

Turcotte spotted a familiar face coming out of the room and changed his direction to walk beside Larry Kincaid, the NASA and JPL representative.

Kincaid had a file folder tucked under his arm. "I'm going to get these pictures from Hubble updated."

"Mars?"

Kincaid nodded.

"Cydonia region?" Turcotte narrowed it down to the spot where the Airlia base had been discovered.

"Yep."

As they reached the end of the hallway, Turcotte put a thick forearm across Kincaid's chest, halting the other man abruptly. "You got a secret or you going to tell me why you're being so quiet?"

Kincaid paused. "No secret." He held up the file. "They're doing something on Mars. I just can't figure out what."

"A weapon?"

Kincaid shook his head angrily. "You military guys— that's all you ever worry about—'is it a weapon?' That's what Majestic spent all those years concerned about: whether the Airlia artifacts could be used as weapons. Whether the Russians would find an Airlia weapon. And when we did find an Airlia weapon—or I should say the Germans did—we kidnapped it and used it to build a nuclear weapon to kill other humans. But nobody worried about the bigger picture."

"Is that a no?" Turcotte asked, forcing a smile on his face. He'd worked with men under stress before and he knew that things could unravel quickly.

"Too much coffee," Kincaid paused. "I don't know what it is, and I'm having a hell of a hard time getting more information. We're getting the shaft from our own government—they want to pull use of the Hubble from me. What are they going to look at that's more important than alien machines on Mars? We've had our heads in the sand about the aliens forever, and now people want to stick our heads back in there and pretend nothing's changed."

Kincaid took a deep breath before continuing. "I don't know, Mike. They could be uncovering a weapon. Nothing much we can do about it if they are. I would like to at least see what they're doing with the best equipment we have."

"Talk to Quinn," Turcotte suggested. "He can work some backdoors in the classified world, maybe get you the Hubble back."

"I hope so." Kincaid shoved the door open and went into the Cube. Turcotte spun on his heel and paused. Yakov stood there blocking the corridor.

"Do not be so hard on him. He is out of his depth. Overwhelmed. We all are." Yakov thumped Turcotte on the chest with a large finger. "Remember what happens to us when we think with this, rather than with this." He pointed at his own head.

"Don't—" Turcotte began, but paused when he saw Professor Mualama standing in the doorway to the conference room. "What is it?"

"I have translated the first two chapters of Burton's manuscript," Mualama said.

"That was quick," Turcotte noted.

"My studies have been very beneficial," Mualama said.

"Right," Turcotte replied, his tone indicating what he thought of Mualama's answer.

Mualama held his hand out for the door. "You'll find it very interesting. You have to remember that Burton was more known for his translation of others' writing— like the Kama Sutra or The Thousand and One Nights—than his own writing. This manuscript is all in his words, but it appears a large part of it comes from his translation of documents he discovered."

Turcotte went into the conference room, Yakov following. Quinn went to wake Che Lu.

"By the way," Mualama pointed at a picture tacked to the bulletin board, "that's Burton."

Turcotte paused in his rush to get to the computer. Burton was a savage-looking man, with scars etched on each cheek, blazing black eyes, and dark skin.

"He had a spear run through both cheeks when he was attacked at Berbera on his first expedition with Speke," Mualama said.

"Speke?" Turcotte asked.

"John Speke, another English explorer. The two went to Africa several times to search for the source of the Nile," Mualama explained.

There was another picture tacked to the side of the photo. A large stone structure, shaped like a tent.

"What's that?" Turcotte asked.

"Burton's tomb," Mualama said. "It's designed in the form of a Bedouin tent. His wife did that because he had a terrible fear of being enclosed in darkness. There's even a stained-glass window in the structure to let light inside where the body lay. Burton once said that he had horrible nightmares of being trapped inside a mummy's case."

Turcotte nodded, remembering what it felt like to be trapped inside a sub's hatch during lockout. The thought of being trapped inside a coffin, still alive, was more than he thought he could bear.

Mualama cut into his thoughts. "Your computer is all set to project the translation." Mualama had already disappeared behind the computer monitors. Che Lu hurried into the room and sat next to Turcotte, Yakov on the other side.

Turcotte hit the enter key. The screen on the far wall flickered and then the first words appeared.

BURTON MANUSCRIPT: CHAPTER I
MEDINA TO GIZA, THE BEGINNING OF MY SEARCH
1853–1855

I first met Al-Iblis in Medina. The circumstances of the occasion are not important as this is not my story. This story is about the alien creatures, their minions, and how they have meddled with man's history. And the promise and threat they hold for our future.

At that meeting, Al-Iblis never said exactly what it was he was looking for; it was only later that I surmised it was the Grail. He hinted that it was the Hall of Records he was seeking. There are rumors of a place that holds the truth of the time before our time.

He sent me like a bloodhound to track down its exact location and the way to get to it. He expected me to return to him with the secrets. Even now, after all my studies and searching, perhaps the Grail is the same thing as the Hall of Records, but if it is, it is also much more than that. Much more! I believe that the Hall of Records holds the Grail.

Al-Iblis pointed me to the Giza Plateau to look for a man named Kaji. A caretaker of some sort was the impression Al-Iblis gave. I will not dwell long here on Al-Iblis, as he will reenter the story very soon and you will understand him as I have come to.

I traveled to Giza while Speke went on to England. Many view this as the lowest point of my life—as Speke trumpeted finding Lake Tanganyika and claiming it was the source of the Nile, I was nowhere to be found in England, stolen of the supposed glory that should have been half mine.

Instead, I was in the midst of the most amazing experience I had to that point. I met Kaji. The details of how I convinced him to lead me to the Hall of Records are also not important. Suffice it to say he led me into the Great Pyramid, the one named after the Pharaoh Khufu. We descended into the very bowels of that massive edifice until we were below it, in the Earth itself. Kaji used a ring, a special ring, to open secret doorways, all of which led us farther into the Plateau of Giza, which he called the Highland of Aker after an ancient god.

At one point Kaji paused at a split in the way. One path led to a most destructive weapon, one that could destroy the entire plateau. But we went the other way. Deeper and deeper into the Earth. He told me the tunnels were carved during the time of the Neteru, the Gods of Ancient Egypt. At first I thought this ridiculous as the Neteru were considered a legend, a thing of an ancient religion. I now believe him.

He told me we were moving through the roads of Rostau and once more called the plateau the Highland of Aker. We finally arrived at a chamber deep beneath the Earth. Inside was the most marvelous thing I have ever seen. Another huge Sphinx, this one made of black metal, b'ja, the divine metal, Kaji called it. The Black Sphinx was large, if not larger than the stone one on the surface. This one was guarded by a statue of shemsu horus, a guardian of Horus with red hair, red eyes like a cat, mounted on a platform beneath the mighty paws.

We needed a key to get in, Kaji told me. And that was it. We didn't have the key. And he had only promised to show me the Hall of Records, not what was inside. We left, going back along the Roads of Rostau.

But Kaji had deceived me. He had planned for me to die there, under the Earth, his secret still safe. But I foiled his plan, and he was the one who was mortally wounded while both of us were trapped in a chamber deep under the rock.

Before he died, he told me an incredible tale. He told me he was a wedjat, one of the eye, a Watcher. And whom did they watch?

Ones Who Are Not Men. Airlia. Those who had

*come to Earth from the stars many, many years ago.
He told how they fought among themselves and destroyed much in the process. How their minions have
kept the fight all these years since. He told me little
more before he died, but I have been able to find out
more over the years.*

*I escaped. Kaji had told me there was a second
gateway to the Roads of Rostau. I found the secret
passage in the floor of the chamber we were trapped
in. I opened it with his ring. A shaft beckoned. Cold
air came from it and I heard the sound of water flowing, how close I knew not.*

*I had no other choice. I would not die in the dark
with my tale. I would return to England, to my
Isabel.*

*I climbed over the edge. I dropped, falling for a
second, maybe two. It seemed like forever to me in
that dark hole. Then I hit the side of the shaft and
slid. It was curving from the vertical very slightly. I
moved as quickly as I could along the stone, but it
was cut so smoothly, inhumanly smooth as the other
Roads of Rostau we had walked through.*

*I slid for a long time, how long I could not tell you
now.*

*When I hit the water it shocked me. I was sub-
merged, but came to the surface gasping for breath,
only to be immediately swept by the current away
from the shaft into a tunnel. Reaching up, I could feel
stone less than two feet above my head. I prayed the
ceiling didn't drop as the water took me.*

*But it wasn't the ceiling that came down, but the
floor that came up, or rather the water level dropped
as the tunnel must have widened. My feet hit stone as
I tumbled and bounced, trying to steady myself. I was
knocked down again and again, until finally I was*

able to get my feet, push back against the current,
now around my waist, and hold still.

It was dark. A darkness I hope no man ever knows
until the moment of his death. Carefully I moved with
the water, hoping, as Kaji had said, it would come
out at the Nile.

Turcotte stopped scrolling, excited. "That's it!" He spun
in his seat to Yakov. "That's how we're going to get to
her. Through the Second Gateway to the Roads of Rostau, to the Hall of Records."

"My friend." Yakov's voice was a deep, steady rumble.
"Perhaps we should finish reading first. We do not know
for sure that Mister Burton made it out exactly that way."

Impatiently, Turcotte turned back to the screen. He
hit the scroll.

I walked for perhaps a quarter mile. I knew my
pace and had used it in the past when mapping unfa-
miliar territories. Of course, being waist deep in wa-
ter certainly made the measurement questionable.

Be that as it may, it was some time before I real-
ized I was not alone. I cannot tell you how I knew
there was something else in that tunnel with me, but I
have often had this feeling and it has always been
right. Something moved in the tunnel behind me. A
chill ran up my spine, the cold hand of death, as
strong as I had ever felt it.

It—whatever it was—kept pace with me. I could
hear a sound, a light clatter of metal on stone, but
what caused it, I knew not.

I do not know why, but I felt that as long as I moved away from the Duats, as Kaji had called the chambers, it would let me go. But if I turned and tried to return, I was absolutely certain I would be struck down most grievously.

"What is he speaking about?" growled Yakov.

"His imagination was running wild," Turcotte said. "He had just survived an attack on his life. He was in a pitch-black tunnel that led God knows where."

"He was a brave man," Yakov said. "A man who went where others feared to go. He would not have written this if it was only his imagination. He really felt something was following him."

But Turcotte was already thinking ahead. "How far is it from the Giza Plateau to the Nile?"

"I don't know offhand," Yakov said.

"I've been there," Che Lu said, "and it's several kilometers at least to the river."

"Good, we can—"

"Let us finish reading," Yakov once more tried to douse Turcotte's enthusiasm.

I went farther, the water level remaining relatively constant. I shouted, hearing my voice echo against the walls, trying to bolster my spirits. I didn't stop to measure how far apart they were.

After a while, I felt that the threat was no longer close, that it was letting me go unscathed. But the water began to rise, moving more quickly. The tunnel was narrowing. Soon I bumped into the wall on the left. I kept my hand on it and continued to move forward. When the water rose to my chin and the roof of the tunnel was less than six inches above the top of my head and still declining, I realized that I would have to commit myself to fate once more.

I took several deep breaths, then threw myself into the surging water. The water filled the tunnel, top to bottom, side to side. I hit the wall several times, tumbling about until I had no idea which way was up.

I was growing faint, the air in my lungs used, when I felt a change in pressure in my ears. Light, blessed light hit my eyes.

I was out of the tunnel. I could see the surface above, light beckoning. I kicked for it, my head faint. I broke into air, sucking in lungfuls. My nostrils could catch the odor of the city, its foulness never smelling so wonderful.

I was in the Nile, just south of Cairo, north of Giza.

If you are reading this, then you must also be interested in the Hall of Records. It is well hidden. Going down from the Great Pyramid I must admit I was too overwhelmed to be able to give accurate information how to proceed. For that I apologize. An explorer should always keep his bearings.

But when Kaji led me out from the chamber that contained the Hall, I paid strict attention. I do not know how much help it will be, because it is only from the Hall chamber to the room I was trapped in—and there was not a way to open the stone door to the tunnel, but I will you give you what I know.

We went one hundred and twenty paces down the tunnel from the blackness that absorbed all light. On the left was a door, which Kaji opened with his ring. We turned right, two hundred and seventeen paces to

one of the doors that only appeared when he placed
his ring on the wall on the right side. Walk through
that door and then seventy paces to the hidden door
on the right, which guarded the chamber where Kaji
tried to trap me. I have used my pace count on many
mapping expeditions and have found that one hundred
and sixteen of my steps equals one hundred meters.

"If this tunnel he escaped through comes out north of
Giza," Turcotte said, "then this underground river must
begin somewhere south of there. That's how we'll infiltrate, with the current."

"But how will you find the cavern that houses this
Black Sphinx?" Yakov asked.

"I'll find it," Turcotte promised. "I'll reverse the directions Burton gave." He picked up the phone and
talked to Major Quinn in the Cube, ordering him to get
every bit of intelligence and imagery possible on the
Giza Plateau and the nearby Nile, particularly hydro-
graphic surveys of the river. He also told Quinn to begin
working on the request for the support Turcotte thought
he might need.

"But how will we open these doors Burton mentions?" Yakov asked.

"We have to get a Watcher's ring," Turcotte said.
"We had one before; Harrison, the Watcher who died in
South America, but Duncan took that with her to Giza.
We need another one."

"Then we need to find another Watcher," Yakov said.

"They show up when you least expect them," Turcotte said. "They've been—" He paused and turned to
Mualama. "Why did you start following Burton's path
and studying him?"

"I found him a fascinating individual and—"

"How did you find the scepter so quickly?" Turcotte cut him off, angry with himself for not having suspected this before.

"I told you. There were drawings in the manuscript that—"

"But you told us at first you couldn't read the manuscript," Turcotte said. "And now you've been translating it. You lied to us."

"And you kept the scepter secret for a while," Yakov noted, picking up on Turcotte's suspicion.

"Why did you let Duncan go to the Ark and not you?" Turcotte demanded.

"The robes would only fit her," Mualama said.

"You've only done what you wanted, when you wanted," Turcotte noted. He stepped closer to Mualama. "Who are you working for?"

"I work for no one," Mualama said.

"I don't believe you," Turcotte said.

Che Lu came forward between the two men. "We need to work together, not against each other."

Turcotte stabbed a finger at Mualama. "He's the one that's had his own agenda. It stops right now." He turned to Quinn. "I don't want him to have access to anything. The manuscript—anything. Put him under guard."

A panicked look crossed Mualama's face at the prospect of being cut off from the manuscript. "Wait!"

Turcotte turned back to him. "Yes?"

"I can tell you where you can find some Watchers."

"And how can you tell us that?" Turcotte asked.

Mualama reached into his shirt and pulled out a medallion hanging on a chain. The Watcher's symbol was etched onto the surface.

Turcotte's hands balled into fists. "You're a Watcher?"

"I *was* a Watcher," Mualama corrected.

"What happened?" Yakov asked.

"Do you still have your ring?" Turcotte's question was right on the heels of Yakov's.

"I did not have a ring. Only those of the first order have rings. Those of the second order have these." He held up the medallion once more.

"You said you are no longer a Watcher," Che Lu said.

"I was searching for information, and the first order did not approve of that. They wanted me to watch my corner of the planet and keep my mouth shut and my mind closed."

"Why did you turn on the Watchers?" Che Lu asked.

"I was tired of being a second-class citizen," Mualama said. "My ancestors were recruited to be Watchers by the original Watchers, the *wedjat*. There is a hierarchy in the organization, a split between those who claim a lineage to the original *wedjat* and those who were recruited, the first and second orders. And I wanted to know the truth."

"About?" Yakov asked.

"Who the Watchers were. Why we were watching."

Turcotte leaned forward. "And did you learn the truth?"

Mualama nodded. "Quite a bit of it."

"Tell us," Che Lu said. "Who are the Watchers? How did they begin?"

"Will your information help us get a ring?" Turcotte demanded, his mind focused on the upcoming mission.

Mualama rubbed a hand through the stubble of his gray hair. "It began when my wife was diagnosed with breast cancer. She went through it all—mastectomy, chemotherapy, experimental drugs. And none of it worked. When she died, I lost—" He spread his hands, searching for the right words. "I lost all my beliefs. My wife had been a Christian. To the moment she died, she believed she would be going to a better place. But I, who knew of the Airlia, did not know what to believe. I wanted the truth then.

"I had learned from another Watcher, one of the line of Kaji, about Burton visiting Giza. And I had found reports about Burton in Tanzania where I lived. So I began to study him. Then I began to follow his path all over the world, to the many places he had been, trying to discover what he had learned." Mualama shook his head. "It is funny that he found the repository of the Watchers, scant miles from his own home, in his dear England."

"Where?" Yakov wanted to know.

"Glastonbury Tor, near the Salisbury Plain, in southwest England," Mualama said. "Burton traveled there in 1864 with John Speke, his companion from their search for the Nile. The Watchers had tried to kill Burton before, so I imagine he brought Speke for protection. Or, more likely, to make sure someone else knew the truth in case something happened to him.

"During Burton's time as consul in West Africa, an attempt was made on his life after he mounted an expedition in search of the Mountains of the Moon, known to the natives as Ruwenzori, deep in the heart of my continent. It was not the first time such a thing occurred, and it would not be the last. When I learned that Burton and Speke had traveled to Glastonbury, I went there also. Especially given that Speke died the next day, supposedly of a self-inflicted gunshot wound, but I saw the long hand of the Watchers in that death. I as-

sumed Burton and Speke had come close to something
significant to evoke such a response.

"I approached the Tor at dusk, seeing the jagged,
broken finger of the stone tower at the top. I climbed the
long path when I knew there would be no others there,
to see what was to be seen. I knew what to look for, and
using a flashlight, I eventually found the smallest of in-
dentations in one of the old stones on the side of the ruined tower. I pressed my medallion against it, but
nothing happened.

"I continued my search and was about to despair of
finding anything more when I heard the sound of stone
moving on stone. A figure robed in brown came out of
the pitch-black shadow of the tower. He looked like a
monk, with a long white beard and pale skin that had
seen little of the sun. I held up my hand, showing my
medallion to him, and he in turn showed me his ring."

"Where did the rings come from?" Turcotte wanted
to know.

"Patience," Mualama told him. "That will be clear
shortly." The Watcher signaled for me to turn my light
out. "What do you seek?" he asked me.

"I had thought about what to say if I met another
Watcher, and I had decided that the truth was best. I told
him I had traveled far from my home and that I sought
knowledge. It was the right answer, for he smiled at me.
"I am the keeper of our knowledge," he told me.

"I asked him who he was and he told me his name
was Brynn. I knew the roots of the name from my studies of Burton's published writings—it was a derivative
of the ancient Welsh name—it meant 'from the hill.' He
asked me mine. I told him as well as where I was from.
I was not yet considered a renegade—it was that night
that would make me an enemy of the Watchers.

"Have any of you ever been to Glastonbury?" Mualama asked.

He was greeted with a unanimous negative.

"It's a very impressive place. We were over five hundred feet above the land on a mound of Earth that poked unnaturally toward the sky. How such an abrupt hill came into existence in the midst of a vast plain was a mystery that the locals referred to in terms of legend. I had learned to listen to such legends very closely.

"There were legends that in the old days Druids lived on the Tor and sang the eternal song. Constantly rotating people twenty-four hours a day, every day of the year, they kept the song alive, which supposedly kept the Tor alive. I asked Brynn about the Tor.

"He told me 'In the old days the Tor was surrounded by water. The land around us is actually below sea level and this was an island. It was called Avalon.'

" 'That is a place of myth,' I argued. 'Not real.'

" 'Do you feel the Earth beneath you? Is that not real?' Brynn didn't wait for an answer from me. 'This *was* Avalon. Many feet, belonging to people much more famous than you, have stood in this place and felt the ground under them. Arthur was here on his deathbed. Arthur was brought here after his last fight, the Battle of Camlann. Merlin came here many times.'

"Brynn told me more as we stood there," Mualama said. "He told me that before Arthur and Merlin there were others who had been on Avalon. He listed names I had heard of only in legend: Bron, the Fisher-King, who he said ruled from atop the Tor long before Arthur. And before Bron, Joseph of Arimathea came there from the Holy Land. He even told me there were some who believe the Christ-child came with Joseph during one of his early trips to trade tin."

"Ah!" Yakov could not control his reaction.

Mualama looked at the Russian. "I am only telling you what I heard and saw."

"Go on," Yakov said. "It is just that every time I think I have heard so much I cannot be shocked, I hear something more."

"I know how you feel," Mualama said. "Brynn led the way and we slid between broken stone into the ruined abbey, to the remains of the high tower. We stood in the center, the night sky visible directly overhead. Brynn held a hand up, muttering some words that I could not hear. Then he knelt, placing his ring on the stone floor. A large block, six feet long by three wide, dropped down two feet, then slid sideways, disappearing, revealing stairs etched out of the Tor itself, descending into the depths.

"I felt a sense of dread looking into the hole, as if a woolen blanket had been draped over my soul. For the first time in many years, I wondered if I really wanted to know more of the truth, if ignorance might indeed be bliss. What little I did know already weighed heavy on my heart.

"Brynn did not wait on me. He headed down and quickly faded into darkness. My boots echoed on the stone steps. The air was dank and chilly. I could tell from the walls that as we descended we were moving back through time. No one knew exactly when the current Tower had been built, but most agreed it was sometime in the fourth century.

"The stones that lined the stairs were perfectly cut. These stones gave way to the solid rock at the heart of the Tor. The walls were smooth, the tunnel sliced out of hard rock as easily as I could cut butter at the dinner table. Looking down, I could see that the steps were worn very slightly in the center, from generations of Brynn's walking up and down them, I imagined. Still we went down, the path ahead dimly lit from Brynn's and my lights, darkness beyond.

"Brynn had come to a halt on a landing. The stairs did another ninety-degree turn and continued down, but he was facing the stone wall. He placed his ring on it, and another doorway appeared. He waved me to go inside. I stepped through. Brynn followed, the door sliding shut behind them. It was dry inside, but still chilly.

"I gasped as I looked about. I was in a large cavern, about two hundred meters long by a hundred wide. It was brilliantly lit as the small amount of light from our lanterns reflected from the brilliant crystals that lined the walls, ceiling, and floor. Brynn set down his light.

"I asked him where we were. He told me 'This place has gone by many names over many generations. Some call it Merlin's tomb. Others say it is the antechamber to the Otherworld.'

"I asked him what he called it, and he simply replied home.

"I followed. In the very center of the cavern was a large crystal, over two meters tall. We didn't go that way, though. Brynn turned to the right and walked along the wall. He then opened a door, cleverly hidden between two pillars of crystal to reveal a level tunnel cut through the stone.

"We went along it for almost a kilometer before Brynn stopped. He placed his ring against the wall and a door suddenly appeared. The stone slid up. This time Brynn led the way in.

"We were in a small chamber, about ten meters long by five wide. The center of the room was full of wooden desks crammed tightly together. The entire wall on the right was fronted with what appeared to be wine racks, except instead of bottles, the small openings held rolls of parchment. I had seen a similar thing at an old monastery in France—a scriptorium—a room where monks painstakingly copied texts by hand before the days of the printing press, to ensure that copies survived.

"He told me the scrolls were the records and reports of our order, the tale of the *wedjat*. We were underneath the town, where the new Abbey was built. In the old days this was secreted under water.

"I stared dumbfounded, my heart beating rapidly in my chest. Not even in my wildest dreams had I imagined such a treasure trove.

"Brynn waved a hand at the wall. 'They are in various tongues and from many times. I have looked at some and there are few I can read.'

"I moved toward the scrolls, drawn as if by a powerful magnet that was linked to my heart and mind. There was only one other time in my life when I had felt such a way—the first time I laid eyes on my wife.

"Brynn and I sat and talked for a while and he told me what he knew. His line of Watchers didn't watch. They recorded reports from Watchers all over the world as they arrived. He told me that the task was now computerized. His job was to maintain the old records and allow other Watchers access to them.

"From him I learned that for millennia the *wedjat* was exiled from Glastonbury Tor. As he spoke, I eagerly went to the first racks. There was a rolled parchment in the upper, leftmost opening. Carefully I pulled it out. I took it to a desk and unrolled the first piece. It was covered in markings, much like the Egyptian hieroglyphics, but different in many ways. I know now they were High Runes.

"Brynn told me to look below the first sheet. I lifted the parchment and underneath was another page, written in Celtic. He told me it was the translation, done in the Dark Ages by his predecessors.

"I ran my fingers lightly across the first lines. I could feel the age of the paper and thought of the men who had labored here in this cave, translating the story of the history from High Rune to Celtic. I asked him to tell me of the *wedjat*, of the early Watchers.

"The *wedjat* were the priests of Atlantis. They served the Airlia, worshipped them as Gods. They worshipped the Airlia in a temple where no man was allowed. A pyramid, blood red in hue, capped the peak of the temple. Inside, upon a table in the center, was the Ark which held the Grail, worshipped as the bringer of eternal life, health, and knowledge."

"This red pyramid," Turcotte interrupted. "I haven't heard of this. The guardian computers I've seen are all gold." He glanced at Yakov. "Have you?"

Yakov shook his large head. "No. Perhaps that is the master guardian?"

"Perhaps," Mualama acknowledged. "The priests of the *wedjat* were not allowed to touch the red pyramid or even view it, never mind touch the Grail. The Ark remained closed to them. The leader of the Airlia, Aspasia, promised the *wedjat* that if they obeyed and were faithful, the day would come when all that the Grail could provide would be man's. Foremost among them would be eternal life. Immortality, the ultimate gift of the Gods, lay inside the Ark, vested in the Grail. You can imagine how that brought obedience."

"Not too different from many religions," Che Lu commented.

"The Grail held such promise and the *wedjat* worshipped it, but they were forbidden to tap into its power. They were told there would be a time when they would be given access to the Grail and all its bounty, but the time was not now. This went on for generations, each successive wave of *wedjat* believing the promise. Each dying and passing on the belief to their children. As this went on and on, and the Grail was never revealed, there were murmurs of discontent.

"Thus there were those who, despite the comforts of Atlantis and the bounty of the Airlia, were not content to serve. Those who wanted the knowledge and the power of the Airlia themselves, who wanted what the Grail could give *now*, before their own deaths, not content with the promise that it might be given to their children, or their children's children. There were even some among the *wedjat* who felt this way. They felt that if they could have access to the Grail, they too would be gods. But the Airlia were too powerful. Any sign of rebellion was dealt with quickly. Man had his place and the Airlia theirs.

"Then Artad arrived and the civil war among the Airlia began. The *wedjat* and the people of Atlantis fought for Aspasia and many died. And they were betrayed. They learned that their worship and obedience was worth nothing. The Airlia made a truce among themselves. Aspasia and his followers were banished to Mars, and Atlantis was destroyed by Artad. Many of the *wedjat* were killed. A small group remained alive, their mission to convert the locals to worship of Aspasia."

Mualama looked around at the others in the conference. "Could you imagine the sense of betrayal they felt? Their families killed, their home destroyed? They decided to organize themselves, to meet at the northern summer solstices in England, on the Tor. They met some of the survivors of Atlantis and learned some things.

"They were told that just before Aspasia left some of the most fervent of the *wedjat* had been taken inside the temple and transformed by Aspasia and his golden pyramid, the guardian."

"The Guides," Yakov said.

Mualama nodded. "They were given the job of moving the Ark and Grail to a safe place. They established The Mission. They also heard of others, The Ones Who Wait, recruited and changed by Artad to prepare for his return.

"So the survivors decided they would never again trust the Airlia. They would watch and make sure mankind was never again betrayed. A binding oath was taken. Then they scattered to their new homes. The Tor was set up as the repository of their knowledge.

"Brynn told me that the Tor was being phased out. That all the material was being scanned and stored in a computer at the Watcher headquarters. Basically, he was a relic. I think he was lonely. I asked him if he had heard of Burton. He told me his grandfather had allowed Burton in many years ago. Burton had Kaji's ring and had learned much from the Watcher records—even taking some scrolls—before being discovered. He managed to escape before they killed him."

"The rings?" Turcotte prompted.

"All priests of the *wedjat* had been given a ring that allowed them access to places in the temple. The same access technology was built into all the Airlia facilities."

"You still haven't told us where we can get a ring," Turcotte noted. "You've lied to us all along, why should we believe you now?"

Mualama ignored the question. "While Brynn and I were still talking there was a chime. He told me that meant someone had placed their ring or medallion on the wall, like I had. He left to go see who it was. I used the time to look through the documents." Mualama fell silent.

"And?" Turcotte asked.

"The Watchers must have been watching the Tor and Brynn, knowing he was old and foolish. Someone— whoever had come—threw an incendiary grenade into the scriptorium and shut the door. The scrolls began to burn. The room filled with flames and smoke, trapping me behind and the door. I lay on the floor as the room burned. My clothing caught fire but I didn't move, breathing the little oxygen that was left low to the ground. Eventually everything that could burn had done so. I was badly burned. The door opened and someone came in.

"A man knelt next to me. He told me that a painful death was the price I had to pay for betraying my order. He left me to die.

"He underestimated me.

"As soon as he was gone, I got to my feet and followed. I used the pain as a way to focus, to move."

Turcotte had seen men do incredible things while in unspeakable agony, turning the pain into motivation. And he had seen the scars on Mualama's back, which lent more credence to his story. Still, though, the effort required to move in such pain astounded him.

"In the tunnel ahead I could see Brynn in his robe and the stranger. I followed all the way to the surface and waited while they exited, giving them time to start down the Tor. Then I went outside into the night air. I could feel my shirt burned into my back, the cool breeze on the exposed nerve endings. I stumbled down the hill to my car. The worst was sitting in the seat. I almost blacked out. But I could see the headlights come on from their car and I wouldn't allow myself to pass out. I followed them.

"They drove east and I thought we might be going to London, but then they turned north. When the road

passed between stone sentinels, two upright rocks, I
knew where we were: Avebury. We were inside the ring
of stones that surrounds the place. They left the main
road and went onto an old trail. I turned my lights off
and followed. A large hill was directly in front and I
was amazed to watch their car drive right into the hill
and disappear as if snatched up by the darkness.

"I waited as long as I could, but they did not re-
appear. Then I went and sought medical attention. But I
had learned where a Watcher base was: Silbury Hill, inside the ring of circles at Avebury. If anywhere, that is
where you will find your ring."

Turcotte turned to Quinn. "Get a bouncer ready for
me. And all the intel you can get on this hill."

"The manuscript?" Mualama asked.

Turcotte poked a finger in the African's chest. "If the
information you've just given us is true, which we'll
find out shortly, I'll let you continue translating. But if I
catch you in another lie, or you hold something back
from us again, I'm going to make you disappear."

Turcotte left the room, followed by the others, leaving
Mualama alone. The African looked at the pile of papers
and a strange, confused look crossed his face as if he
didn't know where he was. His body twitched as his spine
drew tight, shoving him rigidly back against the seat he
was in. He gasped and his right hand went to the back of
his neck, the source of the pain. He blinked and the confused look was gone. The hand moved to his left ear and
lightly touched it. He pulled the hand back; there was
blood on it. A small trickle was seeping out of the ear.

Mualama dabbed at his ear and cleaned the blood.
He waited, but no more came.

Then he resumed typing.

CHAPTER 6

VICINITY EASTER ISLAND

Using the theory that stealth was better than might, particularly when the opponent had taken out a Nimitz-class carrier, the SEAL commander decided that only two of his men would make the attempt to get under the shield surrounding Easter Island. SEALs worked best in small units anyway, and two was the smallest possible operating element, as the buddy system was an unbreakable code in water operations.

Chief Petty Officers McGraw and Olivetti were the chosen ones. Both were highly qualified men with experience in combat ranging from Grenada to Desert Storm. Between them, they had over twenty-seven years of special operations time.

A three-step infiltration was planned. First, a Chinook off the *Stennis* would fly the two men and a F-470 zodiac to a position five miles outside the shield wall. The chopper would drop them near the island where they would use the boat to get as close as possible to the wall. They would then deflate the F-470, and take it with them as they dove down to the hole in the shield wall. Once through, they would reinflate the zodiac and continue with their mission. To exfiltrate, they would leave the zodiac behind and swim out and signal for the chopper to come pick them up.

The two men knew the location of the guardian underneath Rapa Karu and had maps of the tunnels UNAOC had drilled to get to that chamber. Beyond that, what was going on inside the black shield was an unknown.

Their priority, given to them directly by Captain Robinette, was to first find out what was going on, particularly with regard to the *Washington* and the *Springfield*, then rescue Kelly Reynolds. With these orders firmly in mind, Olivetti and McGraw boarded the Chinook and took off, heading toward the southern horizon.

QIAN-LING, CHINA

The earth was scorched for miles surrounding the black shield that stretched for over three miles in circumference at the base and a mile and a half in height. The dragon paused fifty meters from the shield. Inside, Lexina had a small black sphere in her lap, the surface covered with hexagons. Each glowed slightly, highlighting High Rune markings etched on the surface. Lexina tapped four in order. The shield suddenly disappeared, revealing the bulk of Qian-Ling, the mountain tomb. Over three thousand feet high, it was obvious the hill was not a natural formation as the sides rose uniformly to the rounded top.

Elek pushed forward on the controls, edging the dragon toward the hill. Lexina ran her hands over the black sphere once more, and a large circular opening appeared three quarters of the way up the hill, allowing the dragon access to its millennia-old lair.

Lexina turned the shield back on as they entered the tunnel that angled down to the main storage area inside Qian-Ling. The dragon came to rest on the floor of the large chamber. The back ramp dropped and Lexina led the way off, the case holding the Spear of Destiny in her hand. Elek, Coridan, and Gergor silently followed.

The chamber was huge, with arching beams of black metal supporting the roof. Inside were containers of various sizes, one of which had held the dragon, another of which was open, revealing a large spinning cylinder that propagated the shield wall.

Moving past these, she headed to a doorway which opened onto a wide tunnel, the other Ones Who Wait following. She followed that to a three-way intersection, where she made a right turn and began descending, the others still behind.

She stopped abruptly when a dim red glow lit the main tunnel about twenty meters ahead of her. The glow began to take form, elongating until a ghostlike apparition appeared before her. Lexina knelt, the others following suit, their eyes on the strange image. The legs and arms were longer than a human's, the body shorter, the head covered with bright red hair. The skin was flawless and white, the ears with long lobes that almost reached the shoulders. The eyes were red in red, just like Lexina's.

The figure's right hand came up, palm open, six fingers spread. It began speaking, the voice deep, but the language almost musical. It went on for a minute, then slowly faded.

Lexina put the case in front of her and opened it. She lifted the Spear of Destiny out, holding it by the short haft behind the lance-head. She stood, spear pointing forward, and took a tentative step down the tunnel. Then another step. She froze as a flash of light momentarily blinded her.

Blinking, her catlike eyes adjusted. A steady red beam went from one side of the wall to the other just below the spear point. Carefully she lowered the point until it intersected the beam. Like a multifaceted mirror, the blade reflected the beam in a circle around the tunnel for several seconds, then suddenly the beam disappeared.

With several more tentative steps, Lexina passed the guardian beam and continued down the tunnel, the others following. She kept the spear out in front, not knowing what to expect now that they were past the first trap. Like soldiers walking through a minefield with the point man holding a detector, they moved down the main tunnel toward the bottom level of Qian-Ling.

AREA 51

"Silbury Hill is the largest man-made mound in Europe." Quinn put a photograph on the conference room table for the others to see. "One hundred and thirty feet high covering five acres."

"Reminds you of someplace, doesn't it?" Turcotte asked Che Lu. Upon receipt of the intelligence, Turcotte had called a meeting in the conference room to plan their next step.

"Qian-Ling," she said. "The Airlia had a penchant for putting their bases underground."

Quinn nodded. "No one knows who built Silbury or why. According to legend it was always there. It's always been avoided by the locals, though, even today."

"The Watchers took over some old Airlia outposts," Mualama said. "Just as The Guides and The Ones Who Wait did. I'm sure Silbury is a smaller version of Qian-Ling."

"All right," Turcotte said. "That's where we're going."

"My friend—" Yakov's voice held a note of something that Turcotte couldn't quite place.

"What?"

"What are you proposing we do?"

"Get a Watcher ring so we can then go rescue Doctor Duncan," Turcotte said.

Yakov raised his bushy eyebrows. "Why?"

"Why?" Turcotte wasn't sure he had heard correctly. Then his face turned red and his hands balled into fists. "We're not abandoning her. We're a team here and—"

"My friend—" Yakov held up his hands, as if surrendering. "Listen to me for a second. In Moscow I acted from here," he tapped his chest, "and look what happened. I trusted Katyenka and she betrayed us." Turcotte remembered the incident deep beneath Moscow where Yakov's former lover had turned her gun on them.

"Are you saying—" Turcotte spit the words out, but Yakov spoke over them, quieting him.

"I am not telling you anything about Doctor Duncan. What I am concerned with is the larger picture. Both sides of this alien civil war have tried to destroy us. That is the overriding concern. What does Giza have to do with Easter Island? Or Qian-Ling? Or The Mission? Are threats growing there? We have no clue where The Mission disappeared to, and we know how dangerous it can be."

Turcotte blinked, confused. His mind had been so focused on the mission of rescuing Duncan that he couldn't quite fit Yakov's words. The Russian must have sensed that because he sat down, shoving out a chair for Turcotte next to him.

"We have made many mistakes. I have made many mistakes. Trusting Katyenka was just one of them. There have been others. Let us try not to make any more. Are you with me on that?"

Turcotte forced the anger in his chest to hold, a dike of resolve that was thoroughly saturated. "Yes." The word was torn from his lips.

Yakov nodded. "We are slowly learning some of the truth from Burton's manuscript. Information that would have helped us greatly had we been aware before. We would have known of the Watchers. The Mission. The Ones Who Wait. The Guides. All before they showed themselves to us in ways that took us by surprise. That cost the lives of all those people in South America. That cost your country two space shuttles. That cost me my comrades at Section IV."

Yakov pointed past Turcotte at the computers and Professor Mualama, who was now working on the manuscript, the clicking of keys a constant backdrop in the room. "Burton's manuscript. You see it as giving us the intelligence to find Doctor Duncan. But what is it really about?"

"The Grail," Turcotte said.

Yakov nodded. "Yes. The Grail. I think it is, how do you say, the linchpin to this civil war. Whatever it is—whatever it does—it is very, very important. I think it may possibly be what the civil war among the Airlia was about in the first place. I think the manuscript will give us an idea how important."

"What is the Grail?" Turcotte turned to Mualama. "Besides what we have here, I've read about it in terms of King Arthur and the Last Supper and all that. If it's so damn important, we might as well have everything we think we know about it on the table."

Mualama leaned forward slightly so he could see both men. "The Grail is a very old legend, one that rose from many places.

"It is often tied together with the legend of the Ark of the Covenant. It is said that the Knights Templar, when they ruled Jerusalem during the Crusades, knew the whereabouts of the Ark and the Grail. While legend often leads one to truth, the path is never clear or straight. So the Grail could be anything. Or it could be nothing."

"It's got to be something important for Burton to devote his life to trying to find it," Turcotte said, "and for Aspasia's Shadow to want it so badly."

"I agree," Mualama said. "The ancient legends are very complicated and have many different interpretations. There are indeed some who believe the Ark of the Covenant and the Holy Grail to be one and the same, but not either."

Seeing Turcotte and Yakov's confused expressions, Mualama tried to explain. "The Ark was possibly not an Ark. And the Grail was most likely not a grail or cup. But whatever each was, they could have been the same thing. Or maybe not. Or maybe each are parts of a whole. I think the latter is the reality, but I do not know for certain.

"After all," Mualama continued, "all those objects in their own time were extremely revered. Some of the legends that grew up around them were, as a spy would say, cover stories. Misinformation. Do you know how many different objects each has been described as?" He didn't wait for an answer. "The Grail has been described as a stone from the stars, one description which would seem to be more applicable now, wouldn't it? Of course, before people knew of the Airlia presence here on Earth so many years ago, that was interpreted to mean that it might be a meteorite. But maybe it literally was a stone from the stars brought here by the Airlia.

"There is even a legend that it is a stone that was given to man during the battle between Lucifer and the Christian's Holy Trinity by the pure angels, who took neither side in this war. Or a spin-off on that legend where the Grail was actually a precious stone that fell off Lucifer's crown when he was defeated in his revolt against God and cast down. And remember, Lucifer was an angel first. And he is mentioned in Burton's tale as a name given to Aspasia's Shadow.

"Pushing the Ark legend forward to the time of Christ, there is of course the more common notion of the Grail being the cup from which Christ drank at the Last Supper. Most people these days believe that to be the source of the legend, but it actually predates the time of Christ.

"There is an older Jewish legend—mentioned in the Old Testament and tied somehow to the Grail—about two objects called the *thummin* and the *urim*. These are balls of clear material filled with burning water. They are supposedly made from the fire of the sun. The *thummim* and *urim* were supposed to be buried in a cave with the Ark, or perhaps they were the Ark, who knows? Then again, maybe the *thummin* or *urim* were something entirely different. Maybe the ruby sphere you found under the Great Rift Valley in Ethiopia was one of those balls filled with a burning water? You must remember that early man had limited ways to describe things they had never seen before.

"Another way to explore legends is to examine the languages the legends are told in and their nuances in definition. Another word often used for the Grail is sangreal. Some cut that word in two, San Greal, meaning Holy Grail. However, if you cut it a different way, Sang Real, it means royal blood."

Mualama smiled. "This theory has never gained much light of day because it suggests something the Christians fiercely deny. The royal blood is the lineage of Christ. Those who espouse Sang Real as the true meaning of the Grail say that Christ had a child with

Mary Magdalene. There are those that believe a secret society has maintained Christ's bloodline down to the present day and that the progeny of this bloodline has been involved in many of the world's great events over the ages, and that person is the incarnation of the Grail."

"You're joking, right?" Turcotte asked.

Although Mualama was smiling, his voice was entirely serious. "I am not joking. I am simply relating to you some of the many legends surrounding the Grail and the Ark."

"I think blood does play into this somehow," Yakov added. "Burton mentions it and speaks of vampires in his manuscript. During my investigations for Section IV, I often came across references to blood. There were rumors the KGB ran an experiment for many years involving draining blood from people, searching for a certain strain. We know that the SS used blood from a Guide to inject into each of their top members—what were they seeking by that?"

Turcotte nodded. "Duncan thought that Von Seeckt stayed alive as long as he did because he had a trace of Airlia blood in his veins, even after all these years." He turned to Mualama. "What else do you know of the Grail?"

"There are, of course, the Celtic and Arthurian legends surrounding the Grail. These date from well before the supposed time of Arthur, though. And, of course, Arthur himself and the entire Camelot tapestry is a legend that we don't know how much credence should be attached to.

"In Celtic legend, there is the Cauldron—or Grail—of Awen which could bestow all knowledge on those who drank from it. It is also said the Cauldron could restore life itself.

"There is or another theory that the Grail is somehow

connected with another object of legend, the lance of
the Roman legionnaire Longinus—the spear that
pierced Christ's side on the cross."

"We know that part is true," Yakov said. "The Spear
of Destiny was an Airlia artifact."

"So you agree with the manuscript that whatever the
Ark or Grail are, they are also Airlia artifacts?" Turcotte
asked.

Mualama nodded. "Yes, and very powerful ones hidden after their civil war and presently of utmost importance now that the war is being renewed."

"What do they do?"

"To that, I have no answer. But all the legends, from
all the different sources, agree that the Grail, in whatever shape it is in, brings health, wisdom, and immortality to those who partake of it."

Turcotte thought about it. "But if the Grail is in the
Black Sphinx with Lisa, then rescuing her is one and
the same thing."

"Yes," Yakov said, "but I wanted to be sure you were
thinking clearly. Because that means that she is not the
important thing down there, no matter what your heart
tells you. If it comes down to it, we must get the Grail
before we get her. Do you agree?"

Turcotte looked up, met Yakov's dark gaze, and lied.
"I agree."

CHAPTER 7

SOUTH PACIFIC

Ten-foot waves smashed harmlessly against the wide steel bow as the ocean gave way to the massive object plowing through it. A football field longer than the Empire State Building was tall, and seventy meters wide, the supertanker *Jahre Viking* was the largest man-made moving object ever constructed.

A lap around the huge main deck covered over a half-mile and Johan Verquist was on his sixth circuit as he approached the bow. He ran smoothly, each foot slapping the steel decking lightly, then springing to the next step. He was in remarkable shape for someone seventy-eight years old and reputed to be the third-richest man in the world by those who kept such lists. Each trip the *Jahre Viking* made from the oil fields to the oil consumers increased those riches, but this journey was different.

Verquist paused at the bow and looked to the rear. The bridge was over a quarter mile—four hundred and fifty meters—away. His icy blue eyes surveyed the hundreds on deck—Dennison's flock—allowed up for their hour in the sun, before rotating with the next batch. There were over ten thousand people crammed into the large tanks. He'd had the tanks steam blasted, then converted into multiple-level barracks.

He had one mission and he approached it as he had approached everything else in his life—with single-minded determination to achieve the end result regardless of cost.

The Mission had made him what he was, and when

The Mission called—in the form of Guide Dennison—
to give him orders, he followed them without question.
As further impetus for this mission—after all, what
could they offer a man who had practically everything?
Dennison had also dangled a most intriguing
enticement, of particular interest to Verquist given his
advanced years—the possibility of extending his life.
Dennison had not been specific about how this could be
accomplished, but the possibility was simply too tempt-
ing to Verquist.

The lines around the old man's eyes narrowed as a
group of brown-clad people came toward him, a tall figure in the lead—Dennison. The Guide's face was perfectly smooth, making it difficult to judge his age
accurately.

Following Dennison's instructions, Verquist had
the ship's captain pick up groups of the Progressive—
those who believed mankind's future lay in allying with
the Airlia—off several coasts on the way from the Middle East to this location. Ferry boats, sailboats,
freighters—all types of craft had come out to meet his
behemoth ship and transfer the believers on board.

Verquist turned back to the bow, ignoring the approaching Dennison, and stared out at the deep blue ocean
that stretched to the horizon. The end of the journey was
not far off—Easter Island, where he was to deliver the ten
thousand to their destiny, whatever that might be.

A new world order was coming, and Verquist felt
certain that The Mission was going to be a very important part of that order. If delivering ten thousand people
at the cost of millions of dollars in lost oil revenue was
the price he had to pay to be part of that order, he considered it very cheap indeed. Especially if The Mission's offer turned out to have any degree of validity.

"Mister Verquist." Dennison's voice was as smooth

as his face. Verquist had heard the man "preach" though, and knew there was much more to this man than was readily apparent. After all, he and his other Guides had gotten all these people to give up their normal lives and come aboard to an unknown fate.

"Yes?"

"There has been an outbreak of cholera in hold 3 starboard." Dennison said it as casually as if noting the direction of the wind that blew over the bow. "We have mostly Pakistanis in there. One of them must have been infected before coming on board. Now it's spread."

Verquist frowned. They were a long way from help. "We could radio—" he began, but Dennison cut him off.

"We will radio no one. That is not the solution."

"I don't have the medicine to deal with—" But Verquist was cut off once more, something his former adversaries would have loved to see.

"We have already sealed hold 3 starboard," Dennison said.

"You mean quarantined," Verquist corrected him.

"We've sealed it," Dennison continued, "and now I want you to order the captain to flood it."

Verquist stared at Dennison for several seconds, not quite sure if the man was serious, although in his gut he knew he was.

"I don't think the captain will do that," Verquist said.

"Then do it yourself. The whole is greater than the few." Dennison turned and walked away, his inner cadre right behind him.

VICINITY EASTER ISLAND

The CH-47 Chinook, a double-rotor helicopter, was descending toward the ocean on the north side of the

Easter Island shield wall. The back ramp was down and
the zodiac rested on it, held on board by a nylon strap.
McGraw and Olivetti stood next to it, rigged in their
wet suits, their tanks on board the boat.

The belly of the chopper actually settled into the water, the ramp awash from the slight swell. Olivetti cut the
nylon and the zodiac slid into the water. Both men followed. They clambered aboard the rubber boat and got
the engine started. As they pulled away, the Chinook
rose into the air and headed back toward the *Stennis*.

McGraw was a slight man with muscles like ropes.
He had the nickname Popeye among the teams for his
build and for his willingness to take on anything and
anyone, no matter what the odds. Olivetti was a big,
quiet man with a fringe of hair he was very proud of, ignoring the large bald spot that dominated his crown.

"Ready, Popeye?" Olivetti asked.

"This is some weird stuff," Popeye McGraw replied
as he looked to the horizon where Easter Island was
supposed to be. "Let's do it."

They'd both been given as much information as was
available on what Easter Island had been and what it
could possibly be now. They knew there were three major volcanoes on the triangular-shaped island, Rapa
Raruku in the east, Rapa Aria in the northwest, and
Rapa Karu in the southwest. All had lakes inside their
craters, the only source of freshwater on the island.
There were also only two beaches, the rest of the island's shore being rocky. The one that concerned them
the most was the northern beach, Anakena, the direction
which the *Washington* had been headed when it had disappeared. It was there that the hole in the shield was
supposed to be—directly in front of them. After getting
through the shield wall, their first priority was to check
on the status of the *Washington*.

The next place they were to go was the southernmost volcano, Rapa Karu. Over a thousand feet high, it dominated that part of the island and would also allow them to look to the center where the International Airport was. After checking the airfield, they were to descend inside the volcano, locate the guardian computer—and Kelly Reynolds if she was still alive—and destroy the alien object.

Olivetti checked his bearing on the global positioning system, out of habit, as he brought the prow of the F-470 about. There was no mistaking direction. On the horizon, the top of the black shield was clearly visible now, straight ahead.

GIZA PLATEAU

Lisa Duncan felt stone pressed up against her cheek. She opened her eyes and saw she was lying on a stone floor looking at a white veil. She had to think hard for several moments, her head pounding as if from a severe hangover, before she remembered where she was.

She heard Aspasia's Shadow call for her. She noted the two sphinx heads turn, so she knew someone had entered the chamber. Slowly, she got to her feet, the pounding in her head almost making her ill. She pulled the veil aside and saw him standing in the entranceway.

"You've discovered you don't have everything you need?" Aspasia's Shadow asked.

"I've discovered the Ark is the history of the Airlia on this planet," Duncan said.

"The past is not important," he said. "You're like a child looking in the dark, not sure what you are looking for and if you did find something, not sure what its importance is."

"Where are the *thummin* and *urim*?" Duncan asked.

"Very smart," Aspasia's Shadow said. "I am currently in the process of tracking them down."

"So you don't know where they are?"

"They're in a very secure place," he allowed. "They are in the Negev."

"Israel?"

"They traveled for a long time and were last held by monks in Ethiopia at one of the monasteries on Lake Tanaga. But they were not safe there, and the Israelis took them back to the Dimona archives bunker in the Negev Desert that also houses their nuclear weapons. It is supposed to the most secure place on Earth." He gave an evil smile. "But I have learned over the years that no place is totally secure."

"And if you get them?"

"Then we can bargain. I'll have something you want, while you have something I want. I almost had them once before, long ago, but they slipped through my grasp."

"How long ago?"

"I have been walking this Earth since before the beginning of your human histroy."

"How can you have lived so long?" Duncan asked.

Aspasia's Shadow pointed at his head. "This—the knowledge, the experiences—have lived as long as Aspasia's Shadow lived." He tapped his chest. "This body, this shell, has a life span. I acquired this one forty-five years ago. It will be time to move on soon. This body is failing me."

"I don't understand."

Aspasia's Shadow pulled an amulet from underneath his black cloak. "This is the essence of Aspasia—of me. All that is missing are my experiences since I last updated it a month ago. It is called a *ka*. Think of it as a recording device for one's life, for one's memories. But it is more than that. When the time comes to pass on, as it is called, I will go to The Mission. There the *ka* will be updated to the present, then this body will be destroyed. The *ka* will be used to install my essence into the new body and my life will go on."

"If you can do that, then why do you want the Grail?"

"Because the Grail can do more than that."

"What more?"

"That information I cannot give you."

AREA 51

Turcotte studied the information Quinn had gotten regarding Silbury Hill as the bouncer lifted off the floor and floated out the hangar doors. As soon as it was clear, the pilot accelerated and gained altitude.

"Do you believe Mualama's information?" Yakov asked.

"He has the scars from the fire," Turcotte noted.

"He also withheld telling us he was a Watcher for a long time," Yakov said.

"We need a Watcher's ring," Turcotte said simply. "If there are no Watchers at Silbury, then I won't believe him."

"Do you have a plan?" Yakov asked. The two of them were the only occupants, beside the pilot and co-pilot.

"Not yet."

"Should we knock on the side of the hill and ask them if they can spare us a ring?"

"Why don't you do that?" Turcotte snapped.

"My friend, I think you are not seeing the forest for the trees."

"Look," Turcotte held out a photograph. "See how the side of the hill is indented right here?"

Yakov took the picture. "Yes."

"Remember at Qian-Ling how there was an opening for a bouncer to go in and out on the side of the mountain?"

"Yes."

Turcotte tapped the picture. "That's where we're going to knock."

CHAPTER 8

EASTER ISLAND

Popeye McGraw and Olivetti simply sat in the zodiac, bobbing in the slight swell. As a SEAL they'd traveled all over the world and seen some pretty amazing sights from the interior of whorehouses in the Philippines to the full fury of a Pacific typhoon to the northern lights off the shore of Alaska, but they'd never seen anything like the black wall that shimmered in front of their boat.

"Damn," Popeye said, which pretty much summed it up.

Olivetti spit over the side of the zodiac. "Yeah."

Popeye grabbed his tanks and slid them on. He secured his weapon and equipment bag. "Ready?"

"Yeah."

Popeye did one last position check using the ground positioning receiver—GPR—confirming they were over the spot where they needed to be. He sealed the GPR in its waterproof bag. They turned the valves that connected the five chambers that made up the U-shaped outer hull, opening them to each other. Then Popeye opened a valve cap near the rear and air rushed out. He turned and opened another valve, attaching a hose from a CO_2 tank secured on the floor of the zodiac securely to it.

Both men fit their mouthpieces, turned their backs to the water, sat on the transom, then flopped overboard. They bobbed in the water as the zodiac slowly settled lower and lower. They grabbed the hull nearest them and wrapped their arms over it, helping push out the last of the air. Popeye reached over and secured the valve cap as the zodiac reached less than neutral buoyancy and slipped beneath the waves. Olivetti attached a lead from the lifeline that lay on top of the buoyancy tubes to a line around his waist. Then both men dove.

They had worked together so often that they fell into a pattern as soon as they started diving, angling toward the wall—Popeye in the lead with his nav board held out in front, Olivetti right on his fins pulling the deflated zodiac behind him.

Popeye paused as he saw the black wall just ahead, then went vertical, diving straight down. He slowed as he saw the bottom. A large divot had been carved out of the bottom as if a large hand had scraped along the coral and rock.

Cautiously, Popeye settled down to the lowest point of the divot. There was a gap below the shield wall, about seven feet deep. He looked over his shoulder at Olivetti floating behind him, the zodiac slowly settling to the bottom. There was no question if they were going through.

Popeye finned forward, scraping his belly on the bottom. He went for several seconds, then rolled on his back. He was through. He floated up as Olivetti shoved the deflated zodiac through next. Popeye pulled it through, then the other SEAL followed.

Popeye grabbed Olivetti's shoulder and gestured furiously. Ahead of them was a long gray wall, touching the bottom as it reached toward shore. The *Washington*. It was moving very slowly, the hull edging back into deeper water. Looking closer, the two SEALs could see that a black film covered the hull where it was touching the bottom, fluctuating as if it were alive. They'd heard the reports of how the ship had been taken over and had no desire to get closer.

Popeye jerked a thumb toward the surface. Olivetti nodded and twisted a valve on the CO_2 canister. The zodiac began filling and ascending, the two SEALs following. By the time the boat reached the surface it was almost fully inflated.

Popeye's head burst into the open air and he blinked. The *Washington*'s enormous bulk filled his vision. Something was different about the ship. He'd spent a lot of time aboard Nimitz-class carriers and he didn't doubt his first impression. He scanned the ship from bow to stern, checking for the differences.

The first thing that struck him was that there was no one moving; not a single crew member. A ghost ship, slowly sliding into the ocean from the shore. But then he saw more. The island, which contained the ship's bridge and operations center, was more streamlined. The various radar and communication masts were different too, although Popeye wasn't sure what that meant. The bow, facing inland, was torn and twisted, but even as he watched, he could swear that it was being repaired, centimeter, by centimeter, even though he could see no men working on it. He felt a chill watching the majestic carrier, the pride of the fleet, being controlled by forces he couldn't understand.

He shifted toward the island. Six *maoi* statues gazed out to sea. Popeye rolled on board the zodiac, Olivetti following. They were a half mile away from the carrier, now afloat. Olivetti cranked the engine and they turned to the west to circle around the island. The first part of their mission was complete, although they weren't exactly sure what their report would say.

QIAN-LING, CHINA

The main tunnel widened beyond the scope of the lights Lexina and her comrades carried. From the echo their

feet made on the stone floor, it was obvious they were
entering a large open space.

Lexina froze, seeing a tiny point of light, above and
ahead. The light grew stronger, illuminating the cavern
they had entered. It was over a quarter mile wide and a
half mile long, with the roof over four hundred feet
above their heads, where the glowing orb was now at
full power. The walls were smoothly cut stone, the floor
so flat it looked polished. But it was the center of the far
wall that drew the attention of Lexina and the other
Ones Who Wait.

Two golden doors, inlaid with intricate lettering,
each one hundred feet high and fifty wide, were set in
the wall. Doors worthy of a god. Like moths to a flame,
Lexina, Coridan, Elek, and Gergor were drawn forward,
across the cavern floor. They stopped in front, overwhelmed by the sheer size and beauty of the doors.
Etched into the gold was High Rune lettering mixed
with Chinese symbols.

Elek pointed. "That is the sign of Shi Huangdi, the
first Emperor of China."

But Lexina could make out something in High Rune
that was much more significant. "Artad and his people
are behind these doors waiting to awake!"

"How do we open them?" Coridan asked, always the
practical one.

Lexina continued to translate what she could of the
High Runes, and found the answer, right before them.
"This—" she held the Spear of Destiny "—goes here."
She put the point on a spot at eye level exactly along the
seam where the doors met. The spot she was pointing to
was outlined with black metal, *b'ja*, the metal of the
Airlia.

She pushed the spear, pressing it against the black.
The point slid into the *b'ja* to the base of the tip, then

stopped. Lexina let go and stepped back. The doors seemed to shimmer, then, as if a stone had been thrown in a pond, the gold changed to black in an ever-widening circle. When both doors were completely black, there was a loud groaning, as if the metal were protesting. The seam split smoothly and the doors began swinging outward, the spear staying in the opening.

AREA 51

Professor Mualama hit control-D on his keyboard and looked up as the screen filled with words. He turned as Che Lu came into the conference in response to summons.

"What do you have?" she asked.

"You'll find this interesting." Mualama pointed at the screen.

BURTON MANUSCRIPT: CHAPTER 2

Following the destruction of Atlantis and the departure of Aspasia for the skies and the disappearance of Artad, the Watchers at first thought that the world was free of the direct influence of these creatures from the stars. It turned out they were wrong.

Some of The Guides traveled to the Middle East and established a place called The Mission. There appeared in Egypt around nine thousand years before the birth of Christ, new gods, called Neteru, *of whom Isis and Osiris were the two primary ones. The Watchers eventually learned that these new gods were a different form of Guide who wore the* ka *of Aspasia and some of his other Airlia, being their Shadows on Earth to prepare for their return. These*

*were of an order above that of Guide in a way, be-
cause they had the memories of the Airlia imprinted
on their brain.*

There is a device called a ka. *The word in ancient
Egyptian means soul or spirit. The symbol for it is
two extended arms with no body in between. I have
seen this sign on walls and even carved into statues,
such as the* ka *statue of* Hor Auibre *from the thir-
teenth dynasty.*

*I have talked to scholars about the root of the ka
and there is much that is not known. They feel that
the* ka *means something more than just the soul. It
represents the sustaining power of life, an interesting
term if one thinks about it. There are many represen-
tations of a* ka *being fashioned by the ram-headed
god* Khnum *and it was meant to be a double or twin
of the person from which it was drawn. The* ka *came
into existence when a person was born, and the term
"to go to one's* ka" *meant one died and the* ka *was
passed on.*

The hemu-ka *were a kind of priests that facilitated
the passing on of the* ka. *I was told by Kaji about the
Airlia. But he also talked of Ones Who Were Not
Born of Women, also known as The Ones Who Wait.
Throughout the history I will recount to you, there
will be those who are "shadows" of Airlia from both
sides. How they come into being, I do not know. But
they are not born.*

*This first age of civilization in Egypt was the age
of the rule of the Airlia Shadow gods. As the Watchers received this disquieting report, it was often debated whether they should interfere to stop this, but
they remained true to their rules. Also, it appeared
that this handful of Shadow Guides did not seek to*

conquer or expand their empire. Their mission was unclear for a very long time.

I think, also, that unspoken among the Watchers was the knowledge there was nothing they could do to fight the Shadow Guides, who had the loyalty of their new cast of Guide-priests and the population who followed the priests, as the wedjat themselves had once given their loyalty.

For thousands of years there was peace and prosperity in Egypt—as long as the people worshipped the Shadow Guides under their new names.

It appears that Aspasia was able to rescue more out of Atlantis than was first thought and pass it on to the Shadows. The Grail was reported to be in Egypt along with the master guardian machine and other Airlia artifacts. This guardian machine was the device Aspasia used to transform men into Guides. There was also a machine that was used with the ka to imprint the personality of each Airlia on the human mind, allowing it a kind of immortality.

The guardian has been described to me as a gold or red pyramid of varying heights, from several to twenty feet, which makes me think there might be more than one of these things located at various places around the world. I came close to seeing one in South America, but that comes later.

The ka machine has been a closely guarded secret among the Guides. Wherever it is, The Mission is. For many years it was at Giza—the Highland of Aker, a region named after one of the Shadow Guides.

Extensive tunneling was done by the Shadow Guides underneath the Highland of Aker. The Hall of Records, taken from Atlantis before it was destroyed,

was secreted below the stone sphinx. The carving became a thing of legend among the people of Egypt;
they spoke of it only in whispers and no one wrote of
it under penalty of death. None were allowed to approach close or else they were struck down by
guards. This is why historians today know so little of
the stone sphinx or why it was carved.

Plans were made for more buildings near the
sphinx, but these were not carried out before the end
of the age of the Neteru.

As happened in Atlantis, there were others who
could fight these Shadow-gods. As long as the Neteru
maintained a low presence, they existed. But around
the time of four thousand years before the birth of
Christ, they attempted to expand their empire. Thus
there appeared in Northern Egypt two of The Ones
Who Wait who pretended to be Gods named Nepthys
and Seth. A civil war broke out. The Ones Who Wait
were successful at first, slaying Osiris and Isis, and
the other Neteru, thus ending the first age of that kingdom. But the Ones Who Wait were not able to make
their escape before being slain in turn by the faithful
followers of the Neteru, led by a Guide named Horus.

Thus Egypt passed into the second age, the time of
the followers of Horus, a Guide, not a Shadow.

While all this was happening in Egypt, Watchers
tried to find where The Mission and The Ones Who
Wait were hiding and what they were doing. As near
as I can determine, the Watchers suspected that The
Ones Who Wait had a secret base in Africa, close
enough so that they could keep watch on Egypt and
The Mission, which they also believed was now
somewhere not far from Egypt. Having traversed
that harsh land, I know how well hidden those bases
might have been.

The Watchers searched for the base for many years. Several Watchers who went on that mission were never heard from again.

"Interesting," was Che Lu's comment as she read. "There has always been speculation among those who dared to think that there were ages to the kingdom of Egypt before that of the pharaohs. Even staunch Egyptologists are at a loss to explain how the kingdom sprang, apparently fully formed, into existence and then didn't progress for over three thousand years."

"It still doesn't tell us where The Mission is," Mualama noted, "or what the Grail is."

"But it does say there was a master guardian computer at Giza," Che Lu said. "That confirms the message that Kelly Reynolds sent us from Easter Island. If we can find this master guardian, perhaps we can control the other guardians. This may be very important."

"If it's still there," Mualama said. "This is talking about a time over twelve thousand years ago. Much has happened since then."

"This possible Airlia base that's mentioned," Che Lu continued. "I think that I might have something that will help with that. Nabinger had a page of High Rune symbols that he believed were coordinates for Airlia bases, but he couldn't line them up with anything. The problem he had was that he was using our number system based on tens, while I think the Airlia system was actually based on units of twelve. I believe I've been able to correctly translate the coordinates, but I have not had a chance to apply it to a map."

"Perhaps someone here can help you with that,"

Mualama suggested. He scrolled down. "You'll find
this very interesting."

*If Aspasia left behind some of his people in
Shadow form to walk the Earth and try to regain the
glory of Atlantis in Egypt, what of Artad's group?
Where did they go?*

*I eventually found the answer to that buried
among the many parchments I pored through and
translated over the years.*

China.

*I have not had the opportunity to travel to that
land, so all I know of it I have gathered from the
Watcher scrolls and written histories that I have
been able to find, merging the two to find some sem-
blance of the truth.*

*According to the Watchers there were "white peo-
ple" in western China around 9,000 B.C. This was a
small enclave of The Ones Who Wait.*

*Around five millennia before the birth of Christ,
large numbers of Chinese people began settling in
the Yellow River Valley. This was possible because
two things, previously unknown, became prevalent—
agriculture and animal husbandry. While I do not
mean to say that man could have not invented these
on his own, I find it curious that in different places in
the world these two advances came about at roughly
the same time. I believe this was due to the diaspora
from Atlantis and also the influence of The Ones Who
Wait and The Mission.*

*As in Egypt, within an amazingly short period of
time, civilization began to flourish in China. The first*

Emperor—a myth to historians, a fact to Watcher records—was called Shi Huangdi. He was also known as the Yellow Emperor or the White Emperor, depending on which account one reads. He was also considered to be the "Son of Heaven." He is credited with inventing writing, yet there are some scholars who point out that the characters used were so advanced they must have come from an earlier type of writing—obviously High Rune writing from Atlantis.

Mathematics also was "invented" under Shi Huangdi. It is interesting to note that the first number systems used in China were based on factors of six.

According to Watcher records, Shi Huangdi was a Shadow of Artad or even, perhaps, Artad himself.

Shi Huangdi's empire was barely on its feet when it faced assault from The Mission. An Empress named Chiyou—a Guide, according to Watcher scrolls—attacked him from the south. It is written in Chinese legend that a decisive battle was fought at Zhuolu. It is said that Chiyou rode a dragon into battle, one which let out a thick fog all over the field of combat, but that Shi Huangdi was able to lead his troops out of the fog and into victory using his "compass chariot."

Chiyou was killed and the dragon captured, but Shi Huangdi was forced to relinquish the kingdom to humans, just as had happened in Egypt. He also left plans for a massive building project—the Great Wall of China, which was constructed by the first human emperor. I do not know why the Wall was built, although perhaps it is simply as it appears, a defensive line against barbarians, allowing China to develop in relative peace.

Another event of great interest to me occurred later in China's history. Artad was reported to be buried in a great tomb, somewhere in the western part of China, equipped with many security devices. A special key was needed to open this tomb, when, according to legend, Shi Huangdi would return.

Apparently an attempt was made to rob the tomb in the seventh century A.D. The Watcher who was responsible for keeping an eye on the tomb reported it and the robbers were foiled by the Emperor's men. To avoid the possibility of anyone getting to the lowest level and opening Artad's cavern, the Emperor decided to remove the key to that tomb from China. This key was in the form of a spear, housed in a long black box. There was also a large metal container containing another artifact that was shipped with it.

The Chinese sent these materials with a massive naval expedition led by Admiral Cing Ho. They traveled around Indochina to the Middle East.

"'The power and the key,'" Che Lu said. "That was what was on the marker that was found in Ethiopia by Turcotte and Duncan. Written in Chinese."

"The power was the ruby sphere that Turcotte used to destroy Aspasia's fleet," Mualama said. "And the Spear of Destiny was with Cing Ho. I wonder how it ended up in the hands of the Nazis?"

"Colleagues of mine found Caucasian mummies in western China," Che Lu said. "Those who reported this were ostracized and their findings kept secret. We must keep this information to ourselves. It will not endear us with those in power in Beijing to give them this information that our civilization came from outsiders."

"Consider it another way," Mualama said. "Perhaps this information could be used to sway the people of China away from their Isolationist stance once they realize that their history was manipulated by the Airlia. A war is coming in which all countries and all people are going to have make a decision which side they are on. The only way they can make that decision properly is to have this information," he tapped Burton's manuscript. "I think neither side can be trusted."

"Artad did not hurt my country," Che Lu said. "He helped it grow."

"Are you sure of that?" Mualama asked.

Che Lu considered Mualama. "Are you certain you trust what Burton has written?"

"There's no reason not to," Mualama said.

"There's really no reason to, either."

"Why would Burton lie?"

"Why does anyone lie?" Che Lu did not wait for an answer as she supplied her own. "To advance their own cause."

"What cause could Burton have had?"

"That is the question we need an answer to," Che Lu said. She stood and walked out of the room, Mualama's dark eyes following her.

AVEBURY, ENGLAND

The Atlantic crossing had taken less than an hour at the extreme speed the bouncer was capable of, but right now it was barely moving as they drew closer to Avebury. Through night-vision goggles, Turcotte could make out the rings of stone that surrounded the area, monoliths raised by ancient people, most likely as warnings against approaching Silbury Hill, as the *Moai*

statues had been carved and placed on the shores of
Easter Island.

Looking ahead, Turcotte could see the dark hill rising like a cone out of the middle of a large field. There
was no doubt it was an unnatural formation, given the
smoothness of the sides and symmetry of form.

"Are you ready?" he asked Yakov.

The Russian shrugged. "No. But that won't stop you."

"We grab the first person we see and take their ring.
It's simple."

"Simple," Yakov repeated. "Nothing is ever simple."

They were about a quarter mile from Silbury Hill,
still approaching at the same steady rate. Turcotte
grabbed the shoulder straps, buckling them securely
over his chest. Yakov did the same. The pilot lined the
bouncer up with a very slight depression near the top of
the hill on the western side.

The bouncer was now less than a hundred feet from
the depression. Turcotte looked about, but there was no
sign of activity. The closest lights were from a house
over two miles away. The depression in the side of the
hill was slightly larger in diameter than the bouncer,
which fit with Turcotte's idea that it was similar to the
one in Qian-Ling.

The forward edge of the bouncer touched the hill. It
was a question of an irresistible force against an im-
movable object and which would give first as the pilot
tweaked the controls. Turcotte had faith in the strength
of the bouncer after seeing how little damage had occurred to one that had crashed.

The pilot used the craft's edge as a large spade as it
dug into the depression. Dirt and rock fell away, tumbling down the hillside. There was a loud screech, and
the pilot paused as they all looked forward. A line of
metal had been uncovered.

"Airlia," Turcotte said.

"Now the real test," Yakov said. "Also, I think those inside have heard us knocking now."

Turcotte shrugged. "What are they going to do about it?"

The pilot lined up once more, placing the edge of the bouncer against the metal door. He increased pressure on the controls. It was an eerie contest of power played out in silence, as there was no sound of an engine from the bouncer's system.

"It's giving a little, I think." Turcotte was watching forward when Yakov grabbed his arm.

"There!" The Russian was pointing to the right. A Land Rover with its headlights off had appeared from out of the hill itself, racing off into the darkness.

"Like rats off a sinking ship," Turcotte said. "Go after them," he ordered the pilot.

The bouncer easily closed on the Rover, still blacked out, but visible in their night-vision goggles. There was a flare of red as the driver braked, then spun a turn onto a dirt road that ran between two lines of trees.

"What now?" Yakov asked. "They will be in town shortly."

"Land on top of it," Turcotte ordered the pilot.

"What?" The pilot wasn't sure he had heard right.

"Bring your craft down on top of the truck and stop it," Turcotte said. "Crush it if you have to."

"Mike—" Yakov had his hand on Turcotte's arm.

"They destroyed our shuttle," Turcotte said. "They tried to kill Mualama. They've been playing their games for a long time and the game is over."

The pilot went ahead of the Rover, then turned back, coming down the road toward it just above the trees. The bouncer's edge lowered, clipping through the trees like matchsticks. Yakov and Turcotte couldn't help but flinch as they saw the shattered trunks and tree limbs slide along the side of the craft.

The driver of the Land Rover slammed on his brakes as the bouncer approached, then threw it into reverse. The forward edge of the craft was just above the hood of the truck when the pilot slammed down on it. With a crumple, the Rover was pinned to the ground, stopping abruptly.

Turcotte was already on the ladder and out of the hatch. He slid down the skin of the bouncer right onto the windshield of the Rover, weapon ready. There were two men inside, dazed from their impact with air bags. Turcotte rolled off the windshield onto the ground. He ripped open the door and dragged the driver out.

Turcotte pressed the muzzle of the MP-5 against the chin of the man. He could see the large ring on the Watcher's left hand. His finger touched the trigger and began to pull when Yakov's large hand grabbed the muzzle and pulled it up.

"Get the ring," Yakov said. "That's what we came for."

Turcotte reached down and started to pull it off. The man curled his fingers into a fist and Turcotte overcame that impediment by digging his thumb into the man's elbow, pressing down on a nerve junction. The hand flexed open as the man gasped in pain. Turcotte slid the ring off. The other man was opening the door on his side and Yakov fired a round, causing the man to duck.

"Come." Yakov was on the edge of the bouncer, reaching down for him. Turcotte took his hand as Yakov lifted him onto the craft. They raced up the side and into the hatch. They were airborne before the Watcher was on his feet.

CHAPTER 9

DIMONA, NEGEV DESERT, ISRAEL

Simon Sherev believed in the sanctity of the state of Israel much more than he believed in God. In fifty-two years of service, he had conducted countless undercover operations as a member of the Mossad and fought in four wars as a reservist assigned to the paratroops. He had killed men, women, and children when it was called for in order to accomplish the mission, and the mission always supported the sanctity of the state.

Sherev was a realist, a man who saw the world for the brutal place it was. Power mattered. Nothing else. As a child his father had told him the story of Archimedes, the Greek who had claimed he could move the world if he had a fulcrum point and a long enough lever. Sherev never forgot that. He also never forgot that Archimedes, while coming up with a good theory, had been spitted on the end of a Roman sword while absorbed in his calculations. Ideas were never enough.

Sherev's corner office on the top floor of the administration building inside the Dimona compound literally sat on top of Israeli's ultimate power—two dozen nuclear warheads, safely ensconced in a bunker a half-mile underground. The existence of those warheads was one of the best-known "secrets" in the world. Sherev had been part of the team that had "leaked" information about the bombs—after all, there was no point in having such fearsome weapons if no one knew you had them. They were the reason—beyond the pressure of the Americans—that Saddam Hussein had never turned his tanks west toward Jerusalem, and Sherev was in charge of making sure those twenty-four reasons remained secure. Even a madman like Hussein understood the concept of power and leverage. In fact, Sherev often contemplated the advantage a man like Hussein—with no conscience—had in the world of power struggles. Nice guys did indeed finish last in Sherev's experience.

The underground complex below the nuclear plant also contained the archives for the state of Israel. With Jerusalem such a volatile location and not far from the border with Jordan, those items deemed valuable in one way or another were sent to Dimona to be secured.

Now he was facing a situation that had just been presented to him by the man sitting on the other side of his desk concerning two items in the archives. Hasher Lekur was a powerful man in his own right, a member of the Parliament who had consolidated many of the right-wing groups into a powerful political movement. The fact that he had been granted access to see Sherev on such short notice, here in highly classified Dimona, said much about his connections.

"I don't understand," Sherev said. "What is the importance of these two stones, the *thummin* and *urim*?"

"They will help us get rid of a major problem."

"What problem?" Sherev asked.

"Hussein."

"How?"

"We give my contact the stones, he ensures Hussein dies. That is the deal."

"When will this occur?"

"It is already occurring."

"How are you sure your contact will keep his end of the bargain?"

"That is his business," Lekur said. "He is a man of great means and his reach is long."

"Who is this man?"

"I cannot tell you that."

"Why does he want the stones?"

"That is not our concern."

"It is my concern," Sherev said. "I am responsible for the Archives."

Lekur steepled his fingers. "The deal is already done. The Premier approved it two hours ago."

"You made a deal, but you don't know what you bargained away, do you?"

BAGHDAD, IRAQ

The daily intelligence briefing was a requirement, but ever since the Gulf War the time and the location were always changed, to keep the Western intelligence agencies from being able to pinpoint the President's location.

Farik Hassid sat in the same spot for over three thousand of these briefings. As a member of the Tikrit Tribe, the same village where Saddam came from, he had a favored status on the intelligence council. As the chief of staff for intelligence, he had learned long ago to walk the fine line between giving actual intelligence and telling the President what he wanted to hear. He focused most of his efforts on rooting out internal dissension than external threats to the country—after all, what more could the world do to Iraq that it had not already done?

He was irritated when his aide-de-camp, a young man also from the same village, the son of an old friend, entered the conference room while the head of the secret police was giving his daily assessment.

Hassid leaned back in his chair as the aide leaned, lips close to his ear, and whispered, "You have a call."

Hassid turned in anger, but the next words froze his heart.

"It is a message from a man named Al-Iblis. The caller has the proper code."

Hassid swallowed, willing his heart to start. He stood, trying to be as inconspicuous as possible, and followed his aide out the door. He took the cell phone the aide had hidden in a pocket.

"Yes?"

"Al-Iblis requires your services." The voice on the other end was cold and flat.

"Verify that you speak for Al-Iblis."

"Tark."

The word hit Hassid's chest like a knife.

"Fana."

The second code word was the twist of the knife. Abandonment and annihilation. The man spoke for Al-Iblis.

Hassid forced his throat to work, his lips to move. "What is required?"

The order was short and to the point. When the man was done, Hassid could no longer feel any part of his body. He was numb.

"You will comply." It was not a question. The phone went dead.

Hassid slowly dialed the number he had been given. A voice answered in English.

"My name is Farik Hassid. I am the chief of staff for intelligence for the state of Iraq. Stay on the line. It will be worth your time, I assure you."

The voice demanded to know if this was a joke, but Hassid ignored it and placed the phone in his dress uniform breast pocket, still on, facing outward. He turned to his aide. "You are dismissed."

"Sir?"

Hassid ignored him as he walked to the conference room door. He pulled it open and entered. As he walked past his seat, every eye in the room turned to him, wondering what urgent matter could have pulled him out of the meeting.

Hassid went to the end of the table where the President leaned back in his seat, awaiting his report.

Hassid felt nothing. He was past feelings, past any concern of life. He lifted his left hand as if he had something to say, while his right jerked his pistol out of the holster. Hussein's eyes grew wide, his bushy eyebrows raised in shock as Hassid pointed the gun directly at the President's face. He pulled the trigger, a blossom of red appearing in Hussein's left cheek. Hassid kept firing until all but one round was gone and there was nothing left of the President's head.

"Saddam Hussein is dead!" Hassid yelled in English, then he placed the hot muzzle against his right temple and pulled the trigger as the rest of the staff rushed toward him.

DIMONA, NEGEV DESERT, ISRAEL

Lekur checked his watch and pointed at the television mounted in the corner of the room. "Turn on CNN."

"Why?"

"Just do it."

Sherev bristled at being ordered about in his own office, but he pressed the button on the remote. It was the top of the hour. And the lead headline was the apparent assassination of Saddam Hussein in a suicide attack in Baghdad by a member of his inner military staff, less than two minutes ago. A tape of a phone call to CNN headquarters was played, the sound of gunfire, yells in Arabic, and a voice saying in English that Hussein was dead.

"How did this happen?" Sherev turned back to Lekur. He wondered how CNN could have received the report so quickly and if all of this was a setup.

"I told you my contact's reach is long. He has fulfilled his half of the bargain, trusting that we fulfill our part. Bring me the stones."

Sherev leaned back in his hard chair. "The stones have been examined several times by scientists. They are not natural. Do you understand what that means?" He didn't wait for an answer. "They were manufactured a long time ago. And now we know who made them—the Airlia. The United Nations Alien Oversight Committee has queried every government for Airlia artifacts. Of course, like us, no one has been forthcoming, willing to give up whatever pieces they have. Now you want us to turn these two stones over to some mysterious contact you have?"

"What can *you* do with the stones?" Lekur asked. "What have you done with them other than lock them in a vault and let them gather dust? Religious icons." The politician shook his head. "What a waste. I am not concerned with the Airlia. I am concerned with the safety of my country, and the largest threat to that safety has just been killed. I consider the stones a small price to pay for that. I don't care what my contact wants them for. They were worthless to us; now they have become valuable."

Still, Sherev hesitated. He knew it was indeed a great coup for Hussein to have been killed. The Mossad had tried to accomplish the very same thing for two decades without success. So had the Americans. A powerful coalition of nations had not been enough to remove the one man who was the greatest threat to stability in the region. Now it was done.

Sherev turned it around. If this contact of Lekur's could get to Hussein, then he could get to anyone. There was an underlying threat to this deal that Sherev felt sure Lekur had not seen yet.

"My assistant will take you to the Archives." Sherev spun his chair about, looking out at the desert. He heard the door close behind Lekur. Then he turned back to his desk once more and picked up the secure line to Mossad headquarters.

AREA 51

"What is it?" Che Lu had just walked into the conference room and caught Mualama staring off into space.

Mualama was startled. He tapped the manuscript. "Burton discovered the truth about Ngorongoro."

Che Lu sat down across from the African. "I noted that no one asked you what you were supposed to be covering when you were a Watcher. Was it Ngorongoro?"

Mualama nodded. "I told you we were second-echelon Watchers, recruited by Wedjat. So much was lost over the years. I think the core of the Watchers no longer trusted those in the second echelon. And—" he pointed at the screen "—now I know why they never contacted me, or my father, or those before us."

"What do you mean?" Che Lu asked.

"What we were watching." Mualama shook his head. "It is best if you read it."

BURTON MANUSCRIPT: CHAPTER 3

The Horus-Guides ruled Egypt for over a thousand years. The stone sphinx grew to be an enigma among the people of Egypt, the reason for its existence—to mark the location of the Hall of Records below—forgotten. The "gods" were remembered, but became myth, a religion, not the reality they were. It is the same way we view the legend of Atlantis in our modern world.

The peace did not last forever, though. It was time for The Ones Who Wait to take action, and when they did, the reaction from Aspasia was fierce and deadly. I have seen with my own eyes the results.

Their base was eventually discovered by the Watchers. It was in a mountain, part of a pair known as the White Sisters in central East Africa. At first I thought they might be speaking of the Mountains of the Moon, the Ruwenzori, which I have searched for myself—legendary mountains said to be covered in snow and hidden in clouds even though they lie on the equator.

But in an old church in Somaliland, I saw etched in the wall the image of two massive peaks, both snowcapped. I recognized one of them to be Kilimanjaro, the queen of all African mountains. The other was a mystery to me, because although there are other peaks near Kilimanjaro, none come close in height, yet in this drawing, the other was just as tall. So I traveled south to that land taking scrolls with me.

From one scroll, I learned there was a Watcher who traveled to the same place, around three thousand two hundred years before the birth of Christ, acting on the report of a traveler who had come down the Nile River with a strange tale of a black metal forest growing out the side of a tall mountain. The tale was strange enough, but the reference to black metal much like the b'ja made it worth investigating.

I can only imagine how difficult that trip was for him, as over five thousand years later, I encountered so much trouble getting there. He traveled across Europe to the Middle East, and then into Egypt. The Horus-Guides still ruled there, but he made safe transit with the assistance of other Watchers already in place in that kingdom. He then traveled along the east coast of Africa and suffered much until he arrived at the place where he was to strike inland. It did not take him long to see the first of the White Sisters, Kilimanjaro, covered in snow far on the horizon. Soon he saw the second, farther west, the one the base was located in where the strange forest grew.

I do not know if word of his journey and destination was picked up by The Mission. From what I have learned, it is apparent that both sides had spies, who for varying reasons passed information to the other side. Or perhaps what was going on at the The Ones Who Wait's base simply reached such a level that it was discovered by The Mission on its own.

Certainly the watcher's report about what was being done to the mountain backed up the rumor. From a long distance away, the Watcher reported seeing along the northern slope a vast network of black, like a spiderweb, covering most of the surface. Beasts of metal stalked among the web, working, continuing to build. Such beasts were written of in other places and were known to do the bidding of the Airlia and their followers.

The Watcher circled to the north and hid to watch what was happening and try to understand its purpose.

The second week he was there, a strange thing happened. A small glowing sphere of gold flew by. Watchers in other scrolls reported seeing such things. They also are tools of the Airlia. It circled the mountain and then disappeared.

Two days later sky ships came. Nine black forms long and lean, like knives against the sky. They too were made of b'ja, the sacred metal. A golden light crackled on the tips of the sky ships, then jumped down to the ground and into the mountain.

The top of the mountain exploded. A blast of air hit the Watcher even though he was miles away, knocking him off his feet and tumbling him about as the sky darkened from the dirt blown into the air. The sky ships departed, but the end of the mountain continued. Red, boiling earth flowed out of what remained.

I have seen the results of this. I have been to what was once the other White Sister. It is now called Ngorongoro Crater. It was once a peak as high as Kilamanjaro. Only half the mountain and the crater remain today.

Whatever The Ones Who Wait had been up to, it had failed.

"My family was recruited by this Watcher to keep an eye on the remains of the base," Mualama said. "But we weren't told what it was. Just to watch and report."

"Some of this base must still exist, though," Che Lu

said. "The dragon machine went there after getting the key from Turcotte."

"It is possible, but neither I nor anyone else in my family saw anything for as long as could be remembered."

"You did the right thing by leaving the Watchers," Che Lu said.

"I didn't leave them," Mualama said. "I betrayed them. What if they are right? What if the course of action they have tried to follow for so long is the right one? To be neutral. To support neither Artad's or Aspasia's side. If they are right, then I may be the greatest traitor ever by giving the Watcher headquarters to Turcotte."

"I think you overestimate your role and underestimate the active role the Watchers have played," Che Lu said.

"Perhaps," Mualama said.

"Are you all right?" Che Lu pointed at his ear.

Mualama reached up and his hand came away with several drops of blood on it. "An infection I picked up in Africa. Quite irritating."

EASTER ISLAND

Popeye McGraw felt the sand on his belly. He lay in the surf and slowly looked from side to side. Nothing moving on the beach. The towering *Moai* statues on the slope of the volcano were all turned inland. He wondered why these looked to land, while ones on the beach at Anakena looked out to sea.

"Damn," Popeye muttered to himself. He could feel the age of those statues. He'd grown up in Maine where old burial mounds existed, dating from the earliest inhabitants of that land. He knew these statues predated those. He'd always felt a shiver as a kid when he'd walked those mounds.

They'd left the zodiac offshore about five hundred meters, just inside the shield wall, held in place with the sea anchors. They had debated whether or not to beach the craft, but decided it was more secure leaving it offshore. The cruise around the west shore of the island to the southwest tip had been uneventful. Nothing moved along the rocky cliffs that made up the shore.

Olivetti was behind him. Popeye felt the tug as his partner pulled his fins off. Then Olivetti crawled next to him and slightly forward. Popeye returned the favor, removing his partner's fins and looping the straps over his non-firing forearm. Olivetti glanced over his shoulder at Popeye, who nodded.

The two SEALs stood and dashed inland. They made it to the base that supported the *Moai* and stuffed their fins in their packs.

Popeye looked up the steep slope of the volcano. "Ready?"

"Born ready."

GIZA PLATEAU

Duncan realized her hands were shaking as she hooked up the wires from the Ark to the crown. She still had a headache from her first experience, but the draw was too great. She connected all three leads, then placed the crown on her head.

Immediately, she was no longer in the Hall. She was in a large, enclosed space. The floor was black metal. The walls curved to meet a hundred meters overhead. Bouncers rested in metal cradles. Eighteen of them.

She knew that she was in the hold of the mothership.

Airlia moved about, preparing the bouncers, moving equipment. She saw the Ark on a cart. An Airlia was carrying the Grail, placing it inside. Then rolling the Ark over to one of the bouncers. The Airlia was treating it as a piece of equipment, not an object of veneration.

Her attention was drawn to one side of the cargo bay as two large doors opened. She could see out, noting that the mothership was hovering about a mile above the planet's surface. Bouncers began leaving the hold, going about their missions. Looking down, Duncan saw water extending to the horizon in all directions.

A Talon spacecraft passed by between the mothership and the ocean. Something about what she saw disturbed Duncan; something wasn't right.

Duncan started, feeling a lance of pain in her temples. She grabbed the crown and pulled it off. She felt as if every ounce of energy had been drained from her body. She set the crown down and sat with her back to the Ark's stand. Her eyelids drooped, her mind shutting down. Just before she fell asleep, her mind replayed what she had seen. The Talon was racing toward the horizon, the sun glinting off its black skin—no, that was it, she realized with alarm. There were two suns in the sky, one large, like the one she knew, but there was a second smaller, red one close to it.

CHAPTER 10

AREA 51

Major Quinn had to almost run to keep up with Turcotte as he walked across the hangar toward the elevator. "Did you get the ring?"

Turcotte held it up briefly, then asked his own question. "What do you have?" Yakov followed behind, walking more slowly.

"We got a team to help you on the Giza mission."

"Who?"

"A mixed Special Forces–SEAL team from Space Command." Quinn pointed toward one of the walls that crossed the large hangar. "They're in there."

Turcotte abruptly changed direction. Quinn opened a door in the partition and they entered a corner of Hangar 1. Satellite imagery was tacked to a large piece of plywood, the corresponding map sheets covered with acetate pinned next to the pictures. Several men in black jumpsuits stood in front of the maps, marker in hand, comparing them with latest downloaded photos of the same sites.

One of them, a tall man with a shaved head and large black mustache, turned at the sound of the door shutting behind Yakov. He came striding over.

He snapped a salute. "Lieutenant Graves."

Turcotte returned the salute, then extended his hand. "Mike Turcotte."

Graves nodded. "I heard we're going after the sons-a-bitches who took out our men on the shuttle. Every man here is a volunteer and eager to kick some ass."

Turcotte felt at home, having been in this type of planning situation many times before in his Special Forces career. It was called "isolation," where the team was given its mission statement and the intelligence data needed to plan the operation.

"The last time you tried this mission," Yakov said, "it did not go well."

Graves frowned at the Russian and Turcotte quickly introduced Yakov.

"What do you have on the underground river?" Turcotte asked.

Quinn pointed at one of the boards as they walked across the room. There was a series of satellite imagery tacked on it. "There's a KH-14 always on duty over that area, supporting our peacekeeping force in the Sinai. I had a buddy at NSA do a complete spectrographic workout of Giza and the Nile."

"We're looking for an underground river running from the Nile, below Giza, and back to the Nile," Turcotte said.

Quinn didn't hesitate for a beat. He tapped a color-filled picture. "Thermal. High discretion." Quinn tilted his glasses, peering at it. "There. See the change. Something's going on in the river on the west bank—right there. Then see how the shoreline at the spot is a little cooler, then follow the line looping around to Giza and back to the Nile. That's your underground river."

"How come no one's seen this before?" Turcotte asked.

Quinn gave a short laugh. "This is top-secret, top-of-the-line imagery. Like we're going to give it to someone? And there was no strategic or tactical interest in the Nile and Giza before this."

Turcotte ran his fingers over the photo, noting the slight change in temperature on the shoreline, a cooler spot where water ran underneath the bank. "That's how we're getting in."

"What do you think we should do for infiltration?" Graves asked.

Turcotte picked up a marker and circled the location where the underwater river branched out from the Nile, two kilometers below the Giza Plateau. "Water drop right here. Then we go into the tunnel."

"Drop from a bouncer?" Graves asked.

Turcotte had given that matter some thought on the flight back from England. "They aren't rigged for that. We'll take a bouncer to Israel to save time, but we'll go in by conventional means from there."

Major Quinn spoke up. "I've lined up an MC-130 out of Germany to meet you in Israel."

An MC-130 was a specially modified C-130 transport plane, designed to be able to fly in all types of weather and at low level, below radar. Turcotte tapped the map. "We'll go in low on the C-130 and parachute at less than two hundred feet with multiple drogue chutes rigged for underwater."

Graves frowned. "Scuba? Why not use what we're trained on?" He pointed to the wall where black suits were lined up, like an army of drones.

"TASC-suits?" Turcotte asked.

"What's that?" Yakov asked.

"Stands for Tactical Articulated Space Combat suit," Graves explained. "Each suit is self-contained." He looked at Turcotte. "If you're going with us, you'll have to run through the mentor program to learn how to operate the suit, which takes about two hours. And then you're going to have to learn to actually use them in action, which isn't exactly—"

Turcotte cut him off. "But they give us an advantage, correct?"

"Yes, sir. A lot of advantages. You'll be completely armored, stronger, and the weapons are extremely accurate when using the suits aiming system. You have a built in rebreather so we can infiltrate directly into the water."

"And I can learn to use it in a basic mode quickly, right?"

"Yes, sir."

"Great."

Graves turned back to the map. "Once we go into this underground river, do we have any idea where we're going?"

Turcotte pointed at a surface photo of the Great Sphinx. "As near as we can tell, our objective is directly below that."

"Does the river run to it?" Graves asked.

"Not directly," Turcotte admitted, remembering Burton's account. "We're hoping we get some more information before we go wheels up. We do have directions once we go up the shaft that Burton came down. That shaft intersects with the river." Turcotte ran through the account Burton mapped from the Hall of Records chamber to the one he was trapped in. "If his pace count is one hundred and sixteen steps per hundred meters, we can use that to approximate the location of these doors."

"And the ring which helps find these doors and open them?" Graves asked.

Turcotte reached into his pocket and pulled out the Watcher key.

"And exfiltration?" Graves asked.

Turcotte had been expecting that. It was something every special-ops man asked when given an assignment, and something that was rarely given in the mission briefing as higher commands always were much more concerned about getting the men in, then getting them out.

"Helicopters from the peacekeeping force," Turcotte

said. "They can come in from South Camp and retrieve us. But we have to be in the river, ready to be picked up an hour before dawn. If we're later than that, forget about getting out by chopper, and it's a long walk."

"Roger that," Graves said.

"And Easter Island?" Yakov asked. "Qian-Ling? What is going on there?"

"Let's go down to the conference room for that," Turcotte suggested. He slapped Graves on the shoulder. "Keep planning and get my suit ready to be rigged." He pulled one of the large-scale images of the Giza Plateau off the board.

"Yes, sir."

Turcotte, Yakov, and Quinn headed for the elevator.

"Uh, sir—" Quinn paused.

"Yes?"

"There's some interesting material in the folders you took from the Russian Archives."

"Such as?"

Quinn opened a folder. "The file which held the photo of Mount Ararat . . . *was* the search for Noah's Ark. Hitler sent teams around the world looking for the place it supposedly came to rest. Naturally, Mount Ararat was one of those places."

"Did they find it?"

"It doesn't appear so."

"Why would they be looking for Noah's Ark?" Turcotte asked.

"Perhaps it is something else," Yakov said, "as all other legends have turned out to be."

"What else do you have?" Turcotte was studying the Nile imagery, committing it to memory. Quinn closed the folder. He had one more that he hadn't opened yet. Quinn hesitated, fingers running along the edge of the manila folder.

"Well?" Turcotte pressed as they reached the elevator.

"I was checking CIA case files on the Watchers, seeing if I could find another ring. When I pulled what they have now, it was cross-referenced with some other files, um—" He paused.

"What other files?" Turcotte checked his watch.

"It's just a list," Quinn said, "of people the CIA thought needed watching; targeting people who they suspect had some sort of connection with The Watchers or The Mission or The Ones That Wait. You have to understand that they did this in a rush after the revelations of what was here."

"And?" Turcotte was surprised at Quinn's sudden reticence. The elevator doors opened and they got in.

"Doctor Duncan's name is on it."

"For suspicion of what?" Turcotte snapped.

"Just as requiring further investigation," Quinn said.

"Why?"

"I don't know." Turcotte took a step toward the smaller major.

Yakov put out an arm across Turcotte's chest. "Easy."

"It's bull," Turcotte said. "Clowns In Action—I worked with them before and they couldn't—" He caught himself. "We've got more important things to do."

As he walked out of the elevator toward the conference room, Quinn gave Yakov a questioning glance. The Russian merely shrugged his large shoulders.

EASTER ISLAND

Popeye McGraw stared down at the Easter Island International Airport as Olivetti recorded the scene on a digital recorder.

"Damn," Popeye said.

The fact that Olivetti said nothing in response indicated the depth the effect of the scene below had on the larger SEAL.

A strange collection of people and equipment were all over the airfield and the surrounding area. Six-legged machines stalked about on their tasks, while people moved around as if in a stupor. Various aircraft from the Washington lined the runway in different stages of either assembly or disassembly, it was hard to tell.

"They ain't normal, those people," Olivetti muttered.

Popeye raked the area with the binoculars, checking everything. There were several clusters of people staked out next to the runway, heads all pointing inward as mechanical robots walked by, spraying something over them.

He could see the entrance to the tunnel that led to the guardian computer chamber. A squad of marines with M-16s stood there. Popeye twisted the focus. The men had blank expressions, but their hands held the weapons tightly.

Popeye had often boasted in bars that a Navy SEAL could kick butt on a dozen marines. But that was in a bar. Automatic weapons were a great equalizer.

"What the hell is going on?" Popeye muttered. During the mission briefing, they'd read the report about the people who had come to Easter Island on the Progressive trawler who had been taken over by some sort of black cloud. Popeye pulled the glasses away from his eyes and rubbed a hand across his forehead, smearing the camouflage paint.

Olivetti waited patiently.

"The crater," Popeye said.

Olivetti didn't even nod, but hoisted his pack

containing various gear and his tanks onto his back. They turned away from the airfield and headed farther up the slope of Rapa Karu.

Kelly Reynolds twitched. Consciousness seeped into her brain. She had no idea how long she had been out. For just the slightest of moments she was home in Nashville, snug in her bed, buried under a down comforter.

That image was ripped asunder as the flow of data through the guardian cascaded over her. She knew where she was, she just didn't know what she was anymore. How long had she been here?

She paused her racing mind. What had woken her? The torrent of data was a river pouring past her, and it was like trying to find a slight disturbance in the flow.

She began searching.

Popeye McGraw and Olivetti went over the lip of the crater, their wet suits soaked with sweat, but their breathing almost normal. They'd done things in training that made the climb look like a weekend jaunt. Two hundred feet below, the surface of the lake filling the crater was totally smooth. They didn't even pause, but began clambering down.

Within a couple of minutes they reached the water. Packs were dropped and cached under some rocks, tanks were put back on, and they slid into the water.

Working off the information they had been given in their mission preparation, they searched for the tunnel entrance at the bottom and found it relatively quickly.

They swam into it, navigating by feel through the darkness. Both men had been in dark water before, and they moved forward without fear.

Kelly Reynolds saw what the guardian had noted. A woman, one of the ones brought by the *Southern Star*, among the third wave infected by the nano-virus, had caught a glimpse of a light reflecting off glass high on the flanks of Rapa Karu. The woman, a former nurse from Australia, of course, had no idea of the import of what she had seen. She's simply continued on her task of dragging food supplies for other humans from the UNAOC supply depot.

But the guardian, capable of two billion calculations per second, had reacted differently. Within three seconds, the event had worked its way through various layers to the forefront of the computer's attention. None of the nanovirus slaves were on the slope. Neither were the mech-robots.

The conclusion—an unknown variable.

The guardian didn't know what it was, so Kelly didn't either. But the guardian began reacting.

The two SEALs headed toward a small dot of light. It grew brighter as they approached, and in a minute they surfaced inside a cavern. The light came from a glowing orb on the ceiling. They swam over to a lip of rock on one side and got out of the water. A tunnel was cut into the wall in front of them. They secured their weapons and headed into it. The ground sloped up slightly, then turned to the right. It was lit by thin strips of glowing material set into the ceiling.

They entered a cave, about a hundred meters wide and long. The walls were of rock, except for the far one, made of black metal with control panels built into it. Their eyes were focused on what was in the forefront. The body of a woman was splayed against a twenty-foot-high golden pyramid. Near it, a hole was cut in the floor of the cavern into and out of which a steady stream of small robots flowed.

Slung over Olivetti's shoulder was a satchel containing explosives. He'd already prewired several different charges, and already mentally calculating what he would need to destroy this chamber and the pyramid.

Both men started, swinging the muzzles of their weapons about as something moved to their right. A young boy dressed in brown walked out of the shadows.

Kelly Reynolds saw the two SEALs through the guardian. She fought to open her eyes, to be able to control her lungs and mouth. To shout a warning.

"Are you all right?" Popeye McGraw asked the boy.

There was no answer as the boy came forward, now less than twenty feet away. He was pale and thin, a ghostly stick figure in the chamber's glow.

"How did you get here?" Popeye asked, his finger still over the trigger, eyes shifting from the boy, to the pyramid/woman, to the unceasing line of robots.

"My parents," the boy said in a cracked voice.

"Please help me." He held up his hands as he continued to walk toward them.

"Where are your parents?" Popeye asked.

"The machine," the boy whispered as if the pyramid could hear. He reached out a hand and Olivetti instinctively lowered his weapon and reached forward with his left hand to the boy.

Flesh met flesh and Olivetti cursed, trying to jerk his hand back from the sharp burning sensation searing his palm. But the boy's hand was like a vise as the nanovirus tore through the child's flesh and bore in the SEAL's palm, infiltrating his veins, racing for the brain.

"Get him off me!" Olivetti had let go of his weapon and was trying to peel the boy's hand off with his free hand.

Popeye had the boy in his sights, his finger on the trigger.

"Get him off!" Olivetti spun about, the boy airborne but still keeping the grip.

The flesh in Olivetti's arm crawled as the nanovirus swarmed up it, underneath the skin. The boy let go and turned toward Popeye, dead eyes reflected in the glow of the orb.

McGraw pulled the trigger, the rounds smashing the boy onto the floor. Along with the blood, a black stain poured out of the wound and headed across the floor toward McGraw—the nanovirus seeking a new host. Olivetti dropped to his knees, hands pressed against his temples.

"Run!" The voice was barely audible.

McGraw turned, surprised. It came again—from the woman on the pyramid.

"Run!"

Popeye turned and dashed back down the corridor he had come in.

QIAN-LING

The huge doors were wide open, but the light from the chamber could not penetrate the blackness behind the doors. It was not solid, but rather as if the air itself had lost all ability to allow light to travel through it. A straight wall of darkness.

"What is this?" Gergor asked.

Lexina was puzzled. "I don't know."

Gergor stepped forward and reached out with his hand toward the darkness.

"Don't do that!" Lexina ordered, but Gergor ignored her. His fingertips touched and he turned to look at her. "It's not solid. It's warm. There's—" A look of surprise passed over his face, which quickly changed to one of terror as the black around his arm turned bright red, spread down the arm, and enveloped him in less than a second. He screamed as skin disintegrated.

Within another two seconds there was nothing left of Gergor but his clothes in a small pile just in front of the once more smooth black wall.

Carefully Lexina knelt and felt the cloth, searching. She found Gergor's *ka*.

CHAPTER 11

AREA 51

Equipment check was an integral part of any special forces isolation, and in this instance, it was essential due to the radical nature of the equipment being used. Turcotte and the members of Graves's team were in the isolation area. Turcotte was toweling off, having just finished his fitting for his TASC-suit.

The suits were in the back of the isolation area getting last-minute updates from the Space Command techs. Each was black, the external material a ceramic polymer that provided protection against small arms up to 7.62 mm. Under the armor, the suit was complex. Battery-powered strips of IPMCs—ionic polymer metal composites—added power, magnifying the wearer's own strength.

The inner layer was airtight, fitting against the wearer's clothing and skin. The suit was designed to be used in space. A backpack contained both the computer that operated the various systems and a sophisticated re-breather that could sustain oxygen for over twelve hours. If operating in a safe environment, a valve in the back of the helmet could be opened to allow outside air in.

The helmet was the most advanced part. It was solid, with no visor to the outside world. Flat screens on the inner front portrayed whatever the wearer directed. Numerous mini-cams were on the external armor, from the two where the eyes would be pointing forward to give a normal front view with depth, to ones pointing straight up, down, and back. They were necessary because the helmet fit onto the body of the suit tightly, allowing no movement.

While Turcotte had his doubts about where some of the technology used in the TASC-suit came from, the Space Command people claimed the helmet and control system came out of two Air Force programs. DVI—Direct Voice Input—allowed the wearer to give commands verbally to the computer. This considerably streamlined any process and made use of the suit much easier. The second program was VCASS—visually coupled airborne systems simulator. The helmet screens not only relayed the picture from whichever external cameras were voice-activated, but could also relay information from the computer such as its occupant's location when in contact with ground positioning satellites.

"Scary, isn't it?" Graves asked.

The immersion in the black tank, then having foam pumped all around his body to get a mold, had been unnerving. The worst part was being unable to move for the period of time it took them to confirm the sizing.

"What about weapons?" Turcotte asked.

Graves led Turcotte over to a table. "We've got some kick-ass stuff. This is the Mark 98. It fires a depleted uranium round for kinetic energy impact."

It was three feet long, a thick cylindrical shape that tapered to the end where the tube was about an inch in diameter. At the other end, there were two pistol grips: one about six inches from the flat base, the other eighteen inches in with a trigger in front of it. The non-firing end ended in a flat plate. The entire thing was painted a flat black.

"You can fire it either attached to the suit arm or detached." Graves grabbed the two-foot-long cylinder and loaded it into the top of the gun. "Want to give it a try?"

Turcotte picked up the heavy gun and aimed out the hangar doors into the desert.

"You have a laser aiming sight," Graves said, "that is turned on when you activate the gun's main power—the switch is there. When you're wearing the suit, you'll get an aiming point on your screen that's one hundred percent accurate."

Turcotte turned the gun on and aimed at a small boulder on the edge of the runway. He pulled the trigger. There was no report as it fired, but a loud pinging sound. The rock disintegrated as the round smashed into it.

"It'll go through any body armor made," Graves said. "High tension, pre-loaded, ten rounds per cylinder. Pulling the trigger releases the spring. The barrel is electromagnetically balanced so that the round goes right down the center, never touching the walls and thus not losing any velocity and staying true to target. That's why you have to turn the gun on—to charge the barrel and to rotate the cylinder. It fires the rounds as quickly as you pull the trigger, which unfortunately is not as fast as you can pull the trigger. It's as fast as the weapon will allow. The trigger locks up until the barrel is set. The cylinder also rotates, aligning a new round. You can fire once every second. When the system is attached to the firing arm of the TASC-suit, the suit's power system will allow you to handle it with more ease than you can here.

"We also have the Mark 99." He tapped another gun that looked just like the Mark 98. "The only difference with this one is that it can fire a high-explosive round. Better than the M-203 grenade launcher and more accurate. Combine that with the fact the suit can take hits from small arms up to and including 7.62mm machine gun fire, we've got a big advantage over the bad guys."

Turcotte was pleased with that. "Communications?"

"Integrated secure SATCOM."

Turcotte considered that. Not much help underwater or underground. "What about among team members?"

"FM capability."

That would restrict them to line of sight. Better than nothing, Turcotte allowed.

"Let's run you through your suit orientation," Graves said.

Down below in the Cube's main room, Larry Kincaid was staring at a computer screen feeding him live images from the Hubble of the surface of Mars. Quinn had managed to wheedle more live time off of the scope, but Kincaid had a feeling he was going to get shut down soon.

The mech-robots directed by the guardian on Mars had uncovered something, of that there was no doubt. Something that had been destroyed long ago and covered with rubble. There were still mechs at the site, but only a fraction of those had cleared away the rubble. The imagery wasn't detailed enough to know exactly what the object was or what they were doing. All he could make out was a network of black metal. And it was moving.

Kincaid stared at the imagery for several moments. Where the hell were they going now? He typed in commands to be relayed to those controlling Hubble. As long as he could, he wanted to keep an eye on what was developing.

Kincaid picked through the many papers on his desk

until he found the translation that Mualama had done of
Burton's manuscript so far. The account of Ngorongoro
intrigued him—most particularly the part about the
black network of metal that had been constructed on the
side of the mountain and destroyed.

He pulled out a photo from the "face" at Cydonia
and looked at what had been uncovered. It appeared to
be the remnants of a black network of metal.

QIAN-LING, CHINA

"It's moving." Elek's observation didn't register with
Lexina for several seconds.

"What is moving?" she asked.

"The wall." Elek pointed at Gergor's clothes.

Lexina wasn't sure what he was indicating until she
realized that the gap between the clothes and the wall
was larger than it had been before.

"It's going back, very slowly, but it is going back,"
Elek said.

Lexina felt a tremble of excitement. They'd simply
been in too much of a rush. It was working after all. She
looked up at the shimmering black surface. Soon what
they desired would be revealed.

EASTER ISLAND

Another flight was taxiing down a runway on the opposite side of the world. An F-14 Tomcat reached the end
of the Easter Island International Airport and slowly
turned to face the long expanse of concrete. A man sat
in the cockpit, but he was not a pilot. He had been

chosen at random from among the thousands of humans
who had survived the nanovirus experiments. He was
there to throw the right switches when ordered to by the
guardian. The alien computer was going to fly the
plane.

With a jerk, the brakes were released and the F-14 accelerated down the runway. Using information culled directly from the Naval Flight Center master computer, the
guardian followed correct procedure and the plane's
wheels lifted off the runway a half mile short of the end.
It arced upward, afterburners kicking in. It headed directly for the inner curve of the black sphere when the
guardian began a hard right bank over edge of the island.

Too hard. The wings lost their grip on the air and the
plane slid sideways. The guardian tried to compensate
and almost pulled it out, but the engine stalled and the
F-14 dropped like a stone. The man in the cockpit
watched with dead eyes as the ground rapidly approached, his hands at his sides, no attempt to pull the
eject lever.

The F-14 hit the western slope of Rapa Karu crater in
blossom of explosion.

Within minutes, a cluster of mech-robots were gathered around the flames waiting. As soon as the wreckage cooled they would go in, retrieve all the pieces, and
bring them back to the nanorobots at the edge of the
runway. The nanorobots would then rebuild the plane.
The man was a loss, but humans were more easily replaced than machines for the guardian.

The data from the flight was analyzed, flight toler-
ances adjusted.

On the runway, another F-14 moved into position.

Two hundred miles to the north, Captain Robinette, the commander of Task Force 79 by default, was looking at satellite imagery forward from fleet command at Pearl Harbor. There was no missing the huge ship and the broad wake that spread out from its blunt bow.

"ID?" He asked his operations officer, Command Lesky.

Lesky had an identification book open. "The *Jahre Viking*. 564,763 deadweight tons."

Robinette whistled. "What's the plot on this?"

"One hundred and eighty miles west of Easter Island, bearing directly down on the island at eighteen knots." Lesky waited a moment. "Should we prepare a strike to interdict?"

"If that thing's loaded with crude, do you know what kind of ecological disaster that would make?" Robinette said. "Besides, you know what it would take to sink that thing? We'd have to breach every hold or else the oil would keep it afloat."

Robinette picked up a tighter shot of the tanker's deck. There was a cluster of small objects. The next shot was more focused. Groups of people. Hatches were open. "It's not carrying crude. It's carrying people." Robinette looked up. "Contact Pearl and ask them what they want me to do about this."

"Yes, sir." Lesky relayed the order.

"What about the SEALs?"

"Nothing yet, sir."

Popeye McGraw was in the center of the lake that filled Rapa Karu's crater, treading water. He had surfaced a half hour ago and could have been over the rim and down to the shore by now if he had tried. But what he saw when he broke the surface had stopped him. The rim was lined with people. Hundreds of them. All staring down at him with lifeless eyes. He knew what would happen if he tried to climb up. He didn't have enough ammunition in his weapon to kill all of them. Plus, a SEAL never abandoned a buddy.

He knew what would happen next, and he waited.

When the hand from below grabbed his ankle and pulled him under, Popeye had his pistol ready. He had a brief glimpse through the water of Olivetti's blank face as the man pulled himself toward him.

Popeye McGraw put the muzzle against his comrade's forehead. "I'm sorry, buddy." He hesitated pulling the trigger, looking into his friend's eyes. And in that moment, the nanovirus flowed over his hand, freezing his nerves, infiltrating his system.

McGraw's last free thought was that he had failed his buddy, his mission, and his country.

CHAPTER 12

AREA 51

"Our mission is to infiltrate operational area Aker—the Giza Plateau—and secure both Doctor Duncan and any alien artifacts we come across, with emphasis on finding the Grail." Graves slapped the pointer on the acetate covering the small-scale map of the Middle East. "We will depart this location at 0500 Zulu time via bouncer for transport to an Israeli military airfield located here at Hazerim, ten miles west of Beersheba. There we will crossload onto an Air Force MC-130."

Turcotte followed the pointer in Graves's hand as the team leader continued the briefing. It was standing operating procedure (SOP) for a team to present a briefback—their operational plan—at the end of isolation to their commander in order to get final approval of the mission and plan. Turcotte was a believer in following SOP. It reduced the possibility of screwups, and routine also reinforced men's confidence. Turcotte leaned forward and followed the tip of the point as Graves drew it west, bisecting the Sinai Peninsula.

"We will fly low level across the Sinai to the Gulf of Suez. At that point, the MC-130 pilots have several possible routes to the target and they will decide the safest one to take depending on electronic intelligence of Egyptian air defenses at the time. All routes put us over the drop zone, DZ Nile, located here, two kilometers upstream on the Nile from the underground river which we have designated as Route Alpha."

Turcotte held up a hand, causing the captain to pause. "Two klicks upstream? Why so far?"

"I've talked to the navigator for the MC-130 on a secure SATCOM link," Graves said. "He says they go any further to the north, they will most definitely be spotted. It gets crowded very fast as you move north toward Cairo. As it is, they think they have a small window to get us over the river with a steep bank, a long enough flight over it to get all of us out, then they will have to bank hard again to get over the desert and out of sight."

"How long will it take us to cover two klicks swimming?" Turcotte was trying to remember the times he'd done what special forces called maritime operations. Two kilometers was going to take a little while, even wearing the TASC-suits.

"We won't be swimming it, sir," Graves said. "The TASC-suits have fittings for propulsion units. Based on other operations we've conducted underwater using the suits, we can make it to the opening of Route Alpha in under ten minutes."

Turcotte caught the note in Graves's voice. He knew that the captain had everything locked down from the second they took off in the bouncer to the moment they entered that tunnel, but from there this mission was an unknown. And that bothered the officer. Turcotte now knew why Yakov had been hammering at him to slow down, to read the translation of Burton's manuscript, to gather intelligence. For just a moment, Turcotte considered whether they should scrub the evening's mission and delay it for twenty-four hours. Then he thought of Lisa trapped somewhere under the Giza Plateau and he knew they had to go.

"Continue with the briefback," Turcotte ordered the team leader.

The operational briefing was depressingly short.

There was a lot of "playing it by ear" once they got in the tunnel. So much so that even Turcotte had to acknowledge the scarcity of good intelligence. Exfiltration was also iffy with no backup to the helicopters from the peacekeeping force.

To balance the lack of planning and intelligence, Turcotte felt they had an advantage with the TASC-suits. Duncan had been told that the suit had taken four billion dollars and fifteen years to develop under a covert research program funded by the black budget. She'd confessed her concern to Turcotte that Majestic-12 and Area 51 had a lot to do with the technology that went into the suit—appropriated Airlia technology.

The briefback was over and Graves was waiting for any questions.

Turcotte only had one. "Are we all set?"

"Yes, sir."

"Good. Let's get the gear ready for loading." He noted that Yakov had entered the room for the latter part of the briefback. The Russian came over to him once it was done.

"The professor has translated more of the manuscript."

"How much?"

"Another chapter."

"Is it important?"

"We don't know what's important or not yet," Yakov said.

Turcotte stretched out his back, feeling the strain of memorizing flight routes, emergency rally points, primary and alternate exfiltration points, code names, call signs, radio frequencies—all the details needed for the upcoming mission.

Turcotte bowed to the inevitable and followed Yakov to the elevator. The descent was made in silence, each man left to his own thoughts. Yakov wasn't going with them, despite his protests. He was too large for any of the TASC-suits. Besides, Turcotte wanted him here at Area 51 to monitor everything that was happening.

Che Lu was sitting in her seat and it appeared to Turcotte she hadn't moved since last they were there, although he knew she had been working with Quinn on Nabinger's coordinates. He assumed she hadn't come up with anything since she didn't say anything.

Mualama was at the computer, and he silently pointed to the screen where the opening of a new chapter was displayed.

Burton Manuscript: Chapter 4

After so many years of inactivity by The Mission and The Ones Who Wait, the destruction of the base at Ngorongoro triggered a burst of activity by both sides.

First—Egypt. Probably fearing retribution, The Mission removed their Guides from Egypt, ending the Second Age and ushering in the time of the Pharaohs, humans who took over the reign.

The long reach of The Mission was still present, though, as the plans for the Highland of Aker that Isis and Osiris had drawn up almost six thousand years earlier were revived. The Pharaohs built the massive pyramids we still see today on the Highland. The purpose of these was uncertain to Watchers at the time, although the best guess was that they were to guard the entrances to the underground passageways. When they were first built, they were covered with a sheathing of white limestone that could be seen for many, many miles.

"Nabinger told us the purpose of the pyramids," Turcotte said to Yakov, who was also reading his copy. "They were a beacon, sending a radar signature from their smooth, flat surfaces into space."

"But think what that means," Yakov said. "The Mission had no other way to communicate into space."

"Maybe they were trying to get ahold of Aspasia on Mars," Che Lu suggested.

"But if they had access to a guardian," Turcotte said, "they wouldn't need to do that."

"But maybe they didn't have access anymore," Yakov said.

"Remember the message Kelly Reynolds sent here?" Turcotte said. "The vision of the top of the Great Pyramid being removed—maybe that was the master guardian." He shook his head. "But that doesn't make any sense."

I learned from Kaji that there were six major chambers—Duats—cut underneath the Highland of Aker. But even the Pharaohs and their priests were not aware of this. It was no longer the priests of the Neteru or the Horus-Guides that watched these chambers, but the line of Kaji. The rings they had from their time as the wedjat still worked on the doors of the Airlia. It is obvious that The Mission did not trust the pharaohs to guard their secrets, as much as they trusted secrecy, and the Watchers stepped into the vacuum. The Mission was aware that the Watchers did this. Why else would Al-Iblis have sent me after Kaji? But they did not fear the Watchers, so they were not concerned.

With Egypt abandoned by The Mission and The

Ones Who Wait base at Ngorongoro destroyed, where did the two groups go? This was the issue that plagued the Watchers for hundreds of years.

The first hints came with the development of civilization in China, far removed from the cradle of the Nile and the Middle East. It seemed too much of a coincidence that such great strides were made in that far-off land so suddenly.

I believe, based on what I have learned, that The Ones Who Wait set up their new headquarters somewhere in that land. The Mission remained somewhere in the vicinity of the Mediterranean, its influence felt throughout the civilizations that began to arise in that area.

A new phase of the Airlia civil war was ushered in, with both sides extending their tentacles into human civilization, trying to guide it in the way each deemed best for their side.

However, through all this, the Grail, I believe, remained inside the Hall of Records. To discover more, I had to travel to the Middle East.

After translating the information about the First Two Ages of Egypt, I once more traveled to that country to see how much of the tale I could confirm. After all, there was the slightest of possibilities that the scrolls could lie, or perhaps even be fiction. If I had not seen the Black Sphinx with my own eyes, I might have had more doubts.

I learned that during the time of the Third Age, the time of the Pharaohs, between what Egyptologists call the Second Dynasty and the Third, that The Mission once more tried to implement change in Egypt to fulfill the original plans of the Guide-Shadows of the First Age. It was with the Third Dynasty of the Third Age that the first pyramids were built. These were built by men, without the assistance of the Airlia, but with the aid of plans drawn up by Osiris and Isis during the First Age.

The first pyramids were practice in studying how to build such structures. I have seen the pyramids of the Third Dynasty at Saqqara in Egypt—the step pyramids of Djoser and Sekhemket. During the Fourth Dynasty, the size increased as the art was being perfected. The bent pyramid of Sneferu at Dahshur was the precursor to the implementation of the plan on Giza.

When the pyramids of Giza were constructed, the Watchers were uncertain why they were built. Indeed, consulting the foremost experts alive today on the subject, I have learned they still are unsure of the reason for such a massive construction project. One of the great mysteries is that there is nothing written about either the pyramids or the stone sphinx in all the writings that have survived from that ancient kingdom. It is as if such a thing was forbidden, which I believe to be the case.

But I learned through one report from a Watcher a most interesting thing. When the Great Pyramid of Khufu was constructed, the capstone was of a different material than the rest. It was red in color.

And that capstone was removed by a flying disk during the Fourth Dynasty of the Third Age, shortly after the Great Pyramid was built as Egypt was reaching the peak of its power and expanding its empire in all directions. These flying disks were mentioned here and there in other Watcher documents. Obviously, they must be a craft of the Airlia.

With the removal of that capstone, it seems as if The Mission faded from influence not only in Egypt,

*but around the world for a long time. And the king-
dom of Egypt slowly began to decline in power also.*

*I believe this capstone was one of these alien ma-
chines. Where it was taken, I do not know.*

*However, despite the removal of the capstone, the
Ark and the Grail remained in Egypt, hidden in the
Hall of Records, forgotten by all but the Watchers
who guarded it.*

*I believe from what I have read and seen that The
Mission moved its influence to the northern side of
the Mediterranean, to Greece and across the Atlantic
to the Americas, in Mexico. The rise of the Greek
City states and the Olmecs in Mexico foretold the
growing influence of The Guides among humans.*

*There is also the issue of these pyramid machines—
it appears several were located at various points on
the planet and early civilizations grew up around
them.*

*The Ones Who Wait fought back in a different and
disturbing manner. Instead of trying to establish
states and armies at this time period, The Ones Who
Wait worked at manipulating men across national
and regional boundaries through the power of faith.*

*That this was effective can be seen through the fact
that they managed to remove the Ark from Egypt. This
event has been recorded, but little significance has
ever been placed to it in terms of historical reality.*

*In 1,200 B.C. a member of an obscure tribe called
Israelites managed to secure a place of power in
Egypt. There are legends how this occurred, but the
fact remains it happened.*

*One man, Moses, then gained freedom for his
people by scouring the land with curses—events
which The Ones Who Wait could certainly have*

helped orchestrate. Or, and this is what makes it so difficult, he could have been a Guide. Or even just a man interfering in things beyond his conception.

I do not mean here to deny the existence of God or his power, but only to tell what I have learned. The truth, which I have searched for all my life, is the truth I have found, not the truth others have found. Perhaps there is a divine power behind all things, even these alien creatures and their followers, but I do not proclaim to know.

Moses gained his people's freedom, but just as important, he gained possession of the Ark, in which was held the Grail. He took it out of Egypt for the first time in over ten millennia and thus the tale becomes more interesting.

The chapter came to an end.

"Do we have any idea where the master guardian was taken?" Che Lu asked.

"If we did, we'd be there," Turcotte said.

"The grid system I have from Nabinger might have that location," Che Lu noted.

"But you haven't been able to align, right?" Turcotte pointed out.

"Not yet."

"You might want to ask Larry Kincaid for help," Turcotte said. He checked his watch. It was time to be going. "If you get any more details on the chambers of the tunnels, forward it to me by secure satellite link," he told Yakov.

"Good luck," the Russian offered.

The acid drip of adrenaline was coursing through Turcotte's veins and burning his stomach. He was ready to go.

CHAPTER 13

QIAN-LING, CHINA

Lexina stepped dangerously close to the dark wall. A rounded, black circle of metal had appeared from behind the veil about four feet off the ground. The circle grew larger as the wall slowly withdrew until it was four feet in diameter, then the metal began going straight back, revealing a tube.

"Do you think that is Artad?" Elek asked.

Lexina placed her hand on the end of the tube. "I don't know. But we will shortly."

Lexina paced along the black wall trying to control herself. Many lifetimes of waiting were slowly being fulfilled as the wall slid back centimeter by centimeter.

AREA 51

"The world is a very strange place," Che Lu said. "Who would have thought a year ago there would be a Russian agent and an old Chinese woman sitting inside the most secret place in America?"

She was in the conference room with Yakov. Her attempts to align the grid system with the planet had failed so far, but she felt sure she would eventually get it. When she'd been informed that the next chapter of the manuscript was ready for review, she had put that work on hold. She had not been able to find Larry Kincaid who was meeting with NASA officials over use

of the Hubble. She settled down into the chair next to
the Russian.

She removed a small leather pouch that was tied to
her belt and opened it. Holding it a few inches above the
tabletop, she let the contents spill out with a clatter.

"There have been stranger things happen," Yakov
said. "What are those?"

"Oracle bones," Che Lu said. "They are what led me
to Qian-Ling. They were sent to me by a dear friend
who is now fighting in Western China." She picked one
up, a piece about six inches long by three wide. "See
the markings—a version of High Runes. They were
found around Qian-Ling by peasant farmers digging in
their fields."

"And their purpose?" Yakov asked.

"They tell the future," Che Lu said. She gathered the
bones in her wrinkled hands and tossed them.

"What do they say?"

Che Lu gathered them, placed them in the bag and
drew the string tight. "They were just a tool used by the
Emperor's soothsayers. I studied them with an old
woman—older even than I—who could read them."

"What did they say?"

"Several things," Che Lu said sharply.

Yakov chuckled. "So it goes with soothsayers—give
several answers and something is bound to come true."

"Let us hope not in this case," Che Lu said.

Yakov's smile vanished. "What did they say?"

"Betrayal. Fear. Death. Darkness."

"You are right. Nothing good can come of that. But
you are also right in that it is just random chance that
determines the fall of the bones."

Yakov checked the clock on the conference room
wall. Fifteen more minutes and the team would be landing in Israel. Even if they did find anything useful, time

was running out for them to be able to get it to Turcotte. Once the team went through the second gateway of Rostau, they would be out of communication until they reemerged.

The screen lit up with the beginning of the next chapter.

"Let us read," Yakov said to Che Lu, holding a chair out for her to sit.

BURTON MANUSCRIPT: CHAPTER 5

Around 1200 B.C. the tribes of Israel began their Exodus from Egypt led by Moses. Here I must give the "accepted" version of what happened next. According to the Old Testament account, they crossed the Red Sea when it was parted by the power of their God. The pursuing Egyptian forces were drowned when the waters fell back in place.

According to biblical sources, this group wandered in the desert—mostly in the Sinai—for forty years. Such a journey seems strange. The desert there, which I crossed going from Arabia to Egypt, is indeed large and desolate, but not that expansive. It is written that they were led by a column of smoke or cloud during the day and a pillar of fire at night. It seems that such guidance could have been more direct, except for the explanation that this was a punishment for the worship of false idols while Moses was away from them on Mount Sinai.

It was here that he received the Ten Commandments from the one God he worshipped and was directed to make a container for the tablets on which the commandments had been written. It was to be two and a half cubits in length, a cubit and a half in width, and a cubit and a half in height. {A cubit is the length from a normal-sized man's elbow to the end of the middle finger. A little less than a foot and a half. But the cubit was different for many societies, so we must allow flexibility.}

The Ark was to be made of wood, gold-plated on the inside and out. The lid was also to be of gold, with two carved figures of cherubim facing each other. There's some debate over what exactly a cherubim is. Some say it is a sphinx-like creature. Others claim the two cherubim weren't separated but were male and female and carved in an erotic embrace, although orthodox religious scholars don't like that interpretation.

According to tradition, Moses got these basic instructions and he passed them on to a man named Bezaleel who was the most skilled workman available. The ark was built with four gold rings on each bottom corner, so that poles could be placed through for transport. Once completed, the tablets were put inside, and the Ark was covered whenever it was moved in public.

However, I believe that this is a description of an object that already existed and was taken secretly by Moses out of Egypt. It is at Mount Sinai that Moses chose to reveal this Ark to the people. The Ark that Moses had on the Exodus was the Ark of Atlantis, containing the Grail. I feel the transition from Atlantean Ark to Ark of the Covenant is an example of either myth supplanting reality or a deliberate misrepresentation of facts to hide the truth, something I have run across quite often in my study of the Airlia effect on our history.

The first part of this story comes mainly from the Christian and Jewish writing. However there is another body of study that I have perused regarding this journey—the Kabbalah, of which there are several interpretations, some strictly orthodox, others leaning toward the fantastic. I have culled from all these versions some interesting information that sheds light on the Grail.

Kabbalah is defined most commonly as "received knowledge." Over the centuries it has been considered an occult theosophy of rabbinical origins. It is similar in many ways to sufism, a desire for knowledge, to look beyond the apparent and find the ultimate truth of our world. Unlike those religions that promise revelation after death, those who follow the Kabbalah path seek that truth in this life, and, some say, ultimate life before death, transcending the limitations of time and space.

Delving deep into the various accounts, I have found that most branches trace their roots to the same event—the Exodus at Mount Sinai.

For over a thousand years the Kabbalah was handed down verbally before being written, leading to many interpretations. It is reported that while they were stopped at Mount Sinai, four men were called upon to partake of something "unworldly."

Three of these men were identified—a rabbi and two noted men of the tribes. But the fourth is only labeled the "Other." They entered a chamber in the mountain through pillars of marble and gazed upon what was inside. One of the men was killed instantly, overwhelmed by what he saw. The Other directed the two survivors to partake of a "libation" that would bring them to the fourth level of the soul, the chayyah, which is the life force itself.

I believe this Other wanted them to partake of the Grail. He promised them eternal life if they did so and knowledge beyond anything they could imagine.

I believe this Other was a Guide, sent by Aspasia's Shadow, to determine if the Grail was being carried in the Ark and if it was indeed the Grail of Atlantis.

Fortunately, both men refused to partake. The Grail was returned to the Ark and the Other disappeared. The Ark was brought to the Promised Land.

But this hint of such a "libation" led to different interpretations in both the Torah and the Christian Old Testament throughout the ages.

Regardless of what happened at Mount Sinai, the Ark, Grail enclosed, traveled to Israel. In 1040 B.C. during the reign of King Samuel, the Ark was captured by the Philistines. It is said to have caused great troubles for the Philistines and they were unable to open it. They returned it to the Israelites, where it was kept for a while in the town of Baala.

In the fourth year of his reign, King Solomon began building a temple fit to house the Ark and the Grail. The head architect was a Phoenician named Hiram Abiff. Seventy thousand men were employed to bring wood from Jaffa to Jerusalem and even more, eighty thousand, to quarry the stone needed for the construction. It took seven and a half years to build—why such a monument for a people that worshipped one God who asked for no idols to be built to him?

Hiram Abiff is rumored to have sent a report about what he was doing and what the Temple was designed to hold—the Ark and the Grail—to his king in Phoenicia. Hiram Abiff was killed by Solomon upon completion of the Temple to keep the secret, but it might have already been too late.

This report made its way through the Muslim World and when they conquered Spain, it went to the center of knowledge they established at Toledo. There it was uncovered by a man known only as Kyot, a sort of sorcerer, a master of a little-known runic language which sounds very much like the High Rune language.

With the secret disclosed, action needed to be taken to preserve both artifacts. On top of that, internal dissension among the tribes and external forces constantly threatened the temple and its precious contents.

The successors to Solomon make it seem less like a kingdom devoted to God than one committed to power. And what was the power they were fighting over?

After Solomon, due to the turmoil that overtook the state, one legend has it that the Ark was taken by Solomon's son and the Queen of Sheba to Africa, to the Kingdom of Axum, where it has remained to this day. The Ark went south as a ruse to hide the location of the more important piece—the Grail, which remained in Jerusalem, being too valuable and powerful for the priests to part with in their struggles.

I will not go through the various deceptions, assassinations, alliances, and betrayals that boiled in Jerusalem for the next several hundred years.

In 587 B.C., the Babylonians seized Jerusalem and razed the temple, taking the people into captivity. It is written that Jeremiah, a prophet, hid the Grail on Mount Nebo in the Abaraim Mountains. That is the last time the Ark or the Grail is mentioned in the Old Testament. A sect grew, the Essenes, who kept knowledge of the Grail's location a secret. It is possible the Essenes were a group of Watchers.

And then the Romans came.

At first, the Romans came not as conquerors, but

*as allies. They were invited into Jerusalem, the lesser
of the many enemies that had to be dealt with.*

*As expected, the Romans assumed more and more
power, making the state a Roman vassal. And as expected, the Jewish people eventually rebelled.*

*And here you must bear with me. For I think there
was a rebellion of another sort. That the inner priest-
hood, those who watched the Grail in secret chambers
and kept it safe for hundreds and hundreds of years finally reached a state of desperation. I believe some of
these priests were renegade Watchers, for as you will
see later in my account, this was not to be the last time
the Grail was sought as a solution to a current problem by those men who knew where the Grail was, hoping it could be used in their struggle, and perhaps the
ultimate solution to stop both The Mission and The
Ones Who Wait by renegade Watchers.*

*A figure arose in the land who became a leader,
not by force of arms, but by preaching love and
peace. He had knowledge beyond anything ever seen
before.*

*And the Romans helped their lackeys kill him. But
it was said he could not die.*

*Whether it was God or access to the Grail that
brought this about I do not know and do not pretend
to tell you.*

*It did not achieve the immediate desired result but
it did change the course of man from then forward.
History will give the final answer to this.*

Che Lu pushed her chair back. She pressed her hands
against her eyes and held them there. Yakov was silent.
There was no longer the clack of Mualama's key-

board—he too was sitting still, looking at the words he had translated.

"Well." Yakov's voice shattered the silence, but no one went further than that. No one could. What they had just read was so overwhelming in its implications that there was another long silence.

They were all surprised when Che Lu spoke. "Nothing is as it seemed. Nothing." She looked at the others, dismay all over her face. "Who are we? Where did we come from?"

"More importantly," Yakov said, "who should we trust?"

"I think we should trust Artad," Che Lu said. "From this journal, it appears he tried to do good."

Yakov shook his head. "Not entirely. It looks to me as if both sides were manipulative and deceitful."

"A war is coming," Che Lu said. "Do you think we should align with Aspasia's Shadow? Everywhere he has been, his influence was negative. Artad was only trying to stop him."

"Why think a side has to be chosen?" Mualama asked. "Perhaps we have to fight both sides and be true to our species."

"Artad unified China and led the building of the Great Wall," Che Lu argued. "That is a far more positive thing than Aspasia's Shadow is credited for."

"We shall have to see what the rest of the manuscript has to say," Mualama said.

HAZERIM AIR BASE, ISRAEL

The runway was blacked out, allowing the bouncer to arrive unseen except by the commando guards wearing night-vision devices. They had the airfield surrounded, guarding against attack out of the surrounding desert.

Turcotte watched through his own night-vision goggles the floor of the bouncer as the pilot gently set down the large containers holding the team's equipment, released the lines, then floated the craft to the side and set it down. He was the first one out of the hatch, the rest of Graves's team following.

A small group of men waited for them on the tarmac next to a dim light, just in front of the Combat Talon. Turcotte recognized the flight suits of the talon crew, but there was another man dressed in unmarked khakis also in the group.

The tallest of the men in the flight suits stepped forward as Turcotte approached. "Colonel Maher, pilot in command."

Turcotte took the offered hand. "Mike Turcotte, mission commander."

The colonel didn't bother to introduce the rest of his crew, instead ordering them to get the aircraft ready to take off. Graves's team was already carrying the cases containing the TASC-suits and other gear over to the open back ramp of the aircraft.

That left the unidentified man in khaki, who finally spoke. "My name is Sherev."

"We appreciate being allowed to use the airfield," Turcotte said.

"That is not why I am here. I am from Dimona."

Turcotte recognized the name and what was thought to be stored there—nuclear weapons. "What can I do for you?"

"There is a problem we have, that appears also to be your problem." Sherev paused, as if considering what to say. "Someone in my government has given up two items that I think have something to do with your target."

Turcotte waited, hoping Sherev would get to the point.

"I would not have allowed this to happen if I had known who was involved on the other end," Sherev continued, "but I was cut out of the loop. It was only after the items were given up that I discovered who we were dealing with. Have you ever heard of a man named Al-Iblis?"

Turcotte felt a chill come over his body. "What did you give him?"

"Two artifacts from our archives at Dimona. They are known as *thummin* and *urim*. They are two stones, the exact nature of which we never ascertained."

Turcotte remembered Che Lu mentioning those names. "When did he get them?"

"They were delivered to an intermediary in Jordan four hours ago. We were not able to track them further."

"Why?" Turcotte asked. "Why did you do this?"

"Al-Iblis had Saddam Hussein assassinated as his part of this bargain. There were those in my country—powerful people—who felt the loss of two stones that were apparently not worth anything was an excellent trade."

"They were wrong," Turcotte said.

"I feared so. That is why I am here."

A whine split the air as one of the Talon's four turbo-prop engines came alive. Turcotte's nostrils flared wide as the familiar smell of burning fuel wafted over him.

"What can you do for me?"

"I got you this airfield and you'll get counter-electronic-warfare support from our experts all the way into your drop zone and we'll cover the plane coming out," Sherev said. "We have a bit more experience than your Air Force in infiltrating Egyptian airspace."

"That will help. We'll have an AWACS flying support so your people can coordinate through it."

Sherev handed a small slip of paper to Turcotte. "That's how you can get ahold of me via secure SATCOM."

A second engine started.

"How did you know the deal was bad?" Turcotte asked.

"It has been my expereince that no one offers something of value unless they can get something more valuable in turn."

"So what are these stones?"

"They are Airlia artifacts," Sherev said. "The rabbis believe they are an important part of the garments the High Priest wore when attending the Ark of the Covenant."

The third engine was powered up, the noise making it difficult to talk, the wind blown back from the blades causing them to lean into it.

Sherev shouted. "It seems as if legends are coming alive."

Turcotte nodded, anxious to be going.

Sherev grabbed his arm. "Have you ever wondered why there has never been peace in this part of the world?" He didn't wait for an answer. "There are evil forces about—these aliens and their human servants, I think they have spent much time here causing us grief. It is time we got rid of them. Anything you need, you call me."

"I've got to get going," Turcotte said.

Sherev nodded. "Good luck."

Turcotte ran up the back ramp to the MC-130. The crew chief immediately pressed the button that initiated the hydraulic arms, raising the ramp. Members of the team were opening cases in the rear half of the cargo bay. The front half was separated from them by a thick curtain. It was in that section that a large part of what made the MC-130 different from regular C-130 aircraft was housed. Rows of equipment manned by electronic warfare specialists filled the space. They could find enemy radar and defeat it. They could also help the pilot fly in limited visibility at extremely low level, below the probing fingers of radar.

Turcotte had chosen the MC-130 because it was the best chance they had of getting into the Nile undetected. The two pilots, along with the navigator in the cockpit, were the best the Air Force had.

A hand on his shoulder got his attention. Graves leaned in close so he could be heard above the roar of the engines. "We need to start rigging. Time to drop is only a little over an hour away."

Turcotte nodded. He staggered and grabbed ahold of the red cargo webbing lining the skin of the airplane as the plane began moving, taxiing toward the end of the runway.

Circling at thirty thousand feet over the Mediterranean, the Airborne Warning And Control System (AWACS) was a modified 707-320B full of electronic equipment rather than passengers. The thirty-foot dome radar on top of the fuselage was able to "paint" a complete picture of the airspace for four hundred miles in all directions, once every ten-second rotation.

Colonel Mike Zycki was the AWACS commander and his plane's abilities were supplemented by a secure link to the National Security Agency (NSA), which tied him into the network of spy satellites that Agency oversaw.

"We've got Area Five One Six on screen," one his officers reported. "Wheels up from Hazerim."

"Status of Egyptian air defense?" he asked his electronic warfare officer.

"Level four. Not quite war footing, but they're definitely awake, as if they're expecting something to happen. I'm forwarding what we have to Area Five-One Six. I think I can paint them a clear alley to their drop point."

"And out?"

"And out."

"Do it."

AIRSPACE, SINAI PENINSULA

Turcotte slid into the TASC-suit, fighting a momentary feeling of claustrophobia, as the back half sealed against the front half. He'd never liked being in an enclosed spaced. During scuba training, the worst part had been practicing "lock-outs" where he would have to climb into a submarine's escape hatch, then sit inside while it filled with water, before opening the outer hatch.

He felt the inner padding of the suit mold against his body. His fingers fit into the command pads at the end of the arms.

"Power on," he ordered.

The screens on the inside of the helmet came alive and he could see the interior of the combat talon, lit with the red night-lights.

"Low light enhance," Turcotte said.

The screens flickered, then he could see more clearly as the mini-cams on the outside of the suit went to night-vision mode, the computer enhancing the available light. Turcotte had a slightly curved screen four inches directly in front of his eyes that filled his field of vision and on standard view gave him the view that would normally be right in front of him. He could give commands to have the screen display other camera angles.

He also had a small flip-down display halfway between the screen and his left eye that was made of clear plastic on which was reflected whatever data from the computer he wanted. During the testing Turcotte had immediately developed a sharp headache from trying to watch the screen and read the data. He'd talked to Apache gunship pilots who had a similar display built into their helmets and they'd told him it took months to develop the ability to naturally do both. They didn't have months to prepare for this mission. Turcotte felt a moment of doubt, which he quickly squashed.

Carefully, Turcotte stood. They'd attached an interesting appendage to the end of the legs: a flat platform that extended forward about ten inches. It gave stability like feet, but built into the center of each "foot" was a six-inch-wide hole in which a small turbine fan was mounted—the propulsion device once they were in the water.

Power for the TASC-suit came from banks of advanced lithium batteries built into the armor of the suit. To Turcotte that was the major disadvantage—they had four hours of operating power, then they would need to recharge. They had to be in, rescue Duncan, recover the Grail, and be out on the exfiltration aircraft in less than that time. Graves's plan, the best his team could come up with during the isolation, had estimated three hours to do all that. But they were working with a lot of unknown variables, such as the rather glaring question of where exactly the Black Sphinx was located and how to get to it. From experience in Special Operations, Turcotte knew everything always took much longer than one planned.

With the aid of the airplane's loadmaster, a pack was attached to the lower back of the TASC-suit carrying gear Turcotte had specified. Above it was placed the specially designed parachute that would allow them to drop at very low altitude.

Turcotte then had a Mark 98 attached to his left arm. Extra ammo cylinders were strapped along his chest, down to his stomach. He was glad to have the power of the suit, because he estimated he was at twice his normal weight. He checked the hookups to the trigger and sight. The trigger was activated by his left forefinger inside the suit, and the laser sight picture would be duplicated on screen for him.

On his right arm was placed a "hand." It was controlled by moving his hand inside the end of the arm, which relayed to the metal fingers. Also on the mechanical hand, securely fastened to the middle "finger" with wire, was Kopina's Watcher ring.

He was ready to go.

"Area Five-One-Six is in the alley and clear so far," the EW officer told Zycki. He pointed at a spot on his screen. "The only problem spot is this radar site here. They might get an echo from the plane as it hits the Nile."

"Can you cloud it?" Zycki asked.

"Yes, sir. I've got the frequency and I'll run some interference when the Talon gets close."

"Any other unusual activity?"

"We tracked a private jet into Cairo five minutes ago

that was flying low level on an end run around the Sinai. We're not sure what that was about."

"Concentrate on One Six."

Turcotte was amazed at the technology and what it could do. Sitting on the seat, he could look in all directions without moving, just by accessing the various mini-cams on the exterior of the suit.

Looking about the cargo bay was surreal. Not only because he was viewing it on screen, as if he were taking part in a movie, but also because of the mission they were going on.

Black-suited, seven-foot-tall figures moved about, getting rigged, checking their gear.

A voice came over the FM net. "Twenty minutes till drop."

CHAPTER 14

GIZA

Lisa Duncan stirred as she heard the thud of boots coming down the tunnel. She stood, stretched, and felt the pang of hunger in her stomach. Worse, though, was the dryness in her mouth. She was parched and knew that she could not go on without water for much longer.

She went to the veil and edged it aside so she could see. Aspasia's Shadow stood there, a pair of soldiers behind him. One had an intricately carved wooden box in his hands.

"You were here when this place was built, weren't you?" Duncan asked before he could say anything.

Aspasia's Shadow nodded. "I was here. Aker, one of Aspasia's lieutenant's, hollowed out the six chambers. He bore the tunnels to link them. He placed the Black Sphinx in this chamber and directed the carving of the stone sphinx above. This was long before the time your scientists think the stone sphinx was carved. This area was very different then. It was a lush land, fertile for many miles where there is now desert. That was why we chose to come here after Atlantis."

"If you helped build this, how did you lose control of it?"

Aspasia's head snapped toward her, anger in his eyes. "I was betrayed."

"How? By whom?"

"By Aspasia, of course. He removed something I needed to rule. His machine was afraid I would get too powerful while he slept."

"What was taken?"

"The master guardian."

"To Mars?"

"No. It was hidden here on Earth. I have searched long and hard for it, as I have searched for the key to the Grail. And you wonder why I care not for those who still live on Mars? They cared little for me all these years. But now *my* time comes!"

"There are some who won't allow that," Duncan said.

Aspasia's Shadow laughed. "Do you know what you are?"

"What do you mean?"

"What humans are?"

Something was at the edge of Duncan's consciousness, just like it had been when she had first seen the Grail. She knew more than she could bring to her conscious mind, which scared her. How had she gained this information?

"We're intelligent beings who deserve a place—"

"Intelligent?" Aspasia's Shadow laughed again.

Duncan remembered the strange planet she had seen in the vision from the Ark. "I'm standing here, where you want to be. If I'm not intelligent, what does that make you?"

The smile was gone from his face. "Are you ready to negotiate?" Aspasia's Shadow asked, the words echoing in the chamber.

"Are you making me an offer?" Duncan asked in turn as she stepped outside.

Aspasia's Shadow held up a canteen. "Would you like to drink?"

"What do you want in exchange?"

"The Grail."

"You're joking, right?"

"I never joke," Aspasia's Shadow said. "You will not last much longer without water."

"Then I die here, but at least you don't get the Grail."

"Those who you work with don't know who you are, do they?"

"I will not give you the Grail," she repeated.

"Perhaps if I made you a better offer," Aspasia's Shadow said, "you would change your mind."

"There is nothing you can offer me that will get me to give you the Grail," Duncan said.

"Do not be too sure of that," Aspasia's Shadow said. "What if I give you the greatest treasure one can give?"

"And what do you believe that to be?"

His answer was succinct. "Immortality." He signaled and the soldier with the box stepped forward, knelt and placed it on the floor several feet in front of him. He opened the lid, then went back to his position.

Duncan took a step forward without thinking, then halted. She felt the weight of the *essen* on her shoulders, the crown on her head. She could see the two stones set inside the box. "What do you have?"

"The Grail is worthless without these. They were called the *urim* and the *thummin*, long ago by those who really didn't know what the Grail was—just like you. Those names are as good as any. Even I no longer remember their real name."

"The Grail isn't worthless without those." Duncan was trying to collect her thoughts. "It just won't work without them. But the Grail still has value. We are still in a standoff."

" 'Work'?" Aspasia's Shadow repeated. "What exactly do you think the Grail does?"

"Why don't you tell me?"

"If I give *one* of the stones to you," Aspasia's Shadow asked, "will that end the standoff?"

"And allow me safe passage out of here with the Grail and stone?" Duncan knew it was foolish even to ask.

"Of course."

"Now you lie."

"Perhaps. But you will die of thirst if you persist."

"Then the Grail remains safe in here."

Aspasia's Shadow snorted. "For how long? Do you think you wear the only set of priest's clothes? I am sure I can find another set. Or get through the guardians by other means. It will only be a matter of time, and that variable is on my side."

"Then wait for me to die," Duncan said.

"You do not ever have to die."

That gave Duncan pause. "What exactly does the Grail do? I know it is an Airlia machine, but how can it give a person immortality? That is not natural. How can eternal life be manufactured?"

"The Grail does more than just give eternal life," Aspasia's Shadow said. "But turn the question around. Why is there death? Perhaps it is death that has been manufactured? Perhaps it is death that is not natural?"

CHAPTER 15

AIRSPACE EGYPT

"Ten minutes!" Captain Graves's black form was the rearmost figure in the cargo bay. The loadmaster was dwarfed by him, a slight figure in a green jumpsuit holding Graves's static line.

"Go to rebreathers," Graves ordered.

"Rebreather on," Turcotte ordered. The computer on his back immediately sealed the suit's air inlet on the back of the helmet and switched over to the internal rebreather.

"Stand up." Graves gave the command quietly, knowing that each man could hear him clearly through the suit radio.

Turcotte stood, reaching up and hooking his left arm over the steel cable that ran the length of the plane.

"Hook up, loadmaster," Graves said, a departure from the normal procedure. Because each man had weapons attached to the end of their arms, the loadmaster had to go down the line, remove their snap hook from the parachute, and attach it to the static line cable.

Turcotte felt a slight tug as the loadmaster did his. He turned, making sure it was secure.

"Check static lines."

"Sound off for equipment check." Graves gave the next jump command, but then once more he added something. "And I mean all equipment. If your suit isn't working right, now is the time to say something."

Turcotte, the last man in the stick, nudged the man in front. "OK."

The word was passed up the line until the man right behind Graves announced, "All OK, jumpmaster."

Graves turned to face the rear of the aircraft. Turcotte, through the suit's external sensors, could pick up the change in flight speed as he staggered slightly and quickly adjusted. The plane was slowing to drop speed.

"Three minutes," Graves announced.

Turcotte watched the screen just in front of his face as it showed a dark crack appear at the junction of the top of the rear. The crack widened as the ramp came down until it reached a level position with the floor of the cargo bay. Graves knelt, then lay belly down, and slid over, sticking his black helmet out into the one-hundred-and-twenty-five-mile-an-hour wind.

Looking past Graves, Turcotte could see dark desert a hundred and fifty feet below. An occasional light, bright as a flare, dotted the landscape here and there. He knew they were east of the Nile coming in low over the desert.

The plane dipped down even lower and banked hard right. A dark black ribbon lay below. The Nile. Turcotte felt a familiar wave of anticipation. For just a second he remembered his last jump. Over China, also over water. Peter Nabinger was the man next to him, and he'd helped the archaeologist get over his fear. And now he was going where Nabinger had considered his home—Egypt, the center of the mysteries that had consumed Nabinger's life. And the archaeologist had never made it out of China alive.

Turcotte shook his head to get rid of the thoughts and was immediately reminded of the fact that he was encased in a thick, hi-tech suit. The screen in front of him shimmered for a second and he felt dizzy. Then he regained his composure.

"Ten seconds." Graves's voice had gone up, and the shout hurt Turcotte's ears.

"Stand by."

Graves edged forward to the end of the ramp, a hulking figure looking down. The red light above the ramp reflected a deep glow off all the men in front of Turcotte. He blinked as it changed to green.

"Go!" Graves didn't attempt to keep his voice down, screaming the command as if they were on a normal jump and he had to try to be heard above the roar of the engines. But the green light and Graves stepping off into the night sky reinforced the command more than volume could.

Turcotte shuffled forward, barely noticing the strangeness of the suit encompassing his body as he focused on the edge of the ramp. Then he dropped.

The MC-130 had gone up to less than three hundred feet above the flat black surface of the Nile, the lights of Cairo ahead, not far in the distance.

Turcotte dropped like a rock, the weight of the suit adding to his descent. The static line reached its end and pulled out the three parachutes packed in the rig. Their abrupt deployment jerked Turcotte from terminal velocity into a somewhat controlled descent.

"Down view," Turcotte ordered. The flat black surface of the river was just below. In five seconds he hit the Nile and was under water. He cut away the parachute and it quickly sank.

"GPS link and team display on," Turcotte ordered. The dark screen in front of him gave way to a display of the local area. A small red glowing dot in the center was his own position. A dozen other green dots were the rest of the team. A yellow arrow pointed in the direction they had to swim to get to the tunnel entrance—downstream with the flow of the river.

Turcotte oriented himself at a depth of five meters. Gingerly he turned on the propulsion units, while trying to maintain the same depth. It was a case of trial and error as he moved. By the jerky movements of the green dots, the others were experiencing the same learning curve as they traveled downstream.

"Two stones indicate to me that the Grail does two things," Lisa Duncan said.

Aspasia's Shadow nodded. "Ah, you are indeed showing some intelligence."

Duncan ignored the barb. "One is immortality, or at least that's what you claim. What's the other half?"

"That is more difficult to explain," Aspasia's Shadow said. "Is not immortality a great enough gift? Never growing old, never getting sick, having all the time in the world to do the things you've always wanted to do?"

"In a world run by you?"

"Somebody has to run things for you humans. Look at what a mess you've made doing things on your own."

"How much on our own have we been over the ages?" Duncan retorted.

The propulsion unit worked well as Turcotte closed the distance to the tunnel entrance. It had just appeared on his screen as a yellow circle about two hundred meters away. He reached it and waited for the other team members.

"IR lights and IR imaging," Turcotte ordered, switching off the GPS link, which would be cut anyway as soon as they went into the tunnel. The screen cleared and then was replaced by a greenish glow. The infrared lights mounted on his suit penetrated the dark water about ten feet. Turcotte could see the others as they also turned on their lights and infrared cameras. Black forms floating in the water, they waited as each man was accounted for. Turcotte could feel the tug of the water, wanting to draw him into the eight-foot-wide hole in the bank of the Nile.

"All present," Graves finally reported.

"Follow me," Turcotte said. He turned, went into the tunnel, and entered the second gateway to the roads of Rostau. The water carried him along. He hit the side of the tunnel, tumbled, regained his balance and orientation, and continued on.

The tunnel widened and Turcotte could stand, chest deep in the surging water. He stayed on the rebreather, though, uncertain when the tunnel would narrow once more. Burton had not gone this way, so all he could hope was to keep moving forward until he found the shaft Burton had come down. He walked forward, the team following, shifting his screen view to up every two steps, then quickly back to forward as long as he saw a roof over his head.

He was beginning to get the feel of the suit and his gait was getting smoother as he penetrated farther under the Giza Plateau. The tunnel was about fifteen meters wide by three high, the walls showing a smooth cut under the IR light.

"Hold on." Graves's voice was almost a whisper over the team net. "Anyone hear that?"

Turcotte held up his right arm, signaling for everyone to halt.

"Audio magnify to maximum," he ordered the computer.

He could hear the river, like a thunderous waterfall, going by. And there *was* something else. The sound of metal on stone a rapid clicking noise. And it was getting louder.

"Let's keep going," he ordered, heading directly toward the approaching strange noise.

"The change is inevitable," Aspasia's Shadow said.

"Nothing is inevitable." Duncan found that her gaze had strayed from the wooden box to the canteen.

"Your death is, if you continue to deny me what is mine," Aspasia's Shadow swung the canteen by the strap.

"I will not give you the Grail for a drink of water."

"Then how about for this?" Aspasia's Shadow held up one the stones. "This is the *urim*." He knelt and gently rolled it across the floor.

Duncan scrambled to her knees and caught it between both hands. She held it up in front of her, staring into the sparkling green depths of the stone. Her mind and soul were drawn to it with more power than her body would ever desire water.

She knew better. The part of her that was free over whatever was controlling her, knew better. Still, her hands cradled the stone and she felt whatever resolve she had weakening.

Turcotte stopped, signaling for the others to do the same. He'd stepped down the audio feed by stages, yet the clicking noise grew louder until he had no doubt the source was very close. He peered at the screen just in front of his face. He lifted his left arm, the MK 98 held level, just above the surface of the water.

"Aiming," he ordered the computer. A reticule appeared on the screen. As he moved the MK 98, the reticule followed wherever the muzzle was aimed, unless he went too far and it went off screen.

The noise ceased. For several seconds Turcotte stood perfectly still, waiting, the team deployed behind him. He took a step forward. Then another. After four steps the noise came again, not closer, but retreating at the same rate Turcotte advanced.

"Cover me from the right," Turcotte ordered Graves, as he went back to checking the top of the tunnel every other step. The water rushing around his legs and waist was barely noticeable as he continued down. Whatever was making the noise continued to back up until Turcotte suddenly stopped.

The screen showed a circular opening about four feet wide in the roof. He turned as the members of the team gathered round. "We're going up."

Graves stepped forward. "Are we coming back out this same way?"

Turcotte pointed in the direction the noise had come from. "That way should also go to the Nile and you're with the current. Either way. If we go back the same way we came in, we can always go downstream in the Nile itself to the pickup zone."

It was strange, not being able to see the men's faces, to get a sense of what they were feeling. Just dark forms bathed in infrared light. Almost inhuman.

Three of them stuck out thick arms to form a shoulder-high platform. Turcotte clambered up onto the arms. He was able to reach up with both arms and spread them, jamming them between the sides of the shaft.

Using the added power from the suit, he lifted himself into the circular opening. Once inside he braced his legs against one side, his back against the other. Shifting to an up view, he could see that the shaft was not exactly vertical, just as Burton described. Turcotte felt a surge of excitement. He felt they were on the right path.

He began going up by scooting his legs up, then sliding the back of the suit along the stone.

"Down view," Turcotte said. He could see a suited figure—Graves—right behind. "Up view." The shaft extended as far as the IR lights could penetrate.

Duncan felt a tremble in her knees and she forced herself to stay upright, her face calm. The *urim* was in her right hand, the stone giving off an unnatural warmth.

"Why did you give this to me?"

"It is time for us to move on. We cannot stay here forever. Things are happening in the outside world."

"What do you want in exchange?"

"All I want is for you to pull back the curtain and let me see the Ark and the Grail," Aspasia's Shadow said.

Duncan knew there was more to it than that, but she couldn't figure out what Aspasia's Shadow was trying to do. It was difficult to think clearly with the *urim* in her hand, the Grail next to her. Pulling the veil back changed nothing given the weight of the stone in her hand. She reached up and slid the white material aside.

The shaft ended abruptly in stone. Turcotte edged as close as possible, then stopped. "Magnify twofold," Turcotte ordered. "Suit power lock." The suit's muscle magnifiers locked in place, both saving power and keeping him in his place in the shaft.

He scanned the rock, looking for a place to insert the ring.

"Magnify threefold," Turcotte ordered.

It was as if he were searching the surface from just inches away. The slightest of depressions in the smooth surface caught his attention.

"Magnification off," Turcotte ordered. He reached up with his right arm, maneuvering the middle finger, tip bent, ring forward to the depression. It fit perfectly. The stone dropped six inches, then slid aside. Turcotte reached over the edge and climbed into the chamber to be confronted by the mummified body of a man, arm trapped under a stone set in the wall. It confirmed that they were in the right place.

"Who the hell is that?" Captain Graves was the next up through the floor.

"Kaji," Turcotte knelt next to the body. "One of the Kajis," he amended, thinking of Von Seeckt's story.

Brown skin was stretched tight over the skull, the eyes covered with a milky surface. Turcotte wondered why one of the succeeding Kajis hadn't come down here and recovered the body. Perhaps this Kaji's son had not been guided this deeply into the Roads of Rostau, Turcotte thought. Burton also had Kaji's ring.

Turcotte recalled from Burton's tale that he had claimed to have scoured all the walls for a way out and found no place where the ring would work. They had prepared for that in isolation.

"Demo man forward," Turcotte ordered. "Everyone else, back in the shaft."

Metayer, the senior engineer on 055, went to the block that had pinned Kaji's arm. Turcotte helped him remove his waterproof pack and lay it on the floor. Unzipping it, Metayer pulled out a long strip of explosive which he pressed along the stone's seam. He ran out detonating cord with a fuse igniter.

"What about the body?" Metayer asked.

"He's already dead," Turcotte said. "I don't think he'll complain."

"Which side does it go in?" Duncan asked. She had the Grail in front of her, between her knees as she sat on the floor. She felt like a child with a new toy on Christmas morning, sitting on the floor, cloaked in the over-sized robes of the ancient priests. The pull of the Grail was irresistible to her.

"I do not know," Aspasia's Shadow said.

"Don't lie to me."

"As far as I know, the stones have never been in the Grail," Aspasia's Shadow said. "I certainly have never seen it used."

Duncan wasn't sure whether to believe him or not. "Do you know what it does?"

"The *urim* does one thing, the *thummin* another."

"That's not much help."

"I am not here to help you," Aspasia's Shadow said. "I gave you the *urim* so we can end this impasse."

Duncan placed the palm of her hand on top of one end and waited. The end irised open. Reverently she took the urim and placed it in the depression, feeling the tingle as before.

She stared down at it.

Nothing.

A part of her felt relieved.

Metayer held up the ignitor. "I'm all set."

Turcotte slipped over the edge of the shaft and went down, leaving enough room for Metayer to be above him. The demo man followed.

"Fire in the hole," Metayer announced.

"Audio down three quarters," Turcotte ordered the computer. When the blast came, it was muted.

"Audio normal power." Turcotte climbed up behind Metayer. The chamber was full of airborne dust swirling about.

The stone had been knocked out of position and a tunnel beckoned beyond.

Duncan looked up. Aspasia's Shadow stood on the other side of the chamber watching her like a hawk— no, more as a vulture would, she realized. A soldier ran up the tunnel, halted next to Aspasia's Shadow, and whispered something in his ear. Aspasia's Shadow hissed something in return, never once looking away from Duncan and the Grail. The soldier ran back down the tunnel.

Aspasia's Shadow reached inside his cloak and removed a small black sphere. It disappeared inside his large hands, the fingers moving around the surface of it. She briefly wondered what it was, but the lure of the Grail was too strong for her to spend much time on that.

Duncan reached in and removed the stone. The opening closed. She turned the Grail over and placed her hand on the other end. It opened. She lowered the stone in and knew she had it right this time as soon as the *urim* got close. The stone grew hotter, the green light inside blazed brightly, illuminating her and the entire chamber with an unearthly glow.

A shock raced up her arm as she placed the stone in its place. The opening irised tight against her wrist. She tried to remove her hand but couldn't. Her fingers would not let go of the stone, held by an invisible force. Pain radiated through the flesh that touched the stone, lancing into her bones and causing her to cry out. It was as if her hand were on fire. She could feel the flesh peeling back, charred and burned. She had never felt such intense agony.

In her concern for the pain the Grail was causing, she failed to notice that the light had gone out in the ruby eyes of the sphinx head guards.

CHAPTER 16

THE GIZA PLATEAU, EGYPT

Turcotte felt a momentary sense of panic as he entered the tunnel. Was it right or left now? He forced himself to concentrate on the mission. Burton had said the hidden door was on the right, which meant he had to turn left. He shifted in that direction. Seventy paces, which meant about sixty meters. Turcotte had checked his pace count in the suit while in the hangar during isolation. He moved quickly, the team following, each man keeping his own pace count. The last man in line dropped a chem light next to the door, marking the location as it slid shut.

Turcotte stopped where he thought the hidden keyhole should be. "Pace check," he announced over the radio. The report from the rest of the team indicated they all agreed plus or minus about three meters, which wasn't bad. Turcotte placed the ring against the left wall at shoulder level. Nothing. He shifted left several feet, then back to the right when the outline of a door appeared. The door shifted, then slid up.

Turcotte stepped through, weapon leading. He took a quick shift glance in both directions. He turned left. "Let's go."

Like a bear trapped with its paw in the honey pot, Lisa Duncan remained on her knees, frozen. The pain was centered in her hand, but now Duncan couldn't move any part of her body as it radiated through her nervous system, crawling up her arm like an inevitable tide of agony. Every nerve ending vibrated with the feeling of a red hot needle knifing through it from the inside going outward, as if the source were her bone marrow itself. She didn't even blink as, out of the corner of her eye, she saw Aspasia's Shadow walk forward, past the bodies of the two soldiers that had been killed earlier.

"One hundred and eighty-seven meters," Turcotte said.

"Check," Graves replied.

Turcotte put his hand on the wall and began searching for the next door. The last door between them and the tunnel leading to the Hall of Records chamber.

Beyond the pain resonating from her hand, up her arm, and exploding in her brain, Duncan barely felt it as two soldiers grabbed her and began carrying her out of the chamber, the arm with the Grail dangling. Four others picked up the Ark, carrying it by the poles out of the chamber behind her.

Aspasia's Shadow knelt next to Duncan. His long fingers closed around the narrow center of the Grail and squeezed at a certain spot. He carefully removed the Grail from her hand. Then he turned it upside down and a glowing stone dropped out. That end of the Grail closed. He pocketed the stone and then placed the Grail inside the Ark. He threw a white sheet over the Ark, covering it.

Still Duncan didn't move.

A burst of automatic weapons fire echoed into the chamber.

Aspasia's Shadow stood. "It is time to leave." He still had the black sphere in one hand. The surface was divided into small hexagonal areas. His fingers tapped several of the hexes.

The first burst hit the ceiling above Turcotte's helmet, sending chips of stone flying. There was no chance for the soldier to get off a second burst, as Turcotte had centered the reticules on the man's chest even while he was firing. Turcotte's trigger finger twitched and a dart ripped through the man's chest, sending him tumbling back down the tunnel into the darkness from which he appeared.

"We're in the right place," Turcotte yelled, hearing the echo through his own receiver.

"Right behind you, sir!" Graves replied.

Turcotte ran toward the darkness. He paused just before entering and fired the rest of the magazine into the blackness as quickly as the cylinder rotated. He grabbed another cylinder off the bandoleer on his chest and reloaded.

Then he went in.

A soldier staggered onto the landing leading to the tunnel, blood spurting from the stump of his right arm, neatly severed by a dart. The man tumbled over the edge and fell to the ground with a solid thud. The blood stopped spurting.

Aspasia's Shadow yelled commands in Arabic, sending the soldiers he had in the chamber running up the stairs toward the ledge.

Just as the darkness enveloped him, Turcotte heard the beginning of a startled yell over the team radio net. Then it was cut off as if a switch had been flipped. He waded forward through the darkness and stepped into the brilliant light of the Hall of Records chamber. Behind him, the tunnel was as dark, the strange doorway closed behind him.

"IR off, normal light," Turcotte ordered as his screen was overloaded and blanked out for a second.

That's all it took for a three-round burst from an AK-47 to hit Turcotte in the chest, staggering him back a step. The special ceramic/alloy armor absorbed most of the impact, chips flying.

The screen came alive with normal light. The reticules were high. Turcotte drew them down to the lead man coming up the stairs and fired. The steel dart tore through his chest and kept going, taking out the two men directly behind him before hitting the spine of the third man changing direction slightly, flying down into the chamber.

Turcotte took a second to scan the chamber. The Black Sphinx dominated the view, but he was more concerned about finding people. He saw Duncan! She lay unconscious on a tarp, being carried by two men. Behind her was a tall figure in a black robe, and behind him something draped in white also being carried.

"Spread out on the ledge," Turcotte ordered over the team net.

There was no answer.

Turcotte fired another dart down the stairs.

"Rear view."

There was no one behind him. The tunnel went ten meters, then faded into the strange black darkness.

"Front view."

Turcotte fired the MK 98 again, spearing the closest man. He could see the flashes as others fired. Rounds from men on the floor of the chamber chipped stone all about him. Hard thuds on the suit indicated some of the bullets were hitting.

Turcotte took a step back into the tunnel, getting out of the angle of fire of those on the floor. A head appeared coming up the stairs and Turcotte fired, taking it clean off. That bought him some time. Still, no one came out of the darkness.

Silence on the team net.

"Can you hear me?" a voice yelled from below.

"External speaker on," Turcotte instructed the computer. "I hear you."

"You will let me out or your friend will be dead."

"Who are you?" Turcotte needed to buy time for the team to reinforce him. He had no idea why they hadn't come through yet.

"Aspasia's Shadow. You will let me out or your friend will be dead and then we will kill you," Aspasia's Shadow continued. "Be glad I give you this offer."

Turcotte tried to think, to assess the situation. "I'll let you pass only if you give me her in exchange."

"I cannot give you the woman. She has partaken of the Grail. She must go with me to finish the process. If you take her, she will die."

Turcotte had no idea what he was talking about. Where the hell was the rest of the A-Team?

Another head appeared, peering cautiously. Turcotte aimed. A black object flew through the air. Turcotte shifted the reticules, tracking, fired, and the dart hit the grenade in midair.

At the same moment, a terrorist leapt up onto the ledge, firing on full automatic. The rounds impacted on the left side of Turcotte's suit, staggering him sideways. The screen inside the helmet flickered, then adjusted as the left-side helmet mini-cam was destroyed. Turcotte dropped to his knees and fired, killing the man. Warning lights were flickering on the bottom of the screen, informing him that the left front mini-cam was out. Some of his lithium batteries had been destroyed, reducing available power by twenty percent and various other problems that he didn't have time to read or know how to deal with.

"We will kill you," Aspasia's Shadow yelled. "And I will kill Doctor Duncan unless you immediately allow us to pass."

Turcotte kept his aim on the top of the stairs. He switched to FM. "Report? Anybody?"

Silence.

"We are coming up and Doctor Duncan is in front," Aspasia's Shadow's voice echoed in Turcotte's helmet.

Turcotte stood. He could see two men coming up the stairs supporting Duncan, who appeared to be unconscious, between them. Turcotte knew he could take both men down easily, but they might take Duncan over the edge with them. Behind them loomed Aspasia's Shadow.

"If you are thinking of killing me," Aspasia's Shadow began, a second before Turcotte pulled the trigger, "you need to know I am the only one who can revive her. Without me, she dies."

"What did you do to her?" Turcotte demanded.

"I didn't do anything," Aspasia's Shadow said. "She accessed the Grail and now the process must take its course. And I am the only one who can make sure it develops properly or else she dies a most terrible death."

"What process?"

The two men had reached the ledge, less than twenty feet from Turcotte. They paused as Aspasia's Shadow came up behind.

"We will go now," Aspasia's Shadow said, the other survivors from his group on the stairs, carrying the Ark.

"What process?" Turcotte repeated.

Aspasia's Shadow pointed and the men moved

forward. Turcotte held his ground for a second, then stepped aside. "You'll never get out of here."

"I believe we will," Aspasia's Shadow said. He smiled, revealing long, sharp teeth. "Do you know who she is?"

Turcotte was at a loss for an answer, not understanding the intent of the question.

"She is not who you believe her to be," the creature continued. "She has lied to you—or more likely even she does not yet know her true identity." The two men and Duncan disappeared into the blackness. "Do not follow us or she will die." He stepped into the blackness before Turcotte could say another word.

"Damn!" Turcotte cursed. He wondered if Graves and his men would ambush them. He waited a few seconds, so he wouldn't be caught in the kill zone, then dashed into the darkness, the heavy metal thud of his legs hitting the tunnel floor echoing into his helmet.

The blackness grabbed him, and he propelled himself forward, the MK-98 extended, finger ready. He stumbled over something as he entered the tunnel on the other side, hit his knees, forced the muzzle of the weapon up, scanning the screen for targets—nothing moving.

As he got to his feet, he almost fell once more.

"Down view."

Turcotte blinked, trying to make sense of what he was seeing. A black tube, about two feet long. Turcotte took a step back as he realized what it was. The severed leg of one of the team members, still encased in the suit armor.

"Forward view."

The tunnel was littered with body parts, some still in armor, others ripped out of the suits. A head, half out of the helmet, lay to one side. It was Graves, dead eyes staring at nothing, neck cleanly severed. The body was ten feet away, farther down the tunnel, blood pooled

where the head should be. The walls of the tunnel held
large divots where darts had hit, so the team had put up
a fight against whatever had attacked them.

"It's the whole team," Turcotte whispered to himself,
as if hearing the words would make the impact less severe. He counted, trying to add up body parts and suits.
As near as he could make out, every member of
the team was dead.

How could Aspasia's Shadow have done this? He
wondered, but even as the thought crossed his mind,
he realized this had happened while he was in the chamber still talking to the alien creature.

The MK-98 was still pointing ahead, but Turcotte
wasn't aware of where the reticules were, the vision on
the screen too overwhelming. Turcotte remembered
something from the briefing given by the space command representative. He went over to Graves's body,
turned it over, the backpack now accessible. With his
right hand, he pushed a button. A cover popped open,
revealing the master computer. Turcotte removed a
DVD disk. He knew he could put it in his own computer
and have whatever it had recorded from Graves's cameras and mikes played on his screen, but there wasn't
time for that now. He shoved it into one of the empty
ammo pouches on the front of his suit.

He began to run. He left the bodies behind, hoping
that carrying Duncan would slow Aspasia's Shadow
down enough so that he could catch them.

The pressure on the suit leg was so slight that
Turcotte almost didn't register it. He skidded to a halt,
his instincts warning him a second before his mind was
aware. Too late as the trip wire ignited the mine.

Steel ball bearing ripped into the TASC-suit, the con-
cussion of the blast knocking Turcotte off his feet and
sending him flying backward down the tunnel ten feet.

Two SA 365 Panther helicopters blew up sand as they
landed next to the Great Pyramid. Egyptian troops surrounded the area, but none came close as Aspasia's
Shadow and his entourage came out of the Caliph's entrance, carrying Duncan and the covered Ark toward the
choppers.

They loaded, the doors slid shut, and the choppers
lifted, heading to the east.

Turcotte had felt pain like this once before when he'd
been shot in the chest while wearing a protective vest,
except this was all over his body, not localized in one
place. He was in complete darkness, and it took him a
second to figure out why that was.

"Screen on," he ordered. "Forward view."

Nothing.

He tried moving, but the suit didn't respond. The inner,
airtight pressure layer pushed in on every part of his body
except his head, clinging, not allowing him to move. Into
his trapped darkness, Turcotte screamed, the sound reverberating inside the helmet. Then he passed out.

"We've got two bogies moving due west. Takeoff point
just about on top of the Great Pyramid."

"Identification?" Colonel Zycki asked as he came
down the aisle in the AWACS to stand behind the screen
watcher who had made the report.

"Negative ID."

"Signature?"

"Definitely helicopter. Flying low level but fast. They aren't Egyptian, because whoever's flying them has got to have LLTV and extensive night-flying capabilities that the Egyptians don't have."

Zycki considered that. "Notify our Israeli friends and forward them updates on the helicopters."

"Yes, sir."

Zycki turned to another of his people. "Anything yet from the team?"

"No, sir."

Zycki checked his watch. They only had an hour of darkness. He didn't think they could manage an exfiltration from the Nile in broad daylight.

Turcotte regained consciousness and immediately began hyperventilating. He tried to get it under control, knowing that was how he had passed out.

"Status display?" he whispered, hoping the computer was back on line.

Only darkness. He tried to move his arms. Nothing. Legs immobile. He focused his mind back to the orientation he had received. There was an emergency release if all power was lost. Where? He remembered, turning his head as far as he could to the left and sticking his tongue out. It touched a toggle, which he flipped up.

Turcotte bolted upright as the front part of the suit swung away from his body. He rolled out of the suit, savoring the feel of the stone under his hands and knees. He just lay there for a minute. He knew that Aspasia's Shadow and Duncan were long gone. He'd been in too much of a rush. He stood, pulling a flashlight out of the small butt-pack strapped to the rear of the suit.

Turcotte shone the light down on his suit. The mine had ripped the armor in many places. The protection had held—or else he wouldn't be standing right now—but the pellets had ripped into the computer, damaging it beyond repair. Without that working, the suit was just a large pile of high-tech garbage.

Turcotte checked the SATCOM link that was bolted on just above the computer. It was also trashed. He grabbed the DVD disk he'd taken from Graves's suit. He also took the Watcher ring off the right arm. Then he unlatched the MK-98 from the suit. Without the suit's strength augmentation, the full weight of the weapon reminded Turcotte of carrying a fully loaded M-60 machine gun. He fastened a sling from his belt and slung the gun over his head. He took one of the lithium batteries from the suit to power the gun, increasing the weight he was carrying by ten pounds.

Turcotte hefted the MK-98, finger on the trigger. He had no clue which cardinal direction he was going in and when he checked the small compass strapped to his watchband, the needle spun wildly. Turcotte looked at his watch. Dawn was only an hour off.

He reached the end of the hallway. Turcotte used the ring and the door slid open. He stepped through. He then turned in the direction he had come from, where the corridor descended.

"We have an Egyptian jet coming at us at Mach-2."

Colonel Zycki frowned at the report. They were over the Mediterranean, well clear of Egyptian airspace.

"Make commo with it and request the pilot to stay clear," he ordered. He turned his attention to the screen tracking the two choppers. They were over the Gulf of Suez, still heading west toward the Sinai Peninsula.

Inside the cockpit of the American-made F-16 Fighting Falcon, the Egyptian pilot, Ahid, ignored both the warnings from the American plane and the confused orders from his own higher command demanding he turn back to base.

Ahid's eyes flickered down, checking his radar, ensuring he was on course. His hands were perfectly steady on the controls, his face relaxed despite the chatter coming through his helmet.

"Uh, sir, no response from the incoming bogey. We're picking up transmissions from an Egyptian air base and they appear to be calling it back, too."

Colonel Zycki frowned. "What's the vector?"

"Straight on to us, ETA one minute. We're already within Sidewinder range, but no fire indicator."

If the F-16 was seeking to take them down, it would already have fired. So what was it doing?

"Where's our nearest support?" Zycki asked.

"The Israelis could scramble and be here in seven minutes," the man replied.

"Goddamn," Zycki exclaimed. Another game of chicken, he thought. It was a dangerous game, one that had been played for many decades in the Cold War and on into the years since the fall of the Wall. A jet would charge down on the AWACS, trying to scare the occupants. The fact that it worked, the crew of the defenseless surveillance craft feeling like deer caught in

headlights of an approaching craft, was a big reason it
had lasted so long.

Zycki keyed the crafts intercom so he could address
the entire crew. "All right, people, we've got an inbound
bogey trying to rattle us. Let's keep doing our job and
let this bozo go by."

"Fifteen seconds out," the screenwatcher reported.

"We still have tracking on the choppers?" Zycki
asked.

"Yes, sir. They're dry over the Sinai, turning to the
north."

"I want—" Zycki began, but the man tracking the
Egyptian jet slammed his fist on the console.

"It's still coming!"

"But—" Zycki never finished the statement.

Ahid could see the left side pilot of the AWACS staring
out the small cockpit window at him as he rapidly
closed the distance between the planes. His time sense
had slowed everything down so that seconds seemed
like minutes.

He could see the rotodome rotating inch by inch, the
AWACS tail number, the star painted on the side of the
craft, the lack of windows, the gray paint. Ahid adjusted
course very slightly and, for added effect, kicked on his
afterburners.

Then the F-16 hit the AWACS dead-on at over fifteen
hundred miles an hour.

Over two hundred and forty miles away, Aspasia's
Shadow looked down at the desolate desert landscape

below as the lead Panther fitted above the ground at less than fifty feet altitude.

"We're clear of radar," the pilot reported. "The AWACS is gone."

"Head for The Mission," Aspasia's Shadow ordered.

CHAPTER 17

THE GIZA PLATEAU, EGYPT

Turcotte paused and got to his knees. He leaned over, ear to the floor. A faint roar, muted by the stone between him and the river. He had already passed through another doorway and he knew he was getting close to the chamber that held the shaft.

And there was something else, a sound that caused him to halt. A rapid clicking noise, almost in a rhythm, but there was something disconcerting about it. Turcotte closed his eyes and concentrated, trying to identify the sound. Metal on stone, like the rapid tap of a chisel on the tunnel floor. And it was coming closer.

Turcotte stood and began to run, more of a shuffle given the weight and size of the MK-98. He knew this was throwing his pace count off, but he could make out the glow of the chem light on the floor ahead. He reached it and slid the ring key along the wall, searching for the correct spot. Turcotte forced himself to slow down and make sure he was covering every square inch.

Turcotte paused and looked down the corridor. There was a golden glow, but he couldn't make anything more out. It was getting closer. He continued to work the ring, searching. The clicking sound was louder, more ominous, causing him to look once more. He blinked, trying to make sense of what he was seeing. His first thought was that it was the largest spider he had ever seen, legs over three feet long, a round golden body, but there was more to it. Just as many arms on top of the globe as on the bottom, filling the corridor completely, top to bottom, side to side. But the arms were metal, the source of the noise. And the golden orb—Turcotte had seen that before. A foo-fighter, encased in some sort of robotic extension. In the golden glow of the foo-fighter he could see the blood on the metal arms and he knew what had happened to the rest of the team. That meant the MK-98 was useless against it.

Turcotte slid the ring along the wall as the machine approached, now less than twenty meters away. The ring touched the right place, the stone door sliding up.

Turcotte fired. The steel dart hit the foo-fighter dead center and ricocheted off. Turcotte threw the MK-98 with all his might at it and dove into the tunnel, the stone slamming shut behind him.

He could hear the clatter of the metal arms on the wall for several seconds, as if it were scratching at the door, then silence. He didn't wait for anything more to happen and assumed the thing was taking another route. He raced down the tunnel until he came to the stone debris that had been the last door. He entered the chamber. The hole in the floor beckoned.

Turcotte lowered himself into the tunnel. He let go and fell.

VICINITY EASTER ISLAND

The crew of the E-2C Hawkeye felt like sacrificial lambs as they circled five miles to the east of the shield wall surrounding Easter Island. The rest of the Task Force was two hundred miles to the north. A pair of F-14 Tomcats were halfway between them and the fleet, but the jets' mission was to guard the fleet, not support the Hawkeye if there was trouble.

"Look at that," the pilot didn't have to point out what he was indicating, as the ship that was heading toward the island was the largest thing floating anyone on the crew had ever seen.

The combat information officer (CIO) keyed his radio. "Operations, this is HK-12. Over."

The reply from the *Stennis*'s operations center was immediate. "This is operations. Over."

"We have visual on the *Jahre Viking* three miles from the shield wall and she's still heading straight for it. Over."

"Roger that."

The CIO waited for more, then finally asked what they all wanted to know. The answer was apparent from the lack of activity on their radar screens—no strike force winging in from the north—but they wanted the answer in plain English. "What are the orders from Pearl? Over."

"Do nothing. There's women and children on that ship from a half-dozen different countries. You want to be responsible for killing them?"

There was no adequate answer to that.

The bow of the *Jahre Viking* was less than a half mile from the shield wall when a dark cloud came swarming out of the blackness.

His crew thought him quite mad. Johan Verquist had been forced to relieve both the captain and first officer. The junior officer now running the bridge felt the same as his predecessors, but the presence of half a dozen Progressives armed with pistols had been enough to persuade him to follow the orders the others thought insane—head straight for the shield wall that protected Easter Island.

Verquist glanced over at Dennison, but the Guide's eyes were fixed on the black wall. On the broad deck of the tanker, the thousands of passengers were gathered, all facing the same direction. Every square foot of deck space held a person. All were above deck except for those that drowned in the 3-starboard hold.

A cloud came out of the darkness and Verquist started. "What is that?"

"Our salvation," Dennison said. He leaned forward, pressed a button, and spoke into the ship's audio system. "Our rebirth is at hand."

An audible moan swept over the bridge, torn from thousands of lips, a mixture of fear and anticipation. The people began chanting something in a low tone that Verquist couldn't make out.

Verquist couldn't take his eyes off the unnatural cloud that was approaching his ship. "I've done what I said I would—what you asked of me. I want what you promised."

Dennison nodded. "What you were promised is also at hand."

The cloud swarmed over the bow of the ship, over four football fields in distance from the bridge. Screams now mixed with the chanting. Those farther back reacted, some staying in place, others shoving and pushing to try to get away from the rapidly approaching cloud. It was mass panic, but as the cloud slid down the deck, those caught in it quickly became quiet.

"What is that?" Verquist demanded.

"What you were promised. The beginning of it, anyway."

Verquist could now see that the cloud appeared to

be a swarm of flying insects. One smashed against the bridge glass but rebounded, buzzing around, searching for a way in. They were machines, Verquist could see that now, smaller than mosquitoes, almost invisible to the naked eye. They poured through the open side doors to the bridge. Verquist dashed toward the rear of the bridge, through the door leading to his cabin. He slammed it shut and locked it. Screams, quickly cut off, echoed through the expensive wood. Verquist threw himself into the chair behind his large mahogany desk. He pulled open a drawer and wrapped his hand around the pearl handle of a revolver. He pointed it at the door.

They came under the door.

He fired five shots in rapid succession, knowing the futility as he pulled the trigger.

He put the hot muzzle against his temple as the first of the micromachines landed on his skin. His finger twitched, caressed the metal, then relaxed. He loved himself too much to do it. He lowered the gun.

The micromachine let loose its load of the nanovirus and the microscopic machines bore through his skin and into Verquist's bloodstream. He screamed and tried to bring the gun up, but he was too late as the nanovirus poured into his brain.

AREA 51, NEVADA

"It is now daylight in Cairo."

"I am aware of that," Yakov told Che Lu. They were in the conference room, Professor Mualama still behind the computers, typing away. It was an indication of the seriousness of the situation that Yakov had a mug of hot coffee sitting on the table in front of him, the vodka bottle nowhere in sight.

"And your awareness improves the situation in what manner?" Che Lu asked.

Yakov spread his large hands wide apart. "And how does your informing me of what I already know improve the situation?"

"Are you aware the Americans lost one of their surveillance aircraft over the Mediterranean?" Che Lu asked.

"I saw the report Major Quinn sent down."

"And that aircraft was tracking two helicopters that took off from the vicinity of the Great Pyramid?"

Yakov nodded.

Che Lu continued the questions. "What—and who—do you think were on those helicopters?"

To that Yakov had no answer. He knew Che Lu was frustrated. She had been working on the grid coordinate system she thought she had figured out in Qian-Ling, but it was not fitting as she had hoped. Close, but not quite there. Her numbers were slightly off, and she didn't know where the problem lay.

"I have more of the manuscript ready." Mualama didn't even raise his head to announce that. "It's coming up on the screen now."

Yakov walked over and sat down. As soon as the translation appeared, he began scrolling.

BURTON MANUSCRIPT: CHAPTER 6

The Middle East is the crossroads between three continents—Asia, Africa, and the eastern edge of Europe. Because of this, it has seen numerous invading armies pass through.

   *The Jewish state has been conquered many times.
Jerusalem, the home of the Grail and Ark for so
many years, has seen its share of warring armies
sweep over it in a flood of blood.*

   *This small place on the surface of the world has
given rise to the great religions of western culture—
Judaism, Christianity, and Islam, all born in the arid
terrain of the Middle East. Beyond the impact of
these religions and their subsequent spin-off faiths
on history, another important factor needs to be considered.*

   *The Grail is said to do two things—grant immor-
tality and give knowledge. But what knowledge? For
a long time I thought this simply meant knowledge of
the Truth, the* tariqat *that I was upon—the truth of
mankind's past and origins, of the aliens who came
to our planet. But on my travels around the world I
have met many wise men and women, and studied
various cultures. And it came to me, not in a flash,
but like a slow tide of awareness seeping into my
brain so that I cannot state clearly the moment at
which I was aware of it.*

   *This awareness? It is that perhaps the knowledge
the Grail gives is not an accumulation of facts or history, but a different way of thinking. And perhaps
some of that has already made its way into our societies.*

   *Think about it, my friend who reads these words.
The earliest civilizations thought differently than we
do now. For them, life was an endless cycle of birth
and death and birth. Their thinking was cyclical,
more concerned with the whole than the parts. Time
was a wheel that each generation trod upon only to
return to the same place.*

When did that change? Where did this change come from?

I believe it changed with the Jews, and this was continued with the Christians and Muslims. Think about the concept of faith as these religions espouse. Think about the way they change the view of time itself. No longer circular, it is now linear. There is a progression from birth, through life, to death, to an after-life. With such thinking, a new concept emerges—something called hope. Hope for a better life, that things can improve. That life can be better.

And they made another change, one that I do not know the ultimate effects of. These religions focused on one God, and that God was removed from immediate contact with man. Certainly this is better than when men worshipped the Airlia, but perhaps it also saps some of our belief in ourselves? I do not know.

For almost ten thousand years human civilization did not change, but in the past two thousand, it has grown in leaps and spurts. There has been progression. Toward what end I do not know. Whether this is a good thing, I know not either.

But I do believe that the Grail changed these people. Just knowing of its existence changed them and all of us who follow. Think what a powerful icon it has been, and then imagine what the reality of it must be.

Where did the Grail go when the attempt to use it failed?

Joseph of Arimathea, along with Nicodemus, took the body of Jesus and buried it. It is said he also came into possession of the Grail, which had been in Jesus's hands and brought out at what the Christians call the Last Supper. It is at this event that Jesus was arrested—but why at that moment when he had been preaching for so long? Perhaps because he was bringing the Grail out and was going to share of it with his followers? That is my suspicion.

And who would want to stop him and take the Grail for their own? I suspect The Mission, The Ones Who Wait, and the Watchers.

There was a Roman named Tacitus, a military man, whose name I have discovered written in many old documents. I believe this is the name Aspasia's Shadow used during this time. He was in Jerusalem in A.D. 33, and sought to get control of the Grail.

There is another twist that came from this that I have investigated, that of the Sang Real.

There are scholars who believe the Sang Real to indicate that Christ had children and that his bloodline exists to this day, hidden perhaps by some secret cabal of the Vatican. However, it is much more literal than that.

When I was in the Himalayas, I talked to an old monk who told me of a small group of people he called the ubyr. *He said they were men and women who drank the blood of others searching for the elixir of life. In Russia they are called* upyr. *In Eastern Europe they are known as* vampir. *In the many places I have traveled I have asked about such people, and I am amazed at the number of legends in far-flung places concerning them.*

And what do the blood-drinkers seek? Eternal life.

This is what I believe the Sang Real is—the desire to drink of the blood of a person who has touched the Grail and try to gain eternal life out of their blood.

"Remember he wrote this decades before Bram Stoker corrupted the image of the vampire into what is our modern myth," Che Lu said. "In fact, from what Isabel wrote, it appears that Stoker got the idea of vampires from talking with Burton."

Yakov ran a hand through his thick beard. "There are stories that Stalin had his secret police performing experiments on prisoners, draining their blood, searching for some rare strain that would bring longer life. And Von Seeckt told us of the SS's fascination with blood. He was injected with some alien blood in a ceremony of the SS."

"This gives us a little insight into the Grail," Che Lu said. "It must affect the blood somehow, perhaps adding something to it that improves the health and life span of the recipient. And the concept has made its way out into the world and been corrupted by these people who drink the blood of others."

"Perhaps the Grail simply injects Airlia blood into human and mixes them," Yakov said. "We know The Ones Who Wait are human-Airlia clones, so there is some compatibility."

"Do you know how unlikely it is that our DNA could be mixed with that of an alien race and produce a viable life-form?" Che Lu asked.

"That is not my area of expertise," Yakov said.

"It isn't mine either," Che Lu said, "but common sense says the odds would be extremely low of a compatible match."

"But the Airlia have technology we don't know about," Yakov said. "Perhaps they could manipulate the material on both sides to find a match in the middle.

"It is more likely that—" Che Lu began, but then she stopped herself.

"What were you going to say?"

Che Lu shook her head. "I will wait to find out more before I say anything else on this matter. Let us read on."

> Joseph of Arimithea secretly left Jerusalem with the Grail. He undertook a most perilous journey, traveling far to remove himself and the Grail from the reach of the Roman Empire and Tacitus, a most difficult task in those days. He left behind agents who spread misinformation about the location of the Grail, hoping to keep Tacitus and The Mission focused in the Middle East while he took it far away.
>
> He finally came to Britain, an island that had resisted Roman invasion for many years and, truth be told, a land with little to offer a conqueror. A land where the Watchers had established their headquarters after the destruction of Atlantis. I read his report on his arrival in England, one of the Watcher scrolls, and there is no doubt Joseph was a Watcher, trying to put right what had been thrown askew by the appearance of the Grail in the Middle East.
>
> It seems that Joseph's decision to leave the Middle East was a wise one and his agents did a most credible job of making The Mission believe the Grail was still there—perhaps too good of a job, as Tacitus continued to press his search using the Roman army as the blunt force to do so.
>
> In A.D. 67 Jerusalem was overrun by the Romans under the command of Titus, with his military adviser Tacitus at his side, after fierce fighting. It is said that over a million Jews were killed or sold into slavery. The Temple was destroyed, taken apart stone by stone, the city ravaged.

But the Grail was safe and disappeared from sight
for several centuries, protected by the Watchers at
Avalon.

Che Lu cleared her throat to say something, but she was
saved from doing so when Major Quinn entered the
conference room. "We've had to stand down the exfil
choppers. There's no way they can make it near the Nile
without being spotted, especially since we've lost the
AWACS ability to jam radars. Our government is
protesting the destruction of the plane and the loss of
the crew to the Egyptians, but it's a confused situation
to say the least. The Egyptians are countering that
we've invaded their country twice now."

"What can we do?" Yakov asked.

"I've managed to get a live feed from a surveillance
satellite over the area. We can try to keep track—that's
about it."

CHAPTER 18

THE GIZA PLATEAU, EGYPT

Turcotte slowly splashed his way down the tunnel, the water of the Nile urging him along. His shoulders were slumped and his step was heavy. The men he had led were dead, Duncan was gone with Aspasia's Shadow, and the Grail and Ark were with him. The mission had been a complete failure.

When the clatter of metal on stone came from behind, he found it difficult to increase his pace. The clicking noise was getting closer and the ceiling was sloping down, the channel growing tighter. In the dim glow of the flashlight he could see the little airspace he had now was completely gone in twenty meters.

The noise from behind had stopped, but he was caught between the foo-fighter sentry and the water-filled tunnel ahead. He moved forward until his face was turned up, pressed against the rock ceiling. It occurred to Turcotte that something might have changed in the past hundred years since Burton went this way, but he didn't care.

Turcotte took several deep breaths, then he pulled his head down and went with the current, legs kicking to add speed, but the effort felt wasted as the water took control. He was tumbled about, hitting the wall of the tunnel several times.

Just as he thought he couldn't last any longer, he saw daylight above. He kicked, using the last of his air. Turcotte broke the surface, gulped in air, and blinked in the harsh rays of the sun, trying to get his bearings. He tread water, turning away from the sun, and saw the pyramids, the Great Sphinx before them, farther upstream and to the west.

Turning, Turcotte saw an Egyptian patrol boat, forward machine-gun manned, heading straight toward them from upstream. He was too tired to even attempt to swim away, not that he could outswim the boat anyway.

QIAN-LING, CHINA

Lexina ran her hands across the High Runes etched in the surface of the black tube. "It is not Artad's resting place." She turned toward the black wall which had just stopped its slow retreat across the chamber after clearing the end of the tube. "He rests further within. This—" she tapped the tube "—is a guard who must awaken before the wall goes any further."

"How do we open it?" Elek asked.

"We don't." Lexina stepped back. "The process is automated and works on its own schedule. This is beyond us."

"Perhaps if we access the guardian—" Elek began, but his words were cut off as the black surface slid open, revealing a silver material that immediately peeled back in several layers until all that was left was a body encased in a clear material.

"It is not Airlia." Elek pointed out the obvious. The body was human, less than five and a half feet tall; a male with Chinese features. He was dressed in a richly embroidered silk robe, dragons breathing fire swirling about the material. Lying next to the man's right hand was a spear, the head of which was of highly polished metal, a replica of the Spear of Destiny that Lexina had used to access this chamber.

The air inside the tube crackled with electromagnetic static as the field which had preserved the body for thousands of years was slowly reduced in power.

THE MISSION

Every cell of Lisa Duncan's being was in pain. It had started with her hand inside the Black Sphinx chamber. Then up her arm, into her chest, and throughout her body. On the helicopter ride, all she could see was the top of the cargo bay through the haze of tears brought on by the agony as the pain spread through her entire body.

She had no idea where she was, although she was vaguely aware she had stopped moving and been taken off the helicopter. She was on her back, of that she had some sense. But the pain—she had never experienced anything even remotely close to it.

Her brain could tolerate it no longer, and her conscious mind shut down as she slipped into a state closer to a coma than anything else.

Across the room, Aspasia's Shadow looked at her body on the bed. The priestly accoutrements had been removed and were neatly piled next to him. They were inside a small room, the walls carved out of brown rock. The Ark rested on the floor and Aspasia's Shadow's eyes shifted from Duncan to the Grail's container. He was tempted. Such a temptation he had not felt in a long time, but he had waited millennia to gain possession of the Grail—he could wait a while longer to see if it still functioned, to see what it did to Duncan, if the ancient prophecies would be fulfilled. In the meanwhile, he removed his black cloak and dressed in the priest's clothes.

Reluctantly, he left the room. One of the two guards on the outside came inside, standing just inside the door, to keep watch on Duncan. Aspasia's Shadow checked for the third time, making sure the man knew his order—to call as soon as there was a change in Duncan's condition.

Then Aspasia's Shadow went down the corridor and entered another chamber hewn out of the brown stone. In the center a golden pyramid glowed—a guardian computer. A chair, more a throne, was set just in front of the guardian. Aspasia's Shadow sat down and the golden glow encompassed him.

Through the alien computer he made contact with Easter Island to be updated on all that had happened there since he had left The Mission to pursue the Grail. He saw that the forces there were just about ready for action. He issued orders to be implemented as soon as all preparations were completed.

EASTER ISLAND

The rebuilt F-14 did what designers at Grumman had known it was capable of but never expected to see—execute a double digit G-force turn. The fact that the maneuver snapped the neck of the man in the cockpit didn't bother the guardian computer controlling the plane in the slightest. Pilot-less, the plane nosed over and crashed.

Taking the data into consideration, the guardian prepared the next pilot better, enclosing him in a suit it de-

signed to take the forces involved. Another rebuilt F-14
went up and began running through the same tests.

The plane made several more high-G maneuvers,
then lined up on the Easter Island runway and came to a
landing any carrier pilot would have been proud of. It
taxied down the runway and came to a halt beside the
full complement of F-14s that had been captured on
board the *Washington*, all modified to the same specifi-
cations.

A mile off the south shore of Easter Island, the *Jahre
Viking* loomed like a half-mile-long wall. Smaller boats
from the *Washington* had been commandeered to bring
the people who were needed ashore. Others worked at
menial tasks on the ship as a flow of nanomachines did
the bulk of the important work.

The nanomachines were building two huge doors by
the expedient method of removing metal atom by atom.
Behind the doors they were preparing they built a
watertight seam at the same level. The first several com-
partments behind the doors were dissolving, the metal
being used to reinforce the hull around the large open
space being designed inside. The forward quarter of the
ship was being prepared as a large open space, accessible through the doors.

Deep under the Rapa Karu volcano, Kelly Reynolds
became aware of a new presence communicating with
the guardian. A force that was issuing commands to the
alien machine, something she had not experienced before, even when it had been in communication with the
guardian on Mars.

For a moment, the link from Mars spiked in activity,
trying to shut down the new link, but the new connection was more powerful, closer. At first Kelly thought it
was the master guardian reestablishing its control, but

then she picked up the presence of a mind, a human mind, behind the new guardian and she realized that was the controlling force.

Aspasia!

The name echoed in her consciousness. How could it be? And human? Aspasia was Airlia. And he was dead.

In her fear of being discovered and the uncertainty about what was going on, Kelly retreated, releasing her toehold in the data stream and hiding in the shell of what remained of her body.

AREA 51, NEVADA

"It doesn't look good." Major Quinn slapped down a black-and-white photograph on the conference room table. The air was heavy; the only change from before was that Mualama was back at work, his fingers hitting the keys even more furiously than before as he translated. Quinn pointed at the man in the water. "This was taken eight minutes ago. That's Turcotte."

He put a second photograph on top. "This was taken six minutes ago."

They could all see the Egyptian patrol boat next to Turcotte. The next picture showed him on board the deck of the boat, surrounded by soldiers.

"What about the rest of the team?" Yakov asked. "Any sign of them?"

"Negative."

"Can you get someone in Washington to contact Cairo and try to get Turcotte released?" Yakov asked.

"Washington has been screaming at Cairo about the AWACS getting downed," Quinn said. "Now the Egyptians have captured an American soldier, illegally

in their country. Also, they let those helicopters get out
of their airspace. Someone holds a lot more leverage
with the Egyptian government than we do. I think the
time for negotiating is long past."

"What do you recommend?" Yakov asked.

"We need to wait and—" Quinn began, but Che Lu
slapped her palm on the table, getting their attention.

"We cannot wait. The Navy SEALs who went under
the shield wall on Easter Island have not been heard
from. The Ones Who Wait are inside of Qian-Ling with
the key to the lowest level." She tapped the photograph.
"Turcotte has failed in his quest of rescuing Duncan,
and I see no Grail in his hands as this boat picks him
up." She turned to Quinn. "You must get beyond thinking only of your country and think globally. There is a
country, is there not, that would have a very good intelligence system in place in Egypt?"

Quinn nodded. "Israel."

Che Lu was in her lecture mode, as if she were back
at Beijing University. "Very good. And an agent of that
government met Turcotte at Hazerim air base, did he
not?" She didn't wait for an answer. "I recommend contacting that person and seeing what assistance he can
render." She almost shoved him toward the door. "Go!"

After Quinn had exited, she turned to the bank of
computers that hid Professor Mualama. "Do you have
any more of the manuscript done?"

Mualama raised his head, just his eyes peeking over
the top of the monitor. "Yes. It's loading now."

"Does it say what exactly the Grail is and what exactly it does?" Che Lu asked. "That information is most
vital now that it appears that someone has escaped
with it."

"The new chapter speaks of the Grail's travels

and—" Mualama paused. "You will have to determine what more for yourself." His eyes disappeared and she went back to work.

"Sit!" Che Lu ordered Yakov as she scrolled.

BURTON MANUSCRIPT: CHAPTER 7

For just short of five hundred years, the Grail was hidden by the Watchers in their headquarters at Avalon. That none of them succumbed to the temptation offered by the alien device in those successive generations is a testament to the discipline of the order. But it was inevitable that such a powerful icon would once again cause trouble.

A Watcher by the name Myrrdin, Merlin as he is more commonly known, read the same scrolls I have translated. He read of Atlantis, the Grail, the Ark, and the alien creatures who walked the Earth. He learned much of the ancient ways. Indeed, I believe he stole some of the original scrolls that told of some of the powers the wedjat *of Atlantis had and used them to his advantage, presenting himself as a magician to the people of his day. Indeed such things as gunpowder, the use of a compass, which plants to be used for healing, surely the humans of Atlantis had such technology and knowledge as part of their day-to-day life, but they would be wonders to the people of Britain of A.D. 500, toiling in their fields and dying on average before the age of 30.*

Imagine the effect this information had on Merlin?

One can understand Merlin's desire. I have been in the room deep under Glastonbury Tor, surrounded by the scrolls of the Watchers. I too wondered why they kept such knowledge hidden. How would I have felt if I had found information in those scrolls that I knew could help the people around me? Would I have been able to stay true to an ancient oath, or would I have tried to spread the knowledge to do good? I cannot judge.

But there were more than scrolls under the Tor. In addition to the Grail, there were other Airlia artifacts. I found a listing in one of the scrolls, dated A.D. 489, which tells of the Grail, shaped like a golden cup, yet solid on both ends—the first description I read. It also says that the Grail is not complete by itself, that two special stones are needed for it to work. This may have been much of the problem that it caused throughout the years—men could hold the Grail but not partake of it!

It also tells of a weapon, a sword of unbreakable metal, yet lighter by three times than the normal sword of the same size fashioned by the best of current blacksmiths. And the sword had runes written into the handle and blade telling of its power.

You must remember that Britain at this time was a divided land, racked with wars between petty kingdoms, threatened from the north, east and south with invasion.

What harm, this Merlin must have wondered, would there be in using this wondrous sword as a symbol of power to help unite the land? After all, the Watchers didn't even know what it really was.

So Merlin stole the sword from the Tor. He gave it to the one he thought had the best chance of uniting the various factions, Uther Pendragon, one of the two sons of King Constantine.

But the sword was not enough. Fighting continued and Merlin realized he needed something stronger.

The myth is that he disguised Uther, brought him

together with Ygraine, the wife of the Duke of Cornwall, and out of that illegal bond came a son, Arthur.

This is not the truth.

Merlin stole the Grail from the Tor. He had it in mind to allow part of it to be used, the part that brought knowledge, to the next ruler of Britain. But he did not have the stones to work the Grail. And then it was taken from him by one of the many fierce tribes from the north.

This brought about what the Watchers had feared. The Ones Who Wait brought forth one of their own, Arthur, to regain the Grail. I believe Arthur was an incarnation of Artad, using the ka method—his Shadow.

The Mission, of course, responded. Mordred, one of the many incarnations of Aspasia's Shadow again using the ka, came forward to do war with Arthur.

"Is this ka thing connected with the Grail?" Yakov asked as the chapter came to an end.

"Perhaps we will find out later in the tale," Che Lu said. "For now, let us hope Major Turcotte has a plan." She pointed at the screen. "Note, however that Artad, or his Shadow, was King Arthur, while Aspasia's Shadow was Mordred. I think our cause lies closer to what is in the lowest level of Qian-Ling than what is hidden in The Mission."

"Perhaps," Yakov allowed. "But you would have to convince the United Nations Alien Oversight Committee of that, and then all the countries that are aligning as Isolationists, Progressives, or Neutrals." He laughed. "I can just imagine trying to convince those politicians that Artad was once King Arthur!"

"This is a very serious matter!" Che Lu admonished the Russian.

"I know it is," Yakov agreed. "But Artad is going to have to rise from the dead *and* do something quite spectacular to convince people to align with him. And coming alive in the middle of Communist China might not have been the best choice he could have made."

"He did not make that choice," Che Lu said. "Communism occurred long after Qian-Ling was established."

"Yes, but people have short memories," Yakov said.

QIAN-LING, CHINA

The first sign of life was the eyes flickering open. And it was the first indication that the "man" was not completely human. Red vertical irises within red pupils, his eyes stared straight up for several seconds before shifting about, taking in the two figures that stood next to the black tube.

Lexina held her hands up. "Welcome," she said in English, knowing there was no way he could understand, but hoping he picked up the intent.

Lexina, Coridan, and Elek bowed their heads as the man sat up. He adjusted his robe. Then, the spear in one hand, he stepped out of the tube.

The red eyes fixed on the three Ones Who Wait. The mouth opened and the singsong words of the Airlia flowed forth, receiving no comprehension. Lexina felt the frustration of not knowing the Airlia language, another piece of knowledge lost over the millennia they had waited. The creature must have realized that, for it became silent once more. Then it spoke in another tongue, most likely ancient Chinese, Lexina guessed, but it was also unknown to her. Once more, seeing the words making no import to the listeners, the man ceased speaking. Abruptly he turned and strode toward the main tunnel leading up.

"Artad!" Lexina cried out, hoping that one word would be recognized.

The man paused, eyes glancing at the black wall ever so briefly, then continued up the tunnel. Lexina, Coridan, and Elek hurried to follow.

As they entered the main chamber, the man paused, taking in the shield generator, then entered the smaller room that held the guardian. He went up to the golden pyramid and placed both hands flat on the surface. In a moment he was surrounded by the golden glow that meant he was in contact with the computer.

Lexina, Coridan, and Elek stood by, watching and once more waiting.

AREA 51, NEVADA

Larry Kincaid remembered crunching numbers with a slide ruler, something the new generation of scientists thought as quaint as using an abacus. His opinion was that while the technology advanced, the human minds using that technology retreated into specialty niches, losing the ability to think with imagination beyond what the machines could do.

That's not to say he didn't appreciate what modern technology could accomplish. Sitting in a small office just down the hall from the conference room, he had the imagery from the Hubble spread across his desk.

The black smear representing the mech-robots was

still moving across the surface, their path relatively
straight since leaving Cydonia. Occasionally there was
a slight detour as they went around various obstructions
in their path.

And there was something else. A second group of
mech-robots was leaving the Cydonia region. These
were carrying long black objects. Kincaid shifted the
magnifying glass to Cydonia. Part of the black network
had been disassembled. They were moving it. To
where? he wondered.

There was a knock on the door and one of the techni-
cians from the Cube handed him a long cardboard tube
and departed. Kincaid pulled out a large rolled-up paper
from the inside and spread it out on the floor—it was a
mosaic of Mars photographs taken by the first Surveyor
probe years ago.

He located Cydonia. Then he marked each location
the Hubble had caught the mech-robots at. He took a
yardstick and put one end on Cydonia and then aligned
it through the median of those points. He drew a line,
then removed the ruler.

His eyes followed the line from the present location
of the mechs outward. There was no mistaking where
the line led—and where the mech-robots were heading.
Mons Olympus. The largest volcano on Mars and in the
Solar System. It was over fifteen miles high, the equivalent of three Mount Everests. However, its sides sloped
so gently, only two to five percent, that its base was
over three hundred and forty miles in diameter. The entire mountain complex was surrounded by a four-
kilometer-high escarpment.

Why were they going there? Kincaid wondered. The
Airlia seemed to have a fascination with high mountains, he thought, as he remembered the story from

Burton's manuscript about the destruction of Mount Ngorongoro in Africa.

He went to the desk and searched through the imagery until he found what he was looking for—a shot of the Cydonia region, focused on the "face." Mech-robots were still working over the black metal grill-work that they had uncovered. The description from Burton's manuscript from the Watcher who had seen the complex on the side of Mount Ngorongoro had reported the same thing. This one on Mars had obviously been destroyed a long time ago also. And now it was being rebuilt. To what end? And how did that connect with Mons Olympus? Kincaid wondered.

His musings were interrupted by a light knock on the door. Che Lu stuck her head in. "Am I intruding?"

"No, come on in."

She walked around the large mosaic of Mars and took the seat across from him. "I need some assistance." She slid a piece of paper across to him, on top of the Hubble images. "I have checked and rechecked my figures, but I still cannot align Nabinger's grid system with our planet."

Kincaid picked up the paper and scanned it. "What is your reference point?"

"I have used both poles, aligning every point at least once with each, but it doesn't make sense. Then I used Easter Island, Qian-Ling, and Giza in the same manner—as one would expect those to be marked by the Airlia—and there has been no sensible correlation among the three points. I even used Ngorongoro—and still nothing."

"What are you hoping to discover with this?" Kincaid asked.

"I think that the current location of The Mission is hidden among those coordinates."

"The Mission has moved often—according to the STAAR records we uncovered from Antarctica and Burton's manuscript. These coordinates are old. Why would The Mission be at one of these ancient sites?"

"I think this is a listing of where guardian computers were located," Che Lu said. "And given the current situation, it would be logical for The Mission to have relocated from Devil's Island to one of the ancient bases that has a guardian in order to stay in touch with Mars and Easter Island."

"How did Nabinger compile this list?" Kincaid asked.

"From his travels and archaeological studies of the High Runes," Che Lu said.

"So not from one source, correct?"

"Correct."

"Maybe some of these are false locations, then," Kincaid said. He counted. "We have twenty-four spots. If even a few are false, that would make it very difficult to orient the grid. What we need to do is run a computer simulation on the spots, removing them one by one, then the various permutations of more than one. We'll use Giza, Easter Island, and Qian-Ling as three fixed points because we know there were guardians at each of those sites."

"How long will that take?"

Kincaid closed his eyes in thought. "It will take me a little while to develop the program. Then, when you consider the factorials of possibilities, even using the computer we have here, it will take a while to crunch the numbers. Several hours at least, maybe a day."

VICINITY, CAIRO, EGYPT

Turcotte was on his side on the desert sand, hands uncomfortably cuffed behind his back. A squad of soldiers milled about nearby, smoking cigarettes while they waited for the commander to make a decision. He was arguing in Arabic with a man in civilian clothes.

Turcotte found he could not focus or bring his energy level up to face the current threat—of course, there wasn't much he could do in the present circumstances. He'd felt like this before, but never so deeply. He knew he was drained of not only energy, but the ability to produce any more adrenaline. His reserve was tapped out and he also knew it was more emotional than physical. That still didn't change the overwhelming feeling of exhaustion.

Turcotte twisted slightly. He could see the civilian and the colonel. They were outside of Cairo, about forty-five minutes from Giza, as near as Turcotte had been able to tell from the bumpy ride in the back of the two-and-a-half-ton army truck he'd been thrown into after getting captured on the Nile. The colonel had taken charge of them and Turcotte first thought he'd be taken into the city, but the civilian—whoever he was— had appeared and presented some sort of credentials, redirecting them to this location.

Turcotte could see the officer nodding and then heard him barking orders to the six soldiers.

One of the soldiers kicked Turcotte in the side, indicating for him to get up, as the other five deployed in a rough line about ten feet away and began checking their weapons.

Turcotte could see the late-morning sun and feel the warmth of the rays on one side of his face and sand on

the other. He swore he could feel every little grain
pressing against his skin.

The soldier kicked once more and gestured.

Turcotte hardly noticed the pain. He thought of
how many times he had seen the sun come up in so
many different places around the world, and how often
he had simply taken it for granted. To think this was the
last he would see seemed more like a bad dream than
reality.

The officer knelt next to Turcotte. "You must stand,"
he said in surprisingly good English, with a slight
British accent.

"I don't think I'll be giving you any assistance in
killing me," Turcotte said. For some reason, he was
thinking how hard it must have been in the old West to
hang someone in the desert. He tried to focus his
thoughts, but couldn't.

"Show some bravery," the colonel said.

Turcotte didn't think it was brave to stand before a
firing squad. It was the ultimate surrender.

The colonel yelled some more orders and two men
grabbed Turcotte by the shoulders, bringing him to his
feet. His first inclination was to immediately drop back
to the sand, but his training was too strong—that would
indeed be a sign of fear in front of these men.

He thought of running, but the field of fire ensured
that the bullets would easily beat him to any cover or
concealment. He almost laughed. The adrenaline was
back, his nerves were alive and alert, his mind racing. If
only the threat of death hung over every second of life,
then he would always be one hundred percent alive.

"Give me a chance in the desert," Turcotte said to the
officer.

The colonel glanced at the civilian, then shook his
head. "I am afraid not."

"Let me die with a weapon in my hand, then. Even an unloaded one." If he could only get his hands free, Turcotte felt he might have a slight chance.

A ghost of a smile crossed the colonel's face. "Do you plan on going to Valhalla? The Viking with his sword or ax in hand to protect the hall of warriors?"

"I work for Area 51, for mankind," Turcotte said. He nodded his head toward the civilian. "He works for the aliens. He is not even a true human anymore. His mind has been affected by the alien's machines. Do you serve man or do you serve the aliens?"

The Guide barked something in Arabic. The officer drew his pistol and snapped an order. The six soldiers put the stocks of their weapons to their shoulders.

Turcotte's arms strained against the handcuffs. The officer stepped to the side, about ten feet away from the firing squad.

He yelled another word in Arabic and Turcotte flinched, expecting rounds to slam into his chest, but it must have been the equivalent "aim."

Turcotte had had enough. He dropped to the sand, scooting his hands underneath him and bringing them to the front. Then he jumped to his feet and charged the firing squad as if going into a gale-force wind, shoulders hunched, body anticipating the impact of bullets.

There were several clicks—bolts slamming home in their breaches—but no rounds were fired. Several of the soldiers were working their bolts, trying to clear what they obviously thought was a misfire. Turcotte didn't take the time to wonder about this as he grabbed the muzzle of the nearest man's AK-47 and ripped it out of his hands, turned it about, and slammed the stock into the man's head, dropping him like a stone. He stepped back, weapon in his cuffed hands as the other five soldiers surrounded him.

The colonel calmly turned toward the civilian and fired one round, hitting the man square in the center of his forehead, blood and brain splattering the sand behind.

The colonel yelled something in Arabic and the five soldiers half turned toward him.

"Get down," the colonel said to Turcotte in a very calm voice as he swung up a mini-Uzi submachine gun with his free hand from out of the satchel looped over his shoulder.

Turcotte dove into the sand as a spray of bullets cut down the soldiers. Slowly he got to his feet. Turcotte watched the colonel, waiting for whatever would come next.

"We must go," the colonel said, gesturing with the smoking muzzle of the mini-Uzi toward the truck. "I hope you can drive this thing."

"Who are you?" Turcotte asked.

"Colonel Ahid Fassid of the Egyptian army," he said. "Military intelligence. I had to pull quite a few strings to be the one to pick you up at the Nile. Fortunately the regular army becomes very afraid when they see credentials from an intelligence officer of the general staff."

"I don't understand," Turcotte said.

Fassid sighed. "It is the way things are done here. How do you think we have kept the peace for so long? My father and all my uncles died in the wars. We cannot do that anymore. I also work for the Mossad when its aims and mine coincide and no harm will be brought to my country. And the Mossad has done things for me when our aims also have been the same. I received a call from a friend in the Mossad this morning, asking me to keep an eye out for you. This—" he indicated the bodies "—is far beyond anything I have done before. Now I must give up my life here."

"Why didn't their weapons work?" Turcotte asked.

"I inspected them," Fassid said. "And removed the firing pins. Now, let us leave here. A helicopter is inbound to a rendezvous point."

CHAPTER 19

QIAN-LING, CHINA

"My name is Ts'ang Chieh, court official to the most noble Emperor ShiHuangdi, Commander of all the World, the Hidden Ruler whose reign goes from rising to setting sun and beyond." A smile creased the unlined face. "At least that is what we showed to the world in our time."

"I am Lexina, leader of The Ones Who Wait, and these are Elek and Coridan of my order. The machine taught you our language?"

Ts'ang was in front of the guardian, just released from its glow. "To one who knows, the ways of the guardian are many. I have been updated on the current situation. It is most grave. The forces of Aspasia's Shadow are mobilizing. There is much I do not understand yet, but there is danger."

"Does the Emperor sleep below?" Lexina asked.

Ts'ang nodded. "He sleeps."

"Is the Emperor Shi Huangdi actually Artad?"

"In a manner of speaking, he was. The Emperor Shi Huangdi wore the *ka* of Artad, thus he was Artad."

"But the real Artad is here?" Lexina asked.

"Yes. He has slept for almost thirteen thousand years."

Lexina's body was so tense, it was practically vibrating. "Will you waken him now?"

Ts'ang nodded. "It is time."

VICINITY, CAIRO, EGYPT

Turcotte lay on his back in the sand looking up at the clear blue desert sky while Fassid nervously paced back and forth just below the crest of the dune. They were six miles from the site of Turcotte's aborted assassination. Fassid checked his watch for the tenth time in the last five minutes.

"Two minutes before, two minutes after," Turcotte said.

"What?"

Turcotte was tired, emotionally and physically exhausted. He felt rather detached and calm, an unusual state for him on an exfiltration pickup zone in hostile territory. "Exfiltration window in special ops is two minutes before the appointed, until two minutes after. Four minutes altogether. If the exfil aircraft doesn't show in that window, you go to the emergency plan. Do you have an emergency plan?"

"Yes," Fassid said. "I start praying to Allah."

"Not much of a plan," Turcotte noted.

"I didn't have much time," Fassid said. He looked at his watch. "Our window has just opened." He cocked his head. "I hear nothing."

Turcotte couldn't even add up the number of times on training and real missions when he'd listened for the sound of helicopter blades. He estimated that over half of those occasions he'd been disappointed and left standing on the pickup zone (PZ) as the window closed, left to move to an alternate PZ or into an escape and evasion plan. It was why he wasn't even getting up, searching the horizon. If the Israeli helicopter showed, fine. If it didn't, he was certainly better off than he'd been an hour ago when he'd anticipated imminent death. Frankly, he didn't much care.

"Ah!" Fassid was jumping up and down like a

schoolchild as a small helicopter popped up over the sand dune and swung around to come in for a landing forty feet away. It was amazingly quiet, and Turcotte knew why as he recognized the model—the McDonnell-Douglas MDX.

Built around the venerable MD-530 bubble frame, the MDX was on the cutting edge, incorporating NOTAR—no tail rotor—technology, thus eliminating the largest producer of noise on helicopters: the small tail rotor had to rotate at much higher speeds than the main blades. Instead of a tail rotor, compressed air was ejected from the side of the tail boom to keep the helicopter's torque in balance.

"Come on, come on," Fassid grabbed Turcotte's arm.

Turcotte got to his feet and put his hand over his eyes for some protection against the blowing sand. He followed Fassid on board, getting into the backseat. The pilot and co-pilot immediately took off, even before he had the door shut behind him.

The helicopter banked hard, then sped east, less than ten feet above the sand. The pilots kept the craft low and in a couple of minutes they reached the Nile, skimming across the surface of the water, barely missing a scow's mast, then over the desert on the other side, heading toward the Gulf of Suez.

Turcotte reached up and pulled down a headset hanging from the ceiling and put it on. He listened as the pilots called out checkpoints to each other, confirming their escape route. Then a tone chimed, and one of the pilots cursed.

"What's that?" Turcotte asked.

"Radar lock from above," the co-pilot responded. Turcotte leaned against the glass and looked up. Etched against the blue sky were two white contrails from Egyptian jets.

"We know we got picked up on radar coming in," the co-pilot informed him, "and they've scrambled everything they can get in the air to track us down."

"You've got company at eleven o'clock," Turcotte told them. He was amazed the Israelis had continued and made the pickup if they'd been detected. Every helicopter pilot he'd ever met had described the possibility of a battle between a helicopter and a jet as the equivalent of that between a poodle and a pit bull.

"How far until our feet are wet?" Turcotte asked.

"Forty-six miles to the Gulf," the co-pilot answered. "But remember, we gave the Sinai back to the Egyptians in the peace accord."

"And we stationed peacekeepers on the Sinai," Turcotte said. "Can you get me a radio link to South Camp?"

South Camp was located near Sharm El Sheikh, on the southern tip of the Sinai Peninsula and home to part of the multinational peacekeeping force put in place by the United Nations after the Camp David Peace Accords in 1979. Turcotte knew there was a strong U.S. presence there.

"You've got a channel on the MNF frequency," the co-pilot said. "Better buckle up."

Turcotte was slammed against the side door as the helicopter turned perpendicular to the ground and dove into a wadi, now ever closer to the ground, something Turcotte had not thought possible.

"Can you get us over the water?" Turcotte asked the co-pilot, before he keyed the radio. He could see that the two jets were in a steep dive, heading toward them.

"We're sure going to try. We've got a few tricks we can use."

Turcotte keyed the radio and demanded to speak to the senior American officer at South Camp. As Turcotte

talked to South Camp, the MDX began bobbing and
weaving as the two jets rapidly approached.

Out of the corner of his eye, Turcotte saw a missile
flash by, then explode into a sand dune. He felt his
stomach tighten as the MDX spun one hundred and
eighty degrees, abruptly halting forward movement.
The two jets roared past, then the helicopter reversed
once more and continued on course. It took the jets almost a dozen miles to loop around for another pass.

"What are they doing?" the co-pilot yelled.

Turcotte slid the side door open and leaned out. He
could see the two Egyptian planes coming around, very
low this time, at just slightly faster than their stall
speed. "Gun run," Turcotte replied. "Low and as slow as
they can go." He knew that if they were going to fire
missiles again, the jets would be much higher to try to
keep a heat lock. The helicopter must have some sort of
anti-radar device and heat diffusers given that they had
survived the first attack.

"Range?" the co-pilot wanted to know.

"Two miles and closing," Turcotte informed the
pilots.

"They'll wait until they're right behind us before
shooting. Maybe a quarter mile," the pilot said.

"How do you know that?" Turcotte asked.

"We've read their tactical manuals," the pilot said.

"One mile and closing," Turcotte said. "How far to
the coast?" he asked.

"Eight miles."

He knew they weren't going to make it. The two
planes coming dead on for the tail of the helicopter
looked like rapidly approaching darts.

"Half mile," Turcotte said.

"Now!" the co-pilot yelled.

Turcotte felt his stomach slam downward as the nose of the helicopter abruptly lifted. He blinked, realizing he was now looking at the desert floor, then he was completely disoriented as the MDX went vertical and began to loop over.

The two jets went by below and Turcotte was upside down, held in place only by the shoulder straps. His stomach completed the roll as they came around and down, now behind the two jets.

"Fire!" the pilot ordered. A stinger missile leapt from the weapons pod and raced after the jets.

"Fire." Another missile trailed the first.

The Egyptian jets broke, one right, one left, desperately kicking in their afterburners to escape the missiles bearing down on them. They'd played right into the Israelis' hands by coming down to low level and losing the ability to trade altitude for speed.

Turcotte turned from watching the second fireball as he heard a loud, retching sound. Fassid was puking all over himself on the other side of the chopper.

"The Gulf," the co-pilot announced as they cleared a dune and a flat stretch of water as far as they could see appeared ahead.

"We've got two more fast-movers on radar," the pilot said. "ETA six mikes."

"Where will we be in six minutes?" Turcotte asked.

"Halfway across the Gulf."

Turcotte keyed the radio. "Vanguard Six, this is Area Five One Six. Over?"

He felt a wave of relief as he was instantly answered. "This is Vanguard Six."

"Six, do you have us on screen? Over," Turcotte asked.

"Roger. Over."

"Your intercept time to us? Over?"

"Ten mikes. Over."

"Make it six," Turcotte said, "or there won't be anything to meet. Over."

"We'll try."

The pilots had the MDX about twenty feet over the Gulf of Suez, engines maxed out. The interior smelled foul from Fassid's vomit, but that was the least of anyone's concern. Turcotte wasn't scared. He'd always been capable of shutting down his emotions in battle, but on those occasions he'd had some control over his fate. Here he was just a passenger on an aircraft that was either going to make it or go up in a ball of flame, with the latter the more likely event.

"Ship to the right," Fassid reported.

Turcotte looked past the Egyptian officer. A mid-sized freighter flying a Liberian flag was steaming up the Gulf, heading for the Canal. He keyed the intercom. "Can we use the ship for cover?"

In reply the pilot banked the MDX and headed straight for the large bow of the ship.

"Jets two minutes out," the co-pilot reported.

"Guardian Six, ETA? Over." Turcotte asked over the radio as they closed on the tanker.

"Six minutes. Over."

The pilot brought the nose of the helicopter up and they cleared the top of the bow by five feet, banked hard right to avoid hitting the bridge, then were over the large main deck.

"There," the co-pilot was pointing toward an open cargo hatch. The pilot brought the MDX down above the deck of the moving ship, then descended, matching the ship's speed, down through the open hatch in the hold.

They hovered in the darkness of the hole, the only

light coming from the hatch overhead where they could see a few startled crewmen looking down. Turcotte checked his watch. "Time," he told the pilot finally.

They were up, out of the hatch. Five thousand feet up they could see the Egyptian fighters circling. And closer, four Blackhawk helicopters with UN stenciled on the side.

The MDX darted to the east and the four Blackhawks surrounded it. Two above, two behind, preventing the Egyptians from getting to it without shooting them down first.

AREA 51, NEVADA

Kincaid leaned back in the seat and stared the computer screen in front of him. A sphere was rotating quickly, twenty-four red dots glowing along its surface. Stationary on the screen were three green dots representing Giza, Easter Island, and Qian-Ling. One of the red dots would align with Giza, then the sphere of red dots would spin rapidly, as the computer tried to line up another red dot with Easter Island. If there was a hit, the computer was programmed to try to align a third with Qian-Ling, but so far there had been no second hits.

As he watched the computer work in vain, several possibilities occurred to Kincaid, none of them good. One was that these grid points referred to a planet other than Earth—perhaps Mars. Another was that perhaps Che Lu's mathematic assumptions were wrong. Or that using Giza as a fixed point was off base and none of those points referred to Giza.

Kincaid shook his head. None of those possibilities was useful. He'd learned early in the NASA program to make the impossible possible. To do that required looking at things with blinders on. If this was indeed an Airlia grid system of important points on Earth, perhaps they had done something very simple to make it hard to plot.

He heard commotion from the Cube, but Kincaid focused his attention on the problem at hand.

Major Quinn threw the door to the conference room open. "Turcotte has been picked up by an Israeli helicopter and will be landing at Hazerim in twenty minutes."

Yakov looked up from the chess set between himself and Che Lu. "That is news worthy of a drink." He pulled the bottle of vodka out from some hidden pocket inside his large, billowy shirt.

"The Grail?" Che Lu asked.

The enthusiasm dimmed on Quinn's face. "Aspasia's Shadow escaped with it—and Doctor Duncan. Turcotte thinks they've headed back to The Mission, wherever that is now. He said he'd update via SATCOM from the bouncer on the way back here," Quinn said. "He was using an Israeli radio and frequency to tell me what I just told you."

"Some good news, some bad news." Yakov took a drink. "That seems to be the way it always is."

"Anything from Mister Kincaid and his search?" Che Lu asked Quinn.

"Nothing yet. The computer is still doing permutations."

"Let us hope Turcotte has a plan," Yakov said.

HAZERIM AIR BASE, ISRAEL

Major Turcotte had no plan other than getting off the Israeli helicopter without falling on his face. Beyond that, his mind and body were too exhausted and drained to go. He recognized Sherev and watched as the Mossad agent met Colonel Fassid with open arms. His greeting to Turcotte was less enthusiastic.

"Al-Iblis has the Ark" were his first words as Turcotte felt the heat from the tarmac rising like a hot blanket.

"And the Grail," Turcotte added, squinting in the bright sun. "Do you know where he went?"

"Last radar image before the AWACS was destroyed indicated the two helicopters were heading east," Sherev said as he led Turcotte toward the waiting bouncer. "For all we know the choppers had external fuel tanks, which means they could go anywhere in the Middle East. There they could land and cross-load to a plane if they wanted to go farther. One of our listening stations intercepted part of an FM broadcast between the two helicopters which indicated they were heading toward a place called The Mission, which no one seems to know the location of."

Turcotte knew that intelligence agencies all over the world had been trying to find the new spot where The Mission had set up shop after being chased off of Devil's Island in South America.

"Things are very unstable," Sherev continued as they reached the bouncer. "The assassination of Hussein has led to saber rattling in both Iran and Iraq. The fools here thought cutting off the head would kill the beast, but it has just made things more dangerous. The enemy you know is always better than the enemy you don't.

"Your own country is threatening Egypt over the loss

of the AWACS. My country is contemplating mobiliza-
tion of reserves because of what is happening.

"China is still sealed off from the rest of the world,
although intelligence reports indicate their military is
mobilizing. There's fear that the Chinese might invade
Taiwan. North Korea is also mobilizing. Both countries
are hoping that your Navy in the Pacific is so preoccu-
pied with Easter Island that they can act with impunity
in the western Pacific." Sherev shrugged his shoulders.
"The world is getting even crazier than it usually is.
And now we have the Ark of the Covenant and the Grail
both surfacing after being myths for generations and
now lie in the hands of a terrorist.

"I think that what is even more dangerous than the
political maneuverings are the cracks in the foundations
of the major religions. The various clergy are having a
difficult time suddenly reconciling their dogma to the
existence of these aliens."

Turcotte didn't want to get into the real identity of
Al-Iblis with Sherev; he himself had a hard enough time
understanding the creature and its *ka* and being reborn.

"I thank you for saving us." He extended his hand.

Sherev gripped it. "I lost a good mole—" He nodded
toward Fassid. "I hope you two were worth it."

"We'll try to be," Turcotte said.

"Ah," Sherev spit onto the hot runway. "Who knows
what is worth what nowadays." He slapped the side of
the bouncer. "Alien spaceships, the Ark, the Grail, who
knows what will happen next or who is who."

"That's what we're trying to figure out at Area 51,"
Turcotte said. "Thank Fassid for me once more."

"Ah, he gets a nice house, a monthly check from the
government now. He is quite happy that he does not
have to lead a double life. Have a safe journey." Sherev
stepped back.

Turcotte climbed up to the hatch and slid in, shutting it behind him. Within seconds they were airborne and heading west toward the United States.

QIAN-LING, CHINA

Ts'ang used the spear he held to open one of the smaller containers in the large cavern. He removed a black sphere, about eight inches in diameter. Then he led Lexina, Coridan, and Elek back to the lowest chamber.

"I must follow the instructions I was given," he said as they entered it and faced the black wall. "I was put in place to be the first to awaken. Artad is to be the last."

"Who's next?" Lexina asked.

"The Kortad. They must make sure all is secure before waking Artad."

"There is not much time," Lexina said.

"It is the way things must be done," Ts'ang said. "Haste can be more dangerous than anything else." He pressed down on the top of the black sphere. A series of hexagons appeared on the surface. He hit several in a rapid pattern.

The black wall moved swiftly back, revealing row after row of black tube. The chamber was far larger than Lexina had imagined. Over two hundred tubes were exposed before the black wall completely disappeared, revealing a large set of doors made of black metal.

"Artad rests behind those doors in a special vault," Ts'ang said.

He tapped on the black sphere and the lids to all the tubes slid back. The metal foil peeled away, revealing the alien bodies inside. They were identical to the hologram that had appeared in the main tunnel. They were all just short of seven feet tall, with a disproportionally short torso and overly long arms and legs. The heads were half as big as a human's, with bright red hair. The skin was white and unblemished.

Each one had either a spear like Ts'ang, or a sword lying next to their right hands. Lexina wondered about the archaic weapons, but she assumed they had another purpose just as the Spear of Destiny and Ts'ang's spear had served as keys.

"They will be conscious and able to move in an hour," Ts'ang said. "Until then, we wait."

"We have waited for many generations," Lexina said. "Another hour is bearable for us, but I hope it is not too late with regard to Aspasia's Shadow's forces."

EASTER ISLAND

The thousands brought by the *Jahre Viking* had been assimilated by the nanovirus. Food on the relatively desolate island was a major problem at the moment, and the guardian solved that by "shutting down" a large number of the currently unneeded troops. The nanovirus put them into a coma, reducing their bodily functions to bare minimums.

The *Viking* floated offshore, its modifications complete. The massive bow doors slowly swung open, water flooding into the special front compartment built by the nano-techs. Once the water line inside equaled that outside, the submarine *Springfield* slowly made its way inside the huge tanker and was secured in metal brackets specifically designed for it. The doors swung shut, then the water was pumped out.

On board the *Washington*, the modified air wing was in place, and planes lined the deck, wingtip to wingtip.

All was ready. The huge tanker and the aircraft

carrier began moving. From the deck of the *Washington*, a single, modified Hawkeye took off.

PACIFIC OCEAN

Captain Robinette stared at the imagery that had just been downloaded from the KH-14 spy satellite monitoring his area of operations. Two large ships had just appeared from under the protection of the Easter Island shield: the *George Washington* and the *Jahre Viking*. They were moving at flank speed, directly for his Task Force.

Robinette sat down in his command chair and accessed the com-link to the captains of all the ships in his battle group. "Gentlemen. We have contact with the enemy. Prepare your ships for battle. We will advance on the enemy at flank speed. I am launching aircraft for a preemptive strike."

He shut the com-link, then turned to his Commander Air Group. "CAG, I want you to start launching immediately. Everything we've got."

If there was one lesson that had been beaten into Robinette from his first year at the Naval Academy, it was that in modern naval warfare the side that struck first held the advantage.

"What about our CAP?" the CAG asked, referring to the covering air patrol that guarded the Task Force.

"Keep minimum force above us. Everything else gets launched. I want those two ships sunk."

"Sink the *Washington*, sir?"

"Yes. I want you to lead the strike force personally."

"Yes, sir."

As soon as CAG left, one of the radar operators called out a report. "Sir, there's been an aircraft launched from the *Washington*."

"Identification?"

"A Hawkeye."

That made sense, Robinette knew. The Hawkeye was a surveillance aircraft. "Keep an eye on it."

"Yes, sir."

THE MISSION

The body was ready. It had been grown with the utmost care and now floated in a vat of green fluid, a black hose running air into the mouth. The top of the shaved head was covered with a skullcap from which several dozen wires ran to a main line that came out of the tube and snaked over to the command console.

The eyes were open but stared blankly, no spark of intelligence behind them. It was in one of the lowermost chambers of The Mission, surrounded by a bank of alien machinery, the most prominent piece a long black tube built of *b'ja*, the alien metal.

Aspasia's Shadow coughed, pain shooting through lungs riddled with cancer. This was a very bad time to pass on. There was so much that needed to be done, and Duncan still lay in the room next to the Grail, twitching in agony.

But he didn't want to cut it too close. If this body died, he would lose all he had experienced in the past several days and then even more time would be lost trying to catch up. It was a disorienting feeling, awakening in a new body and having lost time that one had in reality lived.

Aspasia's Shadow went to the control console, hands over the lit hexagonal display. He tapped out a sequence, just as he had done hundreds of times in the past. The lid to the black tube swung up easily, revealing a contoured interior designed to fit his body.

He removed the *ka* from around his neck and slid it, arms forward, into the two small holes on the right side of the console. It fit snugly, and a small six-sided section next to it glowed orange, indicating it was in place.

Aspasia's Shadow went to the black tube. He stripped off the priest's garments and crown, carefully laying them on the small stand next to it, and lay inside. The lid lowered onto him, trapping him in utter darkness. Nano-probes slid out of the lining into his brain, tapping into the needed sections. The pain was intense, but there wasn't time to go through the normal preparations which would have alleviated that.

His memories and experiences since the last download were quickly tapped and transferred to the *ka*. Aspasia's Shadow took a shallow breath, never prepared for what came next, because he didn't know what it was going to be like.

Out of small pockets in the lining of the tube, black particles, the size of grains of sand, were expelled onto his naked skin.

He screamed helplessly into the darkness of the tube as the particles dissolved his flesh, muscle, and bone from the outside inward, triggering every pain response the body had. The only positive aspect was that it lasted for barely five seconds before the body was gone.

The console hummed as the data in the *ka* was integrated with the basic profile of Aspasia, then shunted to the figure in the glass tube through the line, into the wires into its brain. The imprinting lasted over a minute.

The eyes blinked, awareness filling them with cunning and malice. The green fluid drained, leaving the

figure kneeling in the tube's floor, trying to get oriented. The tube slid up and the figure tentatively
stepped out. It wiped itself with a towel, then slid on the
garments that had been left.

Aspasia's Shadow, the latest version, turned to leave
the room, but paused. It went over to the black tube and
lifted the lid. Inside there was nothing. A line furrowed
the unmarked brow of the cloned body, as if struggling
to remember something.

Aspasia's Shadow felt the pressure of time and left
the regeneration room. He went deep in the base, to the
lowermost room. A large multifaceted crystal, about
four feet high, was in the center of the chamber. He
walked up to it and laid his hand on the top, ring facing
down.

The crystal glowed brightly from an inner light. In a
complex maneuver that even Aspasia's Shadow
couldn't follow, the outside of the crystal folded on itself in tiny portions along the top, revealing an opening.
He reached in.

His hand came out holding a sword.

THE PACIFIC OCEAN

CAG flew above and slightly behind the strike force.
Spread out below was an impressive sight—twelve
F-14s, twenty-four F-16s, an EA-2C Early Warning
plane, and four EA-6B Prowler electronic attack jets
leading the way. More than enough firepower to take
out both ships. The issue, of course, was who was crew-
ing the ships. CAG could hear the chatter on the inter-
flight net as his pilots discussed this. He keyed his
radio.

"Men. Listen up. You will press home against the *Washington*. I want no one backing off. You've seen the video showing what happened to those people on the rafts heading in toward Easter Island off that trawler. The SEAL team sent in to do a recon hasn't been heard from. If our people are on board the *Washington*, they're not our people anymore. Those ships are carrying a virus deadly to all of mankind. You will press home the attack."

The *Washington* began launching more aircraft as the Hawkeye picked up the incoming flight. There was movement on the deck as some of those who had come on the *Viking* came onto the deck.

The *Viking* was slowing down and the bow doors slowly came open. The modified *Springfield* slipped out. But instead of heading toward Task Force 79, it took a different heading. Where the *Springfield* had been, the nanovirus began construction on a replica of the *Springfield*, which it had spent the last several hours studying.

"We've got bogeys," the EA-2C reported.

"How many?" CAG asked.

"Twenty-four."

"Signature?"

"Looks like F-18, but—"

"But?"

"Something's different."

"What?"

"I don't know, CAG. Just different."

"Great." CAG considered the situation. The bogies were most likely a defensive force sent up to stop the attack. "Checkmate Six," he called for the leader of one of his flights of F-18s.

"Roger. This is Checkmate Six. Over."

"CAG to checkmate. You've got the bogies. Clear our way in. Over."

"Roger."

CAG watched as one of his squadrons of F-18s accelerated, firing their afterburners.

"Where's that Hawkeye from the *Washington*?" CAG called back to the *Stennis*.

"We have it west of your flight at high altitude, closing on our position," the carrier reported.

A new voice cut in—Captain Robinette. "Concentrate on your attack, CAG. I'm sending one of the CAP F-18s to take out that Hawkeye."

The pilot of the F-18 detailed to destroy the Hawkeye was flying with afterburners on toward the slower-moving plane headed directly toward the fleet. He wasn't worried about the confrontation, since the Hawkeye was unarmed. He flipped the switch turning on his 20mm Gatling gun and slowed as he neared the other plane.

The Hawkeye made no attempt to maneuver, coming straight on. At one mile, closing rapidly, the pilot pressed the trigger and held it for two seconds before breaking right. As he passed he could see the tracers race toward the Hawkeye and hit. Chunks of the plane blew off as the 20mm rounds ripped through.

"What the hell?" the pilot muttered as he noticed the

rotodome on top seperate from the body of the plane and continue flying on its own as the plane nosed over and headed for the ocean. He turned hard, circling around. The rotodome was slowly disintegrating, changing from a solid into what appeared to be a black cloud that was spreading out.

The pilot keyed his radio, but there was nothing but static. He changed frequencies with the same result.

"We've lost all communications with Pearl."

Robinette spun his chair around. "Say again?"

"We've lost all communications, sir. SATCOM. High frequency. Everything."

Robinette turned back. There was a clear Plexiglas screen on one side. A sailor stood behind it, updating the position of the strike force and the enemy flight. The two were closing on each other at rapid speeds. A tremor of unease passed through the captain.

The leader of the forward F-18 squadron blinked as the incoming flight disappeared from his radar screen. "Anyone have a lock on bogeys? Over."

"Negative. They're gone. My radar is down!"

Without their radars, the F-18s from the *Stennis* were forced to find their targets visually. This was difficult flying at twelve hundred miles an hour, especially when their targets were approaching head-on at the same speed.

"There!" the squardon commander yelled as he fired his 20mm cannon at a blur he spotted coming at him.

The bogeys were past, F-18s passing each other at a combined speed of over two thousand miles an hour. The startled commander of the Checkmaters whipped his head left and right, barely catching a glimpse of the enemy aircraft. They weren't up to intercept. The path to the *Washington* was clear for the strike force.

Robinette pounded the arm of his chair in frustration. He was blind and cut off from both his strike force and his protective CAP. He could only hope his men's training held true and both did their jobs.

CAG had taken over lead of the flight. Without communication among the planes, it boiled down to a simple tactic—everyone was to follow him and do as he did. He spotted two massive silhouettes on the horizon and knew he had the targets in sight. He armed his bombs as he searched the sky for a protective air cover, but the sky seemed to be clear.

In their abbreviated mission briefing before takeoff, CAG had divided the two targets among his planes. He pointed his nose toward the *Washington* and was relieved to see the planes designated for the *Jahre Viking* break left and head toward their target. Without his aiming radar, and not having to worry about air cover, CAG decided the best plan was to come in low and slow and drop his bomb when he was right on top of the target. He would use the plastic sight bolted to the front of the cockpit reserved for when the radar didn't work.

He extended flaps and reduced throttle. He could make out more details about the *Washington* as he got closer. Planes lined the deck. Some adjustments had been made to the ship, particularly in the radar array and bridge island. Then he saw the people. Hundreds covering the forward part of the flight deck. Men, women, and children. Most of the adults were dressed in Navy uniforms.

CAG hesitated, and that was all it took for him to fly by the carrier, the rest of his strike force following without a single bomb being dropped. The same happened with the force at the *Jahre Viking*.

"Damn it!" CAG cursed as he banked and circled wide, coming around for another run. He steeled himself for what had to be done. With his squadrons right behind him, CAG came in for a second run. He lined up his sight on the center of the flight deck. Then he released the bomb. He banked hard and up, looking over his shoulder as the bomb arced toward the carrier.

Two hundred meters above the flight deck the bomb exploded. CAG cursed as he watched the rest of his planes drop their loads with the same result.

Inside the *Washington*'s cavernous hangar deck, a shield generator, similar but smaller than the ones inside Easter Island and Qian-Ling, spun, projecting a field completely around the carrier. Aboard the *Jahre Viking* was a twin generator, also protecting it.

Alarms clanged and Captain Robinette ran to the wing of his bridge, looking up in the sky. A group of small dots had appeared in the southern sky. He watched helplessly as his CAP reacted, going to intercept.

Unable to use their targeting radars, the F-18s flying CAP had to rely on their Gatling guns. Given that they were moving faster than Mach 1, and the incoming bogeys were flying close to one thousand miles an hour, it was like being in a car going full speed and threading a needle held by someone on the side of the road. They had one pass as the bogeys came in, firing long bursts in the hope of hitting something.

Miraculously, one bogey F-18 was struck in the wing, huge holes torn out of it, but the damage was immediately repaired by nanotechs.

The other eleven bogeys nosed over and picked up even more speed as they branched out, five heading toward the *Stennis* and one each toward each of the accompanying ships in the battle group.

The *Stennis* had only four 20mm Vulcan Phalanx guns for close-in protection. The escort ships were more heavily armed, and as they were on the outside, they began firing first. Unfortunately, they had the same problem as the jets—the Phalanxes were normally radar aimed and automatically fired. In this emergency, they were being manually fired and aimed by eye.

The cruiser *Champlain* scored a direct hit on one of the F-18s heading toward the *Stennis*, the round smashing into the cockpit, killing the human pilot. The plane spiraled down toward the ocean out of control.

From his bridge, Robinette watched events unfold, and before the first explosion he realized what the enemy's plan was. The *Champlain* was the first to be hit, an F-18 flying straight into its bridge, killing the entire command group.

"Kamikazes!" Robinette exclaimed as more F-18s hit his escort ships. He saw one coming in low over the water, directly for his bridge. He could see the line of tracers as one of the Phalanxes tried to hit it. A second later, just before the F-18 reached the bridge, the fuel canister slung below each wing popped open, a fog of black spreading out from each. Then the F-18 slammed into the bridge.

It took the air wing forty minutes to return to the task force. CAG circled overhead surveying the ships. He could see damage on some of them, but they were all afloat. He tried to contact the *Stennis*, but the radios were still out. He did a fly-by, low over the deck, and was startled to see no one moving about. There was no signal officer to wave him in for landing. It was as if the ship were deserted. He could also see the damage to the bridge. He circled once more, the rest of the air wing waiting overhead, fuel levels dropping.

"The hell with it," CAG muttered. He didn't need a signal officer to land. He'd done hundreds of carrier landings and he could see that the wires were ready. He leveled off, reduced throttle, and came in for a perfect landing as his tailhook caught the first wire. He was slammed forward against the restraints as the F-18 came to an abrupt halt.

He cursed as he slid back the canopy and saw no crew members rushing to his plane to clear it for the next jet to land. He unbuckled and climbed out of the cockpit, down to the flight deck. It was unnerving to be

standing there with no one else about when the flight
deck was normally a bustle of activity.

Then he noticed that the damage on the bridge island
was changing, appearing as if it were slowly repairing
itself. A sailor appeared in a hatchway, staggering toward CAG, arms held out. There were others behind
him, their eyes vacant and dull.

CAG turned and ran down the flight deck toward the
rear of the ship. His second in command was coming in
low and level, doing a fly-by to see what was happening. CAG swung his arms, the classic wave-off signal.

CHAPTER 20

Ts'ang Chieh knelt in front of the large black door, backed up by two hundred Airlia in flowing robes. One by one, each Airlia went to the door and inserted his or her spear/sword into a slot five feet off the floor, just to the right of the center seam. The Airlia would then go back to his or her place and kneel.

As each sword or spear was inserted, the door began to glow. Golden bands rose from the floor upward. When the last Airlia slid his spear into the slot, the door became completely golden, bathing all those who knelt in front of it with its glow. Heads bowed as the large doors began to swing open. Lexina prostrated herself, the other Ones Who Wait following suit.

When the doors were completely open, she risked a glance up. A single black tube, resting in a silver cradle, was set on an altar of clear crystal. The top of the tube slid back. Ts'ang Chieh went to the right of the altar, picked up a robe, and stood perfectly still, waiting.

An alien hand grasped the side of the tube, six fingers pulling. A tall Airlia with long flowing red hair appeared, and long legs slid over the side of the tube, touching the ground. Artad stood as Ts'ang Chieh brought forward the robe, wrapping it around Artad's shoulders.

Ts'ang Chieh cried out something in the alien tongue

and the two hundred Kortad replied with one voice. Lexina's body was shaking, tears flowing down her cheeks. This was the moment her people had waited over two hundred generations for.

They were no longer The Ones Who Wait.

AREA 51, NEVADA

On the main screen of the Cube, Larry Kincaid could watch the progress of the bouncer carrying Turcotte as it raced across the Atlantic, but his entire being was caught up in the grid problem Che Lu had given him. The computer had gone through all twenty-four points and then all possibilities for a second hit on Easter Island without success. He'd reprogrammed it to initiate at Giza with the second hit to be Qian-Ling.

He'd already considered the possibility that the guardian computers at those locations had been moved there after the grid points were recorded, but again that did him no good. He had to think of possibilities that might work, not ones that were non-starters.

If the grids had been manipulated by a number code— for example, each one moved slightly—that wouldn't make a difference because the points would still line up. Unless it was a graduated number code where the number change shift depended on the original number, but that seemed very complicated unless it was a set code the Airlia used all the time. In which case, he was again down a dead-end path.

He had a feeling the solution was right in front of him, but he just wasn't seeing it.

"We will be there in fifteen minutes." Turcotte's voice echoed out of the speaker in the center of the conference table. "Have a copy of all that has been translated from Burton's manuscript ready for me, particularly anything about The Mission."

"We'll do that," Yakov said. "We'll see you shortly."

The speaker went dead and the Russian turned to Che Lu. The news that the entire Space Command team had been wiped out and Duncan was in the hands of Aspasia's Shadow did nothing to lighten a mood that was already heavy. "We still have not found anything to help him with. We have an idea what the Grail's effect is, but it is now in Aspasia's Shadow's hands."

The main screen in the Cube showed the airfield above, a video camera tracking the bouncer as it hovered and moved toward Hangar One. Larry Kincaid barely spared it a glance as he focused on the rotating sphere covered with red dots filling the computer screen in front of him.

When he'd first started working in the space program in the sixties, his immediate supervisor had always emphasized what he called "reverse thinking." If an engineer ran into a problem that he couldn't get through within a reasonable amount of time, the suggestion was to try to look at the problem the opposite way one had been approaching it.

What was the opposite of a point on a sphere? Kincaid asked himself.

Then he saw it.

––––––––––

Mike Turcotte's head felt heavy; his thought processes were slow and fragmented, like sand pouring through an hourglass.

"My friend!" Yakov held out a hand to help Turcotte off the edge of the bouncer. "You do not look well."

The hangar was almost deserted, a stark contrast to the normal bustle of activity that had gone on here for decades.

"What have you learned?" Turcotte asked.

"We have much of the manuscript translated," Yakov said. He gestured toward the elevator and led the way as he spoke. "We have learned bits and pieces, but the exact composition of the Grail and the location of The Mission have eluded us so far."

"Easter Island?" Turcotte asked as the elevator doors slid shut.

"Nothing from Kelly Reynolds since the last message," Yakov answered. "The SEALs have not reported back and are presumed lost. And to top all that, contact with the naval Task Force has been lost."

"What about imagery of the Task Force?" Turcotte asked.

"The ships are there," Yakov said. "They just aren't communicating. Most of the air wing of your carrier the *Stennis* is flying north, toward Hawaii. Of course, they do not have the fuel to make it. Your people in the Pentagon are scrambling some tankers to try to reach them, but Major Quinn tells me they will all have to ditch before that happens."

Turcotte tried to make sense of this startling information. "Why aren't they landing on the *Stennis*?"

"Because, my friend, we believe that the nanovirus has taken over the entire Task Force."

"All of it?"

"It appears so."

"Well—" Turcotte was trying to sort through the situation. "That's the Pentagon's responsibility," he finally said.

Yakov's thick eyebrows arched in surprise.

"Aspasia's Shadow is with Duncan. He runs things. We stop him, we stop the Guides and all the rest," Turcotte said.

"So you hope," Yakov said.

"China?" Turcotte asked, trying to change the subject.

"Nothing there to report."

Turcotte leaned against the smooth metal wall as the elevator descended. The words of Aspasia's Shadow echoed in his mind, a ripple of uncertainty and disquiet. "So we don't know how to proceed," he summarized.

"It appears that—" Yakov began, but the elevator came to a halt and the heavy doors opened, revealing Larry Kincaid, a piece of clear acetate in his hand.

"I've got it!"

"Got what?" Turcottle came off the wall as if jolted by electricity.

"The grid system," Kincaid said. "The one Che Lu translated. Some of the points are to throw you off, or maybe there's something there that hasn't been found—but Giza, Easter Island, Qian-Ling—they all line up. And there's other points." He was talking so quickly no one had a chance to get a word in edgewise until he paused for breath.

"The Mission?" Turcotte asked.

"Well, it's probably one of these points, I don't know which one. Let me show you what I have." Kincaid headed for the conference room, the others anxiously following.

As they settled in around the table, Kincaid dimmed the lights and put the acetate on an overhead projector.

A Mercator conformal projection of the planet was illuminated, along with dots all over the surface. Several were starred.

"Giza." Kincaid used a laser pointer to highlight one of the starred points. "Qian-Ling. Easter Island. Tiahuanaco in Bolivia, where Majestic found the guardian it moved to Dulce. Ngorongoro. They are all there, exactly pinpointed."

"How did you do it?" Che Lu asked.

Kincaid smiled. "The points you deciphered were encoded, but it was simple once I uncovered the key. The points you had from Nabinger were where a line, perpendicular to the interior Earth's surface at that spot, was to be projected through the planet to the *opposite* side of the globe."

Turcotte was looking at all the dots. Several were in the Middle East, not far from Giza. As he expanded his search, there were others in Asia, Europe, Africa—any of which could be The Mission, if The Mission was at one of these ancient locations.

"Anyone have an idea which one of these might be where The Mission is now?" he asked those in the room.

Kincaid's smile lost some of its luster. "Well, some of these, like I said, I think are bogus. There's a couple in the middle of the ocean. I just had this printed out, so I haven't really had a chance to check each spot out. I just wanted to be sure I'd figured it out right."

Che Lu was peering at the map. "We must examine each site."

"There's a lot of spots," Turcotte said. "We could—" He was interrupted by Professor Mualama, whom everyone had forgotten about, hidden behind his large computer monitors.

"I think I know where The Mission is." He walked to

the front of the room. A long finger reached out to touch the lone dot on the peninsula between Egypt and Israel. "Here. Mount Sinai."

The location immediately made sense to Turcotte in terms of the direction the two helicopters had been spotted heading by the AWACS before it was destroyed, but he wondered how he had decided on it. "Why there?"

"The Kabbalah!" Yakov said. He turned to Turcotte. "One of the chapters of Burton's manuscript said the Ark and Grail traveled to Mount Sinai after leaving Egypt during the Exodus."

"There's another mention of Mount Sinai in the chapter I just finished translating," Mualama said.

"Let's see it." Turcotte's exhaustion had fallen by the wayside.

The overhead was turned off and the computer screen came alive as Yakov quickly scrolled down to get to the new chapter.

Burton Manuscript: Chapter 8

I was sent to Damascus to fulfill my duties to the Crown. As is my wont, I spent considerable time in the native part of the cities, leaving the foreign section as often as possible.

I became entranced with a woman—as was also my wont in my younger days. I saw her only briefly one evening, highlighted against a second-story window as I traveled the streets to a haven where I spent many an evening, but that was more than enough. Rarely in all my travels had I seen such a perfect form. My interest piqued, I inquired as to the occupants of the house and learned it belonged to a rather important trader.

Under the guise of my consular duties, I called on

the trader the next day. His name was Ibrahim
Al-Issas. The woman was his mistress, I quickly
learned. He sensed my interest in her, and in the way
of that part of the world, offered her to me.

Her name was Kazin, an exotic combination of
Arab and French blood. We had long and interesting
conversations, as she had been a courtesan for many
important men in Damascus for over a dozen years,
and knew much of the inner workings of that part of
the world. I found her intelligence outshone her
magnificent beauty.

She was a student of the holy works ranging from
the Bible to the Torah to the Koran to the Kaballah. I
found her insights into the various writings most intriguing.

One day she mentioned a name that froze the
blood in my veins. We were discussing men of power
in the area, and she said there was a man who
wielded much strength, but always from the shadows,
so far in the darkness that no one rightly knew what
he looked like. She said his name was Al-Iblis.

I told her of meeting Al-Iblis in Medina, although
I did not tell her the results of that meeting. She said
that he ruled from a place called The Mission.

When I inquired if she knew the location of The
Mission, she did a most strange thing. She recited
several lines and told me if I could discover what
work they were from, I would have my answer. They
were:

"Take care not to go up the mountain or even to
touch the edge of it. Any man who touches the mountain must be put to death. No hand shall touch him;
he shall be stoned or shot dead; neither man nor
beast may live."

There was perfect stillness in the conference room. Yakov's finger hit the scroll key, but there was nothing further. Turcotte spun in his chair toward Mualama. "Where's the rest?"

"I don't have it translated yet."

Turcotte's fist slammed down onto the tabletop. "I thought you said this mentioned Mount Sinai? I don't see it."

"You have to know where that quote is from and what it refers to," Mualama quietly replied, a bucket of cold water on Turcotte's anger.

"Where is it from?" Yakov asked.

"The Old Testament," Mualama said. "Exodus 19."

That clicked in Turcotte's mind, connected with what he had just read in the manuscript. "Mount Sinai?"

Mualama nodded. "Yes."

Turcotte spun toward Major Quinn. "I want a complete target folder for Mount Sinai—and I want it yesterday."

"Already on it." Quinn was looking down at his handheld organizer, typing on the small keys.

Turcotte was moving toward the door, barking more orders at Quinn. "I want a bouncer ready to move in five minutes with another TASC-suit, as close as they can get to my size, with an MK-98. And I want whatever fire support you can get us in the Sinai." He pulled his SATPhone out. "I'll coordinate directly with Sherev for ground troops and choppers." Yakov and Quinn were right on his heels.

As the door swung shut behind them, only Che Lu and Mualama were left in the conference room. The old Chinese professor was shaking her head.

"What's wrong?" Mualama asked.

"Men." Che Lu shook her head again. "Always action first, thinking later. I suggest you translate the next chapter of Sir Burton's manuscript."

"I'm sure Kazin was referring to Mount Sinai," Mualama said defensively.

"I agree with you," Che Lu said. "But no one has stopped to think about what we just read. Why would this strange woman so easily tell Burton the location of The Mission, information that has been guarded so tightly for millennia? And the question above that—how did she know where it was? Obviously, Burton didn't stop to think either over a hundred years ago. We need to find what the result of his lack of foresight was, or else history may well repeat itself."

"What are *you* really looking for?" Mualama demanded of her.

Che Lu was surprised at the tone in his voice. "I want to uncover the truth so we may move forward."

"The truth?" A strange grin twisted Mualama's face, as if forced from within. "You work for Artad, don't you?"

"I work for no one. I am like you, an archaeologist who is—"

"Then why are you so anxious that mankind ally with Artad?" Mualama cut her off.

"I just think it would be the wisest course," Che Lu said.

"They question me," Mualama said, indicating the space around him, "but they don't question you. Why did you go to Qian-Ling in the first place? How did you get authority to enter when no one has ever received such permission in thousands of years?" He leaned forward, causing the old woman to step back in fear. "I think you lie too, Professor."

Without another word, Mualama went back to the manuscript. As he turned, Che Lu noted once more a small spot of blood on his ear. She hurried from the conference room, leaving Mualama alone.

CHAPTER 21

THE MISSION

Aspasia's Shadow was as still as the columns of marble behind him. The sword was held in front of him with both hands, point on the floor. The gems on the garments glittered. His dark eyes had not moved for the past ten minutes, focused on Lisa Duncan's form. She had also stopped moving, the slight rise and fall of her chest the only sign she was still alive. Her face had even relaxed, no longer contorted in pain as it had been since she put her hand in the Grail.

He'd known it would take time, but that was a resource that was in short supply. He was receiving continuous inquiries from the Airlia left on Mars via the guardian computer. That was of little consequence to him, although The Mission guardian did indicate that the Mars guardian was doing something on the red planet, the exact nature of which was being shielded. With no talons or mothership available to them, Aspasia's Shadow wasn't overly concerned with the Mars Airlia. The situation had changed, and they would either serve him or be abandoned as he had been abandoned by them.

China was a problem, as it had been for millennia. The shield was up around Qian-Ling, and Aspasia's Shadow had to assume that The Ones Who Wait would be resurrecting Artad. He felt a slight chill of anticipation, something that had been lacking for a long time. He wanted to face down the Kortad Leader and end this once and for all time. He'd fought Artad's Shadow many times, sometimes winning, sometimes losing, but always returning to the truce. Now there could be a final battle with the real Artad.

More important than all that, though, was the Grail.

So he waited and watched Duncan.

HAZERIM AIR BASE, ISRAEL

"We have eight Cobras already in the air, escorting five Blackhawks carrying an assault force." Sherev used the tip of a pencil to point at the map. "They're here, flying low level over the Gulf of Aqaba."

"There's an AC-130 gunship en route from Kuwait," Turcotte said. Cobras were attack helicopters armed with a 20mm machine gun and either Hellfire or TOW missiles, flown by a two-man crew. Its firepower, added to that of the AC-130 Specter airplane, would give them some punch.

"We've picked up your plane on radar," Sherev said. "We estimate it should arrive at Mount Sinai just as my aircraft do."

"How many men on the Blackhawks?" Turcotte was checking the TASC-suit. Sherev had raced out to meet them in an old jeep as soon as they landed.

"Fifty. From Unit 269."

Turcotte knew of 269 from his time in Det-A in Berlin. It was the most elite unit in the Israeli Army, which was saying quite a bit. That meant Sherev was using the very tip of the spear that was the Israeli Army for this mission. Judging the distance to where the choppers were and Mount Sinai, Turcotte knew they had a little bit of time before they had to leave in order to catch up to the aircraft in the bouncer.

"And intelligence on Mount Sinai?" Yakov asked. The Russian had finally shed his bulky overcoat; the dry, warm air of the Israeli desert was causing all of them to sweat. The vest Turcotte had scrounged for Yakov was stretched tight across his massive chest. The MP-5 in his hands looked like a toy.

"It's in the middle of nowhere on the way to nowhere," Sherev said. The pencil moved west and south from the location of the helicopters to the center of the lower portion of the Sinai Peninsula. "I have seen the Mount with my own eyes during the '73 war. We took the Sinai Peninsula from the Egyptians. And we gave it back after the peace accords. But both sides steered clear of *Jabal Mosa*, which is what the locals call it.

"Superstition." Sherev shrugged. "But in reality it is of no strategic or even tactical value. I happened to see it on a long-range recon trying to flank the Egyptian forces. It's not even the tallest peak in the area—Mount Catherine to the southwest is a little higher. Mount Sinai is just about seventy-five hundred feet high.

"There's a Catholic monastery at the base of the mountain. It's been there since the sixth century—the Monastery of Saint Catherine, founded by the Emperor Justinian."

"We know The Mission used the Romans in this area," Turcotte said as he opened the two halves of the suit. "Maybe they put a monastery at the base to distract attention from the mountain. Or maybe it's part of The Mission."

"It's possible," Sherev granted. "But I have imagery taken from overflights, and they show nothing on the mountain." He tossed several photos onto the hood of the jeep. They showed rough terrain, a peak in the center, another in the lower left which Sherev tapped with the pencil point. "That's Mount Catherine. Nothing there either. The only way to get to Mount Sinai on the ground is by using an unimproved road from the coast. Very hard to get to."

"The Airlia had a penchant for hiding things underground," Turcotte noted.

Sherev nodded. "A good place to hide something, as we do at Dimona. You know, Sinai comes from the name of the ancient god that was worshipped by the first people in that area, the moon god, *Sin*. Some Bedouins worship the Mount, most fear it. How do we find an underground base that no one has ever found?"

"I think someone did find it," Turcotte said.

"What is that?" Sherev asked as the suit split into two parts, waiting for an occupant.

"A second chance to rescue Doctor Duncan and destroy The Mission," Turcotte said. He lay down inside and hit the command for the suit to close. The top rotated over and shut.

"Audio," Turcotte ordered. He caught the end of Sherev's question.

"—are you doing?"

Turcotte stood, feeling more comfortable in the suit than he had the first time. He lifted an arm toward the bouncer. "Let's get airborne and I'll get us more information."

AREA 51

Che Lu slowly opened the door to the conference room and peered in. The lights were dimmer and Mualama was a tall, dark form seated near the computer. He wasn't moving and there was no sound of the keys being struck.

"You were right."

The voice startled Che Lu. "About what?" she asked Mualama.

"Burton didn't stop to think either before he raced off into the desert, seeking out what Kazin hinted at."

"Show me," Che Lu said as she turned to the large screen.

BURTON MANUSCRIPT: CHAPTER 9

I traveled with little difficulty from Damascus to Jerusalem. Then I joined a caravan that went south along the shore of the Dead Sea. We went along wadis until we reached Aqaba on the Gulf that bears the same name. That was the convoy's end point. I was told there was nothing worthwhile to the south in either direction—in the Sinai to the west or Arabia to the east.

However, I had little difficulty enlisting the aid of some Bedouins—the only ones who could travel or live in that stark terrain—to lead me into the heart of the Sinai.

Outside the walls of Aqaba I found a small group of twenty Bedouins preparing to depart for the desert. They had traveled to the city to trade for the few items their homeland could not provide them, primarily ammunition for their weapons. They were fierce-looking men armed with guns and swords, well-mounted. I felt at home among them. I had met such men before on my travels—men who lived simply, with strict codes of conduct so they could survive in a brutal land.

As I had done before, I did not tell them of my ultimate goal, but rather simply that I wished to travel to the monastery that was located at the base of the holy mountain. Indeed, I did plan on visiting Saint Catherine's Monastery, as it seemed to me the brothers there would know something of the mountain in whose shadow they dwelled.

The Bedouins took me in, shared their food and tents, and in the morning we departed. Instead of following the coast, as I had done so many times on my treks in Africa, the Bedouins went inland immediately upon leaving the outskirts of Aqaba. They knew their way from watering hole to watering hole, and it most certainly did not make for a direct route. Time meant nothing to these people, only desert and water mattered while they were traveling.

It was a feat I found most amazing, considering the tribe that they sought to reunite with were always on the move and could be anywhere in the vast, broken land we traversed.

But the old man who led us, Taiyaba, seemed unconcerned. He would find his tribe and family, of that he had no doubt. If it was close to Mount Catherine, then he would get me there. If not, he would just shrug and say it was Allah's will that I not go there.

After two weeks, a short time compared to Moses' forty years, I saw the top of two peaks in the western distance. Two days later we arrived at the monastery. The men were anxious. Mount Sinai, or Jabal Mosa, as they called it, was a holy place, one to be feared. They were also anxious to get to their families, which Taiyaba assured them were not far away, to the north and west. How he knew that, I could not tell you.

The building was made of rock and brick, huddled against a high rock wall at the base of Mount Sinai. I was disappointed in the monks. A small group of men, hacking a miserly life out of their rocky home,

they were ignorant of anything unusual about Mount
Sinai. They even debated among themselves whether
Moses had gone up that mountain or Mount
Catherine.

They were worthless. And they were puppets. I
should have seen it in their eyes. As I should have
seen it in Kazin's beautiful eyes. But I was too anxious. Mount Sinai was right there, beckoning, and I
was not paying as close attention as I should have.

Taiyaba offered to go with me up the mountain.

We set out at dawn. There was a track that wound
through the boulders and crags. A single track almost impassable at times.

Two-thirds of the way up we crossed over a spur
and came to a halt. In front of us the way was
blocked by a dozen men dressed in long black robes,
holding long spears. The bright metal glistened in
the desert sun. Beyond the warriors, another figure
loomed, standing on top of a boulder. I had seen
someone like that before, and my heart raced with
fear and anticipation of the coming confrontation.

"Welcome, Mister Burton." The voice confirmed
the identity, sending a shiver up my spine. Al-Iblis.
He came close. "You will now tell me what you
should have long ago."

"I don't—" I began, but he cut me off, leaning
close so only I could hear.

"I want the location of the Grail. And if it is back
in the Hall as I suspect, I want to know where the key
for the Hall is. And I assure you, you will tell me
everything you know." He gestured at his men.

One of the warriors stepped forward and tossed a
purse to Taiyaba.

"You can leave now," Al-Iblis ordered the Bedouin.
"You have been well paid for your guide duties."

"What will you do with him?" Taiyaba asked.

"That is not your concern."

Taiyaba's hand drifted to the pommel of his scimitar. "He has shared my food and my tent."

"You people of the desert." Al-Iblis spit. "I don't care for your customs. This is my place, not yours. I was here before your people were kicked out of whatever land they lived in and forced into the desert. He is mine to do with what I will. You have been paid. Go."

"You lied to me," Taiyaba said. "You said you only wished to speak to him and that I would guide him back to Aqaba safely." He turned back the way he had come. "It is said among my people that lies come back tenfold to the source." He ignored me as he went down the trail and disappeared.

I licked my parched lips, feeling the heat of the sun beating down on me. "Kazin?" I asked. "She is one of you, isn't she?"

His lips pressed together, razor thin in what might have been a smile. "Irresistible, wasn't she? I knew you would fall for her. She is a Shadow, like me. We have had many incarnations over the years. Isis and Osiris. Mordred and Morgana."

"And The Mission has been here all these years," I said.

"No. This is one of many places it has drifted to and from," Al-Iblis said. "For now it is convenient. As it was in the past and will be again in the future. Take him," Al-Iblis ordered.

Two of the warriors grabbed my arms and dragged me along the track. We went about a quarter mile farther to a point where a tall rock, over eighty feet high at least, jutted out of the side of the mountain like the prow of a magnificent ship. Al-Iblis

*waited for us at the base of this spur. He had a ring,
similar to that worn by The Watchers, and he used it
in the exact middle of the rock base. An entranceway,
ten feet high by eight wide, appeared.*

*I knew if I went into that tunnel I would never
come out. But what could I do? The warriors had my
arms tight in their grip. Al-Iblis stepped into the
doorway and was gone, as if disappearing into the
gates of Hell itself.*

*The warriors thrust me forward toward the door-
way. The one on my right cried out and spun to the
ground, blood spurting from a wound in the neck.
The crack of a gunshot followed a split second later.
I dove to the ground, rolling left. More shots echoed
on top of the first, faster than one man could reload.*

*I grabbed the dead warrior's spear just in time as
another came at me. I spit him on the blade like a
fish, the metal punching completely through him.*

*I scrambled to my feet as the war cries of the
Bedouins split the air. Taiyaba came charging up the
trail, followed by half a dozen of his men. The rest
fired from on the rocks.*

*The warriors fell quickly before the sudden on-
slaught of the mighty warriors of the desert.*

"Come!" Taiyaba beckoned.

*I wasted no time, dashing down the trail and join-
ing him. Above us the sky suddenly darkened, clouds
swirled over the top of the mountain. Thunder
roared. Lightning streaked the sky. All within less
than a minute of the rescue, on a day when there had
not been a cloud in the sky. Several of the Bedouin
cried out in fear, but Taiyaba hushed them with a
curse as we continued down the path.*

*"He was our guest!" Taiyaba explained suc-
cinctly.*

I was knocked backward as a lightning bolt hit one of the Bedouins in front of me. When I struggled to my feet there was only a black spot to mark where he had been.

Taiyaba fired his rifle at the sky with another eloquent curse in Arabic, and we continued.

Another lightning bolt, another man dead. By the time we reached the bottom only I, Taiyaba, and two others remained.

We mounted and rode into the desert, leaving the storm behind as it did not seem to be able to move away from the top of the Mount.

I have never been able to figure out why I was spared, but from that day forward the shock that had shaken my core when I saw the Black Sphinx was softened by the thought that there was some power stronger than these strange creatures from the sky and their minions. A power that protected me that day on the mountain.

I have learned many strange things over the years, but that day reignited my faith. Not in life after death, or the various religions I have encountered, or of gods I have heard of, but in man himself. Taiyaba came back for me because of his beliefs. His men died to save me because of what they believed in. I learned that day that a man's belief is a very powerful thing.

Tears were running down Che Lu's cheeks. She was remembering her students in Tiananmen Square, dying for their beliefs. Those she had walked with in the Long March and watched die as they gave their food to others.

The SATPhone in the middle of the desk cut through her sobs with a sharp ring.

Professor Mualama reached over Che Lu's shoulder and hit the on button.

"This is Turcotte. Do you have the location of The Mission?"

"We have more than that—we have the location of the entrance."

AIRSPACE GULF OF AQABA

Turcotte read the words of Burton on the helmet screen as the bouncer skimmed above the light blue water. Yakov and Sherev were reading the same on a laptop.

"We have the entrance," Turcotte said as he reached the end of the chapter. He began to check suit systems.

"I'll relay the information to my men," Sherev said.

AREA 51

Major Quinn had not been to sleep for over eighty hours, and his hand shook as he downed another cup of coffee. He was in the back of the Cube, watching the various developments play out around the world as they were displayed on the master board in the front of the room. Piles of documents, generated and brought into the Cube, and that were no longer being processed due to personnel shortages, littered both sides of his chair.

A thin leather portfolio, the cover worn and aged, caught his attention, crammed in among other folders. He reached down and pulled it out. The swastika on the cover was the first thing he noticed, then he realized it was part of what Turcotte and Yakov had recovered from the Moscow Archives. It contained documents written in German. He realized that it must have been sent to the Cube intelligence section for translation, but given that there was no longer a Cube intelligence section, it had been rerouted back to him.

Summoning up four years of college German and one tour of duty stationed in Stuttgart, Quinn began reading. He quickly realized that the paper in front of him was about *Okpashnyi*, the strange alien creature that Turcotte and Yakov had seen stored both at Section IV in Russia and in the German archives that had been moved from Berlin to Moscow at the end of the World War II. According to this report, both alien bodies had been recovered during a Nazi expedition to Tunguska in 1934. The creatures were composed of a spherical body, head with multiple eyes, and radiating out of the center were several, seemingly independent and interchangable limbs.

First, Quinn found it strange that Germans had been able to search that far into Russia in 1934. Second, and more important, what were the *Okpashnyi*? Were they pets of the Airlia? Then there was what General Hemstadt of The Mission had said to Yakov just before dying—mentioning the word *Tunguska*.

Quinn scanned the document, which was a summary of the underlying after-action report from the expedition. The *Okpashnyi* had been found in the wreckage of an alien craft, origin unknown.

A paragraph near the bottom of the page caught his attention. It listed casualties from the expedition. Five men had died, cause of death not listed except that they had died in service of the Fuehrer.

Quinn thumbed through the documents below,

searching for a report on the casualties, his curiosity piqued. He found the more detailed casualty report buried three quarters of the way into the folder.

The men had been infected by what the writer called an "alien infection" brought on by the discovery that one of the *Okpashnyi* was still alive in the permafrost and the subsequent thawing of it. The five had been shot by their own comrades to keep the infection from spreading.

Quinn hurriedly scanned the other pages in the report, but there was nothing else on the *Okpashnyi* that had been found alive. Only the two that Turcotte and Yakov had seen were listed on the transport manifest back to Berlin.

Quinn sat back in his chair overlooking the Cube, and tapped his fingers rapidly on the report. Something had happened over sixty years ago at Tunguska, something so terrible that it had been stricken from the report.

What the hell was this *Okpashnyi*?

He was distracted from these thoughts as someone yelled out an update on the assault force heading toward Mount Sinai.

CHAPTER 22

THE MISSION, MOUNT SINAI

The heavy wooden door creaked slowly open. Aspasia's Shadow spun about, anger twisting the smooth skin of his face into an ugly mask, the sword half raised in threat. He was processing information from the Easter Island guardian. The attack had been a complete success and he had more than doubled his military power. The next phase of operations was already under way. He had the initiative and he planned on keeping it.

"I ordered no interruptions."

"Sir—" The guard cowered. "There are helicopters inbound. Many helicopters. From Israel."

Aspasia's Shadow cursed. He strode from the room, the sword tight in his grip.

The Cobras led the way, less than twenty feet above the rocks and sand. The pilots had cut their teeth in Lebanon, flying through the streets of Beirut, having RPG rockets fired at them at point blank range. This flight was a "Hollywood" run so far—easy and sweet.

A mile behind the Cobras, the five Blackhawks carried the elite of the Israeli military. Weapons locked and loaded, the members of Unit 269 were hardened soldiers in one of the most war-torn places in the world. They sat in their web seats armed with the new Tavor assault rifles and carrying satchels of demolitions. They

were uncertain what their mission was, but listened as
Sherev's voice came over their unit net telling them
where they were going. Mount Sinai. A door needed to
be blown open at the base of a rock spur.

The place meant something even to those hardened
by the death they had seen and dealt. A place of the
faith of their country.

This wasn't hunting terrorists who set off car bombs
or a punitive raid, or an assassination of an enemy of
the state. This was something unprecedented, even
though they weren't exactly sure what it was.

Sherev's last words hit home. "Our goal is to recover
the Grail and the Ark of the Covenant."

"The *what*?" the unit commander asked, not certain
he had heard correctly.

"The Ark and the Grail. Get them and bring them
back. And the *urim* and *thummin*."

"And anyone we encounter?" the commander asked.

"There is an American woman by the name of
Duncan, being held prisoner. Try to rescue her. Everyone else—kill them."

The SATPhone received an imagery download from the
closest spy satellite. Turcotte had the imagery displayed
on his helmet screen, then he enhanced it.

"The west side," he told Sherev and Yakov.

"I don't see it," Yakov said.

"There's a shadow," Turcotte said. "That must be the
spur. And a thin line indicating the trail."

Sherev relayed the information on the exact location
of the spur to the helicopters. "Lead Cobra will be on
target in three minutes," he informed Turcotte and
Yakov.

Turcotte had one of his radios set to another frequency with which he was talking to the fire control officer of the AC-130.

"Specter," he ordered as the computer switched him to that frequency.

Five thousand feet above the Sinai Peninsula, Captain Debbie Macomber heard Turcotte's call in her headset and responded. "This is Spooky Four-Niner. Over."

"This is Area Five-One-Six. Time on target? Over."

Macomber had two main screens she was concerned with. One displayed the AN/AAQ-117 Forward Looking Infrared Radar and the other the APG-80 Fire Control display, the same as that used by the F-15E fighter. She was seated in a small, enclosed area in the front part of the cargo bay of the modified C-130 aircraft. On one side of her was the electronic warfare officer, and on the other the TV and IR sensor operators, who made sure she saw the targets regardless of light or weather conditions.

"Three minutes. We'll be four thousand feet above highest ground point. Over."

The rest of the large cargo bay held the weapons systems, all pointing out the left side of the craft—a GAU-12 25mm Gatling gun; an L60 40mm cannon; and farthest to the rear, an M-102 105mm cannon. Through the controls on the console in front of her, Macomber could fire all three guns at the same time at three different targets with pinpoint accuracy. Macomber could put a round in every square foot of a target the size of a football field in less than twenty seconds.

She had two primary methods of aiming the guns.

One was to run a computer program using targeting information from the intelligence information which she had programmed. The other was manually, which consisted of her tapping the interactive screen and the guns firing at whatever her finger touched.

Macomber was a graduate of the Air Force Academy who had fought to get this assignment: the first woman assigned to the elite Special Operations Wing that flew the Specters and Talons. She'd fought all her life. Her parents died in a car accident when she was three, and she was raised by her grandmother on a ranch in Montana, a place where most considered it a man's land and a man's job. A picture of her grandmother was taped to the monitor for inspiration.

"Do you have our friends accounted for?" Turcotte's voice crackled in her ear. "Over."

"See them clearly," Macomber replied.

The Cobras were flying single-file in a draw, completely masked from Mount Sinai as they approached. The Blackhawks carrying the assault force were two minutes behind. It was precision flying, the sides of the canyon only a few feet from the tips of their blades on either side.

Since they were masked, they couldn't see the cloud that began boiling out of the top of the mountain.

Turcotte felt the adrenaline kicking in. The suit was tight against his body, and for the first time he felt its power. If MJ-12 under the control of The Mission had siphoned Airlia technology to develop this, he felt it was appropriate it was being used in this assault. He turned and faced Yakov. The Russian gave him a thumbs-up. Sherev had one cup of the radio headset pressed tight against his right ear, listening to his helicopters' frequency. Turcotte could hear all the frequencies overlapping each other in his helmet.

Through the skin of the bouncer, Turcotte could see the rock walls flashing by when he checked the view through his down mini-cams, sometimes less than a couple of feet away. He hoped they had the advantage of surprise. The tail boom of the last Blackhawk suddenly appeared ahead. He braced himself as the bouncer jerked upward over the lip of the canyon.

The Blackhawks were lined up in the canyon, moving at forty knots. Ahead of them were the Cobras, approaching the end of the canyon. Scanning up, Turcotte could see Mount Sinai—and the black cloud that now covered the top of its peak.

"This is not good," Yakov understated.

The lead Cobra came out of the canyon and gained altitude, heading toward Mount Sinai. Behind it the other seven flared up, spreading out.

"Hold the Blackhawks in the canyon," Turcotte advised Sherev.

The Israeli relayed the order. Turcotte switched to the IR, then light amplification, but neither could penetrate the cloud.

Turcotte keyed his radio. "Spooky, can you see anything with your IR through that cloud? Over."

The bouncer was now above the lead Cobra, less than three miles from the mountain.

Macomber had several views of Mount Sinai displayed
in front of her. One was from a TV camera mounted in
the nose of the plane, showing normal daylight view.
Another was from the infrared sensor which normally
could pierce through clouds and fog. But whatever was
obscuring the top of the mountain was not a normal
cloud or fogbank, as it was impervious to the IR imager.

"Negative. I've got nothing."

Yakov pointed. "There's the spur." A finger jutted up
from the side of Mount Sinai, exactly as Burton had described, just below the cloud.

"I'm going to have the—" Sherev began, but his
words were cut off by a bolt of lightning flashing out of
the dark cloud. It struck the lead Cobra dead on. The
helicopter exploded, debris littering the rocky ground.

The other attack gunships scattered. Another bolt,
another helicopter gone.

Sherev was yelling into his radio, trying to coordinate his forces. Turcotte contacted the Talon. "I need
suppression, now!"

Macomber never fired without a clear lock on a target,
given that the Specter gunship had all-weather, all-
visibility capability. But throughout her career she'd
had to work twice as hard as her male peers to be accepted in the elite Special Operations Wing, and that
meant extra preparation. She hit one of the keys on her
board and a computer simulation outlining Mount
Sinai, as it had been mapped by satellite imagery, ap-

peared on her targeting screen overlying the strange
fog. She'd prepared a dozen firing programs and accessed one.

"Firing," she told Turcotte as she pressed the execute
key.

Turcotte saw a string of red lanced down from the
Specter, lashing into the fog even as another lightning
bolt came out, destroying a third helicopter. The string
was a line of 20mm shells. Also firing, the 40mm and
105 Howitzer sent rounds raining down.

Turcotte tapped Sherev's arm with his one free hand.
"We've got to go in now!"

The Israeli's jaw set, knowing what was implied in
giving that order. He keyed his radio. "All units attack,
all units attack. Gunships suppressing fire, assault force
to the doorway location."

The surviving Cobras stopped their evasive maneuvers and headed for the fog, gaining altitude. The
Blackhawks lifted out of their canyon hide and flitted
forward, straight for the rock spur.

Another lightning bolt took out a fourth Cobra. But
the Israeli pilots didn't waver, going right at the source
of their death.

The Cobras began firing, spraying their minguns at
the top of the mountain, adding to the rounds from
Specter. Another Cobra exploded. The Blackhawks
were less than a mile from the spur.

"Go," Turcotte ordered the bouncer pilot. He locked
the suit legs to keep from falling as the bouncer accelerated, racing past the Blackhawks.

A streak of lightning came out of the cloud, heading

for the bouncer. Sherev and Yakov took steps back,
throwing their hands up reflexively as they could see
the bolt come straight for them. It hit.

The alien craft shuddered, knocking Yakov and
Sherev off their feet. The two struggled to get up, but
the floor was canted at an extreme angle, and they slid
to the down side.

"We're losing power!" the pilot yelled. "I'm slowing
us as much as I can."

Turcotte could see Mount Sinai rapidly approaching
as the bouncer lost altitude. He reached down and
grabbed Yakov with one mechanical hand and lifted
Sherev with the arm that had the MK-98. The suit
strength amplifiers strained from the pressure as he
lifted both men off the floor of the bouncer. He flexed
his knees.

They hit and went from forty miles an hour to a dead
halt in a microsecond. Turcotte crumbled to the ground,
even the suit's amplifiers giving way now and the entire
system overloading. But it had been enough to save
Yakov and Sherev, the arms and legs acting like shock
absorbers, reducing the force of the impact. The pilots
were thrown about in their harnesses and knocked unconscious.

Turcotte was in darkness. He tried to move but nothing happened.

Two more Cobras were destroyed in rapid succession
as the Blackhawks closed to within a half mile of the spur.

Aspasia's Shadow was standing in a hemispheric room
deep inside Mount Sinai. The sword was set into another
crystal, this one dark red and only two feet high, directly

in front of him. A golden field emanated out of the pommel of the sword, encapsulating Aspasia's Shadow and touching the equidistant curved walls. On the smooth surface of the walls the 360-degree surface view was displayed, as if he were standing at the very top of Mount Sinai and could see clearly in all directions.

Aspasia's Shadow's eyes shifted to the last Cobra gunship, the closest threat.

A streak of light flashed from the sword pommel to the wall, hitting the image of the Cobra.

A golden sphere was extended on a fifty-foot pole made of *b'ja*, the Airlia metal straight out of the peak of Mount Sinai. A bolt of lightning streaked out of the golden sphere, through the fog.

The last Cobra was destroyed.

In the rear of the AC-130 crewmen used snow shovels to clear the expended brass away from the still-firing guns.

Three digital counters clicked down rounds left in each of the three systems. As Macomber watched, the 25mm clicked to zero and the gun ceased firing, multibarrel smoking. The 40 and 105 kept chunking out rounds, but they too were running low.

Turcotte tried to control his panic.

"Reboot," he ordered, his voice contained inside the helmet.

His heart skipped a beat as nothing happened for several seconds, then the screen flickered and came alive with the scroll of data indicating it was rebooting.

———

Aspasia's Shadow had noted the incoming rounds coming from above, but the Cobras had been a more immediate threat. He now shifted his gaze upward at the AC-130.

On her targeting screen, Macomber saw the glow coming out of the fog and knew they were targeted. There wasn't time to think. She tapped the screen with her right forefinger, right on top of the glow. As the lightning streaked up, both the 40mm and 105mm sent rounds screaming directly in the opposite direction.

Macomber shifted her hand and touched her grandmother's picture as the screen filled with the approaching lightning.

The Specter exploded.

The last 105mm howitzer round that Macomber had targeted struck home, hitting the golden sphere.

Four thousand feet below, in the bowels of Mount Sinai, Aspasia's Shadow cried out and staggered back as the walls flickered with streaks of black and red, the outside image gone.

He reached down and touched the pommel of the sword, willing the ancient technology to work, but the kaleidoscope on the walls continued unabated. Cursing, he pulled the sword out of the crystal and left the room.

On top of the mountain, the strange fog began blowing away with the desert breeze.

———

The data stopped and the screen showed only darkness.

"Forward view, night vision," Turcotte ordered.

He could see the top hatch over Yakov's shoulder. The Russian was struggling to open it.

Turcotte got to his feet. Sherev was waiting at the base of the ladder. The pilot and co-pilot were unconscious in their crash seats in the center of the bouncer. The skin of the craft was solid, all power dead.

"Stand clear," Turcotte told Yakov.

The Russian turned in surprise, searching in the darkness. "I thought you were dead. I cannot get the hatch to budge."

Turcotte climbed up, hooked his weapon arm on the top rung, and with the other applied pressure. The hatch cracked open, letting in sunlight, then fell open with a clang. He climbed out, then reached down and helped the other two out.

The side of Mount Sinai was towering over them, topped with the strange fog. But even as they watched, the cloud was beginning to dissipate.

The first Blackhawk touched down. A dozen Israeli commandos leaped out. Satchel charges in hand, they dashed toward the base of the spur where Sherev had told them the door was.

Aspasia's Shadow staggered as the entire complex shook.

"Come." He gestured to a squad of his men waiting in the tunnel. He didn't head for the surface entrance where the enemy was coming, but rather toward the room where Lisa Duncan was still undergoing the effects of the Grail.

The edge of the bouncer had crashed into the side of the mountain, about two hundred meters from the rock spur. Turcotte could see the Blackhawks landing, commandos leaping off. The three men headed for the commandos gathered outside the opening.

Lisa Duncan blinked. She felt intoxicated, not in control of her body, her head spinning. She tried to reach out with her right hand, to feel something solid, but her arm wouldn't move.

She blinked once more, taking comfort that she did have some control.

"How do you feel?" Aspasia's Shadow loomed over her.

Duncan tried to say something, but no sound came. She saw that he was dressed in the priest's clothes.

"We must be—" the man began, but he was interrupted by a loud explosion reverberating through the rock itself. Aspasia's Shadow straightened. "Take her," he ordered.

The first wave of ten Israeli commandos rushed through the opening they had just blown and were immediately cut down by automatic-weapons fire. The second wave preceded their charge with a barrage of flash-bang grenades. They made it a little farther, killing some of their ambushers, before being pinned down. The tunnel descended slightly and curved, making every foot gained open to new fire from ahead, as Aspasia's Shadow's soldiers and terrorists leapfrogged backward defensively, making the Israelis pay for every yard gained.

Turcotte was like a frustrated attack dog on a leash, Yakov holding him back while those first two groups assaulted. As the third wave prepared to move past the remainder of the second, Turcotte had had enough. He shoved his way past Yakov, catching the Russian by surprise, and dashed after the last man in the third squad.

Sherev was right next to him. "Let my men do their job."

"I can help them," Turcotte said. "Have them follow behind me about five meters."

He strode forward past the point man and was immediately hit with a burst of AK-74 fire, the rounds chipping the armor on his chest. He fired the MK-98, the dart taking out the gunner.

Turcotte began to move quickly down the tunnel, firing his weapon as each new target came into view. The Israelis were close behind as he cleared the way into the complex. He was hit over a dozen times with small-arms fire, but the armor stood up to the damage.

Turcotte dashed around the bend and there was no more incoming fire. He paused as the corridor branched. One tunnel straight and down, the other curved and up.

"I'm going down," Turcotte informed Sherev of his choice. "Split your men. Half with me, half with Yakov, going up."

"I will go with you," Yakov argued.

Turcotte shook his head, hitting the insides of the helmet. "Go with the other force," he ordered. He didn't quite trust Sherev to look out for Duncan's welfare if the Israelis came across her. It was likely they would kill everyone in their path and ask questions later. Turcotte wasn't even sure he completely trusted the Russian, but he couldn't go in both directions and he felt it most likely Duncan—and Aspasia's Shadow—would be deeper in the complex.

He moved into the tunnel, a dozen commandos following.

Yakov and Sherev led their force up the curving tunnel, bodies hunched forward, expecting bullets to come lashing toward them at any moment. Yakov swung the muzzle of the MP-5 back and forth, finger resting lightly on the trigger. The tunnel opened into a large chamber, empty except for several control consoles of Airlia design. There was an opening on the far side.

"There—" Yakov pointed with the gun and they made their away across the chamber.

A door barred the way. Turcotte stepped back while an Israeli demo man placed charges on it. He staggered as the blast resounded down the tunnel, then ran forward through the opening. A large chamber full of bunk beds. And a dead end.

Turcotte cursed and spun about, pushing his way through the commandos crowding in behind him.

As soon as he stepped through the opening, Yakov knew he'd made a mistake. He was in a room about ten feet by ten square, with no other exit. The floor beneath his feet trembled. Sherev joined him and as the next Israeli tried to enter, the entire room began to rise. The commando dove in, barely escaping having his legs

sliced off as the elevator rocketed upward. They passed
several openings, other levels, but the elevator didn't stop
and there were no controls visible on the smooth walls.

Yakov braced himself, the submachine gun aimed toward the open side. "I think we are going to the top of
the mountain."

Turcotte entered the control room to find the remaining
commandos waiting by the open elevator shaft. They
quickly updated him on what had happened. On the far
side of the shaft two cables raced in opposite directions.
One up, one down.

Turcotte didn't hesitate. He jumped across the shaft
and grasped the cable going up. The metal screeched
through the palms of the suit until they locked down. He
was taken along for the ride.

Yakov felt his weight lighten as the elevator slowed and
then came to a halt. A large, circular cavern beckoned.
Sitting in the center was a bouncer, and next to it stood
a tall figure in a multicolored cloak and metal crown, a
pair of soldiers carrying something draped with a thick
white cloth on two poles. Lisa Duncan was held between another two men.

Yakov dashed off the elevator, the butt of the MP-5
tight in his shoulder, Sherev and the Israeli commando
right behind.

"Stay where you are!" Yakov yelled.

Aspasia's Shadow turned. He threw back his hood,
revealing smooth skin, an angular face. He smiled. "Ah,
the large Russian. I have heard of you. Your people are

most formidable. I told Hitler not to invade, but he did not listen. Of course, he did kill many of your countrymen and destroyed his own in the process, so it worked out well in the long run."

"Put the Ark down." Yakov gestured with the gun.

"I don't think so," Aspasia's Shadow said. He gestured and the two men began climbing up the side of the bouncer.

"Stop!" Sherev yelled.

Aspasia's Shadow stepped up and grabbed Duncan, who seemed to be in a daze. He locked her neck in the crook of his left arm, her body between them. A blade appeared in his left, which he laid across her throat. "I've killed many with this. One more won't make a difference to me, but will it to you?"

"No, it won't," Yakov said. He took aim.

The automated elevator reached the top, then reversed direction, heading down.

Turcotte, clinging to the return cable going up, could see the flat white bottom of the elevator coming toward him, filling the entire shaft. There wasn't enough room in the cable channel for him to fit. As another opening approached, he pushed off against the wall, diving into it as the elevator flashed past.

He rolled to his feet and dove once more into the shaft, grabbing the left-side cable going up, locking the TASC-suit glove around it.

"Don't be hasty," Aspasia's Shadow said. He nodded to the two men holding the poles for the Ark. "I've rigged that to blow, and that's what you really want, isn't it? And this." He tapped the garments.

"I'd rather have the Ark destroyed, than in your hands," Yakov said.

"But your friend might not." Aspasia's Shadow indicated Sherev. "He's come here to get his stones back. And getting the Ark, would that not be a major coup for your country, Mister Sherev?"

"We will not let you leave." Sherev edged to the side, the commando with him.

The three-way standoff was upset when Turcotte tumbled into the room, the TASC-suit taking the impact. He got to his feet and pulled the MK-98 off the sling on his back.

"Gentlemen, I hold all the cards." Aspasia's Shadow edged toward the Ark and the side of the bouncer, keeping Duncan between him and the others.

"Let her go." Turcotte's voice echoed out of the speakers on the suit's helmet.

"The Ark." Sherev motioned with the muzzle of his weapon. "Leave it."

A growl escaped Yakov's lips.

Turcotte shifted slightly, seeing the Israeli and what he was doing. "No!" Turcotte exclaimed.

"We can't let him take the Grail." Sherev's jaw was set.

They were both startled as Yakov fired, the round ripping through Duncan's chest and out her back, hitting Aspasia's Shadow, ricocheting off the *thummin*.

Aspasia's Shadow dropped Duncan's body and grabbed the white veil covering the Ark, ripping it off. Immediately the two cherubim heads fired bolts, killing his own men carrying it. The Ark slammed into the floor, the cherubim still firing, a bolt killing the commando and hitting Sherev in the shoulder, spinning him about.

Stunned at Yakov's shot, Turcotte finally reacted, sending a dart at Aspasia's Shadow, ripping a gouge through the robes and along his side, drawing blood. The cherubim fired again, hitting Turcotte square in the chest, staggering him back. Yakov was their next target, the red eyes centering on him.

Acting out of instinct, Turcotte dove to the side, grabbing the Russian and pulling him to the floor, taking the impact of the blasts on the back of the TASC-suit.

"Rear view," he ordered.

Aspasia's Shadow had opened the Ark and had the Grail in his hand. He was carrying it and dragging Duncan with his other hand, blood pouring from the wound on her chest up the side of the bouncer toward the hatch.

Turcotte rolled to his knees, aiming the MK-98. He fired and the dart hit Aspasia's Shadow in the wrist, the sheer force ripping the hand from the body. The severed hand and Duncan slid down the side of the bouncer to the floor.

As Turcotte waited for the cylinder to rotate with the next round, Aspasia's Shadow dove over the edge of hatch, the Grail with him, leaving a trail of blood.

The hatch shut with a clang. Turcotte fired, knowing it was fruitless, the dart clanging off the side of the bouncer. A crack appeared in the ceiling of the chamber, rapidly growing wider. The cherubim were no longer firing, the light gone from the red eyes now that the Grail was out.

Turcotte ran forward and fired again as the bouncer lifted. It was out of the opening and racing away as he reached Duncan.

Turcotte looked down. Her eyes were opening and her lips were moving, but he couldn't hear anything.

"Suit open," Turcotte ordered. The front half swung open and he stepped out, drenched in sweat. He knelt next to Duncan and cradled her head in his arms.

"Lisa."

Her eyes shifted, locking onto his. A half-smile, interrupted by a trickle of blood, graced her lips. "I knew you'd come. I'm sorry. I've screwed it all up."

Then the life went out of her eyes and her body went slack in his arms.

CHAPTER 23

AIRSPACE

The bouncer flight to Area 51 was made in absolute silence. Duncan's body was laid out on the floor, covered with a poncho. Yakov sat cross-legged, a bottle of vodka between his knees.

The Ark was with Sherev. Turcotte had neither the inclination nor the effort to fight the Israeli's claim to it. Given the losses his unit had taken to try to get the Grail and Ark, Turcotte could understand the Israeli's position.

Yakov. The Russian was on the other side of the bouncer, not meeting Turcotte's eyes and not saying anything.

As soon as the pilots regained enough composure, they repowered the bouncer for the trip home.

Through the floor of the alien craft Turcotte could see ocean. They were somewhere over the Atlantic. He'd refused the pilot's offer of a headset. He knew Aspasia's Shadow was gone with the Grail—where, he would find out soon enough.

For now all he could do was try to accept the immediate reality.

"My friend—" Yakov broke the silence, but Turcotte cut him off.

"I don't want to hear anything you have to say."

"I had to try to stop him," Yakov said. "You know that."

"Take out your chess set," Turcotte said.

Yakov pulled the small kit from one of his many pockets.

"Open it and take out a pawn," Turcotte continued.

Yakov did as instructed.

"That's you," Turcotte said. "And me. And her," he indicated the body.

The coastline of the United States appeared and they were zooming across the countryside.

"I'm done with it," Turcotte said. "You took her off the board, well, I'm off the board, too."

CHAPTER 24

MARS

The first convoy of mech-robots reached the two-and-a-half-mile-high escarpment that surrounded Mons Olympus. They didn't pause, but began tearing into the rocky Martian soil, preparing a graded path through the escarpment. The peak of the volcano towered over them on the horizon, one hundred and seventy miles directly ahead and fifteen miles higher.

Back at Cydonia, the remaining mech-robots continued taking apart the remains of the black grid system, loading the parts onto carriers which headed in the direction of Mons Olympus.

CHINA

Two hundred Airlia stood in two rows of eighty, from the last black tube to the exit of the burial chamber. They held gleaming spears or swords in their six-fingered hands, out from their chests in a salute.

In the same singsong language that the hologram in the tunnel had spoken in, Artad asked something of Ts'ang. The Chinese man replied. Without noting the presence of the human-Airlia clones on the floor, Artad strode out of the burial cavern toward the chamber holding the guardian computer. As he passed, each pair of Airlia turned in military precision and followed until only Lexina, Coridan, and Elek were left. Belatedly, they got to their feet and followed like children at an adult function.

PACIFIC OCEAN

The *Washington* and *Stennis*, two supercarriers, steamed in tandem toward Easter Island. Also at the center of the fleet was the *Jahre Viking*. Around them, the escort ships of Task Forces 78 and 79 also were underway. All were under the control of the Easter Island guardian.

AREA 51

The bouncer touched down and a solemn group waited inside Hangar One. Major Quinn, Che Lu, Larry Kincaid, and Professor Mualama stood silently as Turcotte and Yakov carefully carried Duncan's covered body out of the bouncer and onto the gurney that had been wheeled up next to the craft.

"I am most sorry," Che Lu said, taking Turcotte's hand in her small ones.

Turcotte simply nodded, not knowing what to say. Yakov leaned close to Quinn and asked him something. Quinn whispered an answer.

"I will take her to the morgue," Yakov said. He pushed the gurney toward the hangar doors.

"Don't touch her." Turcotte stepped toward the Russian.

Mualama stepped between them. "I will take care of it," he said.

"You neither," Turcotte snapped. "Larry, you do it."

Kincaid nodded and took hold of the gurney.

Turcotte numbly allowed Che Lu to lead him along, the others following as they went to the elevator. The trip to the Cube was made in silence. As the doors slid open, Major Quinn spoke. "We're tracking Aspasia's Shadow's bouncer. It's heading directly toward Easter Island. We—"

Turcotte raised a weary hand. "I don't want to hear it."

"But, sir—" Quinn shut up as Che Lu shook her head. She led him into the same quarters where the two had last spoken, shutting the door on the others.

Che Lu had not let go of his hand. "My friend—" She paused as the phone buzzed. She ignored it. "My friend, I know you feel—" The phone continued to buzz insistently. Reluctantly, Che Lu went over to it and picked it up. Turcotte took the opportunity to lie down on the bunk and close his eyes. He couldn't shake the image of Duncan looking up at him as life faded from her eyes.

He remembered when he first saw her at Dulles International when she had met him on his way to the security force at Area 51. She'd given him his covert mission which had resulted in the cover being blown off Majestic-12 and Area 51. But that was quickly erased by his favorite memory, being with her in her house in Colorado. Watching the sun come up over the high plains to the east. He wondered who would tell her son she was dead, then realized it was his responsibility.

"Mike—" Che Lu gently tapped his arm. "Mike."

Turcotte opened his eyes, his eyebrows arched in weary question.

"Come with me," Che Lu said. "Something important has happened."

He closed his eyes. "I don't care about Aspasia's

Shadow. About Easter Island. Mars. Qian-Ling. Any of it."

"Please."

Turcotte turned on his side away from her.

"Stop it!" Che Lu's voice was like a whip. "You are not that important."

Her words stung. Turcotte swung his feet down to the ground. "What's going on?"

"Come with me."

Turcotte obeyed. They went down the corridor to the elevator. As it lifted, Turcotte flashed back to the elevator in Mount Sinai. What if he had chosen to go up instead of down? If he had been the first to arrive at the bouncer hangar? Could he have stopped Aspasia's Shadow? Saved Lisa? Recovered the Grail? Should he have shot Yakov first as soon as he saw him pointing the gun?

He was jarred when the elevator came to a halt. Che Lu walked directly across the massive hangar, passing bouncers, out into the bright Nevada sunlight.

He wasn't aware where they were going until Che Lu swung a door on a hangar open and the cold air hit his face along with a nauseating medical smell. A hulking figure filled the doorway. Yakov grabbed him by both shoulders, his hands squeezing so hard the pain was intense, startling Turcotte out of his fugue.

"You have to see!" Yakov's voice boomed in Turcotte's head. "You have to see!" He spun Turcotte about.

Duncan was sitting up on the autopsy table.

Turcotte blinked, knowing he was delusional. But the scene was the same. She was sitting, wearing a blood-soaked robe. Her eyes were open. Her head turned toward Turcotte.

"Mike." She raised her arms. "Come here."

Turcotte surprised himself by hesitating. "Who are you?"

A line furrowed the skin on her forehead. "Mike?"

In the back of the room Professor Mualama was watching this miraculous scene, his dark eyes on Duncan, a slow trickle of blood coming out of his ear.

"Who are you?" Turcotte ignored everything but the woman in front of him.

Whatever she was about to say was interrupted by Major Quinn's announcement. "Aspasia's Shadow's bouncer just went under the Easter Island shield. With the Grail."

Robert Doherty is a pseudonym for a bestselling writer of military suspense novels. He is also the author of *The Rock, Area 51, Area 51: The Reply, Area 51: The Mission, Area 51: The Sphinx,* and *Psychic Warrior.*

If you are interested in more information about Robert Doherty, you can visit his website at www. net-trends.com/mayer.